PRIYAMVADA & CO.

SUDHA NAIR

Titles By Sudha Nair

THE MENON WOMEN SERIES
The Wedding Tamasha
Priyamvada & Co.
About That Summer

THE ROMANTICS SERIES
Dr. Heartquaker
The Love Streak
Love Un-Stuck

CLASS OF '11 REUNION SERIES
Flames Of Love
Flames Of Desire

SIGN UP FOR MY AUTHOR NEWSLETTER

Receive an exclusive short and sweet office romance story, LOVE OFFICIALLY, and news, updates, and more, when you sign up to receive my email. Let's keep in touch!

www.SudhaNair.com

1

Prithvi just missed the car on the right, racing him to the last empty parking spot next to his new apartment in HSR, Bangalore.

"Hey," he yelled, slamming the brakes of his Ford Ecosport. He slid the window down and stuck out his finger at the red Maruti, which had grazed the right side of his car as it fled past. "Hey, you!"

But the reckless driver had already dived into the spot, parking badly, and was now jumping out to make a run. A woman, he realised, dressed all in white—white kurta, white dupatta and white churidar. As she sped past, his gaze snagged at the hard-to-miss, mismatched pair of slippers on her feet—one with a large yellow bow on top and the other with two thick lines of beads—before she became a blur. He craned his neck to catch the last of her, her long, unruly curls spilling over her shoulders as she whizzed through the gates of the very building he was going to.

In the back of the car, his mother, Vinodini, deep in slumber, stirred. "What happened?" she asked groggily, and promptly went back to sleep before he could answer.

He cursed and got out, his walking stick—the result of a recent injury—hitting the ground first. The silver paint on the right side of the car was streaked with three long gashes. "Fuck!" He kicked the tyre and scanned the street for an alternate spot, regretting that he hadn't thought to ask for his underground parking number.

On the opposite side, diagonally across, was a spot. If it were only him he'd have parked there and walked back. But with his mother and her wheelchair…he grunted.

A jarring honk from the back startled him and he clambered back in, still fuming. He put the car in gear, and moved it to the side of the road, so that the car behind him could get past. Then he got back out to unload his mother.

His mother was smacking her gums in her sleep as he got her wheelchair out of the boot. Her care-giver, Daisy, sat right beside her, snoring with her mouth open, her buck teeth on prominent display.

"Daisy!" Prithvi called to her. Daisy's mouth opened wider. "Daisy!" he shouted, louder.

The unflower-like Daisy sat up abruptly, wiped the spittle off her cheeks, and looked at him in a daze. "*Entha*, Kuttan Sir? What happened?" She called him "Kuttan Sir" because his mother called him "Kuttan." Daisy was the third certified nurse from the Red Cross in the last six months since his mother's fall. His mother loved the new nurse, the thirty-something, hardworking and honest Daisy, who, to Prithvi's annoyance, smelled oddly of raw fish and burnt coal.

The ten-hour, non-stop ride from Kochi to Bangalore, cooped up in the car with her in the back seat, had suffocated him. But finally, relief! He took in a breath of the cool, fresh air. "We've reached," he told Daisy. "Let's get Ma out. Give me a hand from the other side, will you?"

Prithvi scooped his mother out of the seat while Daisy hitched up her hips.

Vinodini, a one-time actress from decades ago, fluttered her eyelids open, in slow motion, and flashed him a gummy smile. "What was all the commotion?" she asked, smacking her gums, once again.

She reminded him of the old and skinny *Betaal* from the *Vikram Aur Betaal* TV show from his childhood. How much his mother had changed! Her skin was shrivelled, her nails mottled and bent. When he'd left India to study in the US twenty-five years ago, she was still a beauty. Now, a grey bob cut replaced the knee-length black tresses she used to have, and the arms that held on to him with a tight grip were wrinkly.

But she still hadn't lost her theatrical booming voice. "Get my teeth before people see me like this."

Daisy hurried out with Vinodini's precious dentures swimming in a leak-proof jar filled with water. In two thwacks, Vinodini had clamped them into place.

Prithvi slow-wheeled his mother across the street fringed with tall buildings and coconut palms. It was a quiet and green locality. Daisy followed him meekly, Vinodini's bag hitched on to her shoulder. The rest of the bags would just have to wait.

At the entrance to the building, another flight of half a dozen steps awaited them, and Prithvi grunted again. His foot was not that bad but it still hurt sometimes, especially after a long drive like this. Scooping his mother up once more, he made it up using his good leg while she hung on for dear life, her fingers digging into his collarbone. Daisy propelled the rattling wheelchair up the stairs behind him and helped Prithvi lower his mother into it when they finally reached the landing.

A crowd was already gathered at the elevator entrance and it filled up as soon as it came down. There was no space for him or the wheelchair. He waited for the next trip as the elevator went back up, stopped at the fifth and finally returned to zero, the door opening with a clang. A large group stepped out. Something seemed to be up at the fifth floor, where he too was headed. Luckily, the three of them were alone on the next trip.

On the fifth floor, the elevator door opened to the sight of hundreds of slippers, shoes and sandals scattered all over the corridor, from the direction of his neighbour's flat, number 502, all the way to the elevator's mouth.

What a warm welcome, Prithvi thought, cursing his luck, and edged his way out from behind his mother's wheelchair to kick the footwear aside. His gaze caught at a mismatched pair of slippers—one with a large yellow bow on top and the other with two thick lines of beads—stuck beneath a wheel. What the hell! *The one who'd scraped his car was here?*

"Ow!" his mother yelped, shaking violently as he rolled the wheel over the errant pair, crushing one's bow and probably cracking the other's beads.

Served the bloody slippers right for annoying the hell out of him! "Can't help it," Prithvi muttered. "I'm trying to get us through."

Once they were out, Daisy managed to banish the rest of the slippers out of their way.

Vinodini beamed at Daisy, showing off her perfect row of false teeth. "Thank you!"

They made it to their flat, number 503. Vinodini and her favourite nurse were busy discussing the new place as Prithvi unlocked the door and let them in. "What's going on there?" his mother wanted to know. "A lot of people…"

He looked to the right. The door to their neighbour's was open.

Inside, a big crowd was gathered. Laid on the floor in the middle, was a man, wearing a two-piece suit, a crisp white shirt and red tie. His dark hair was gelled and combed back, his eyes were shut and his nostrils and ears were stuffed with tufts of cotton. Swirls of grey from lit incense sticks formed a halo above his head. Sitting on the floor next to him, was a young woman, her face half-hidden. Probably his wife. The late morning light shone harshly on her troubled face. Her nose was red, her face blotched and puffy, and her eyes boring through the inert figure. She was sobbing and jabbing a handkerchief into her dark, teary eyes. She looked so torn and vulnerable, Prithvi couldn't help but shudder.

Suddenly, the woman's glance shifted to the door, to where he stood. She stared for a moment, her doe-like eyes swimming in a puddle of tears.

Then her expression changed. Those miserable, puddle-filled eyes turned fearful, almost horrified. Through her clamped mouth she let out a long, shrill wail. It was a baleful, banshee cry, one that turned all heads towards the door. The next moment, she fainted and fell into the arms of a woman behind her.

Stupefied, Prithvi backed away.

A woman-in-white appeared at the door, eyes red, looking like she'd been crying too. She took in his six-foot-plus frame dressed in black, dark skin, full beard, and her startled gaze traced the long scar that started from his right eyebrow to his cheek and disappeared into his beard. Her eyes grew wide. "Who are you? What do you want?"

"Someone…scraped my car," Prithvi stuttered. So uncouth of him, he realised, instead of, *I'm sorry but what happened here.* A bit too late to behave like a good neighbour.

She swallowed.

It took him a second to realise it was her—*the one who had scraped his car.* "You?"

"Look, my brother-in-law died," she said quickly, sniffling. "This is not a good time to create a scene." She thrust a piece of paper into his palm. "Here!" She stepped back and slammed the door in his face.

Prithvi heard the sound of the lift behind him just then and turned around. Two men wearing badges around their neck emerged. One held a camera. They seemed to be from the media, Prithvi noted, as they strode towards him, their official news crew badges flashing prominently. He clenched his fists and lunged for the nearest fellow's collar. "You bastards won't leave me alone, will you?" He shook the fellow up and thrashed the cameraman who jumped into the fray. A scuffle ensued, in which the camera fell to the ground.

"Stop!" someone yelled. Out of nowhere, two people grabbed Prithvi's hands and held him back. The cameraman and the reporter, still shaken, straightened up and rubbed their bruises.

"You'll go to jail for attacking us," the cameraman said, his eyes smarting.

"Why the hell did you attack us?" the reporter shouted.

"Why the hell are you here?" Prithvi growled in response.

They turned to look at each other in surprise.

"We're here to cover the unexpected death of Dr. Mohan."

The reporter touched his jaw. "He was the HOD of Cardiology at Sakra Hospital."

Prithvi broke free of the holds that had pinned his arms behind him. "Sorry!" He straightened his shirt. "I thought you were here…for me."

The men from the media scoffed and shoved him aside. "*Saala!*" They glared at him as they made their way into flat number 502.

Entering his own apartment, Prithvi realised that he was still holding the piece of paper in his hand. He uncurled his fist. Inside was a five-hundred-rupee note. *What!*

Two pairs of eyes were trained on him when he looked up.

"Such a commotion outside," his mother said. "We were wondering what happened."

"It was the media."

"The media followed you here also?" Her eyes were round like saucers.

It was death, not the media that had followed him here, as well.

Ever since his director had committed suicide, the media had gone berserk.

The wife blaming it on an altercation with the producer, Prithvi, had landed him in trouble. Pretty soon the media was swarming all over his place, camped outside his home in Kochi, day and night, shoving mics under his nose, making it difficult for him to step out or live in peace.

They were hell bent on digging up every angle of the suicide, finding out what the argument had been about. But he had had no argument with his director. There was no sensational story. Just a bunch of lies created by the wife and the media.

But that wasn't the end to his problems. There were protests, black flags, slogans—the works.

Just being the producer had meant hell. An overdose of hell.

He was so tired of all the noise and drama.

A temporary escape to his flat in Bangalore had seemed like the only choice. He'd finally decided to leave with his mother, late the previous night.

He looked at his mother and shook his head. "No, the media was not for me this time. A high-profile doctor is dead, next door."

His mother mumbled something incoherent, before Daisy and she got back to the things they had to do and left him alone.

He sank into the nearest chair, feeling exhausted. He didn't know what to expect in this new place.

2

When Neha came to, she remembered the dark man with bloodshot eyes. For a moment there, the giant at the door had resembled Yama, the God of Death himself, and she'd thought he'd come to take her husband away.

Shweta, the owner of the mismatched slippers and Neha's younger sister, was hovering over her with a glass of water in her hand. "Are you okay?"

Neha sat up and dabbed at the water sprinkled on her face. "Who was it at the door?"

"Just someone who's car I'd scraped as I was coming over."

"Am I getting into trouble?"

"Don't think so. I gave him some cash. Though…," she said, her eyebrows furrowed, "I wonder how he found me…"

Neha groaned and looked at the crowd around her. It felt like the whole room was staring at her, everyone conspiring to exacerbate her tragedy. If only she could be left alone for a bit with Mohan.

The priests called for taking Mohan's body away. "Is there anybody left to come before we leave?" one of them asked the people gathered there.

Mohan was an only child and his parents had passed away a few years ago. Neha's family was here. No, there was nobody left to come. "Where is Ria?" Neha asked aloud, looking for her daughter. "Please call her."

The tall, lanky pre-teen was nudged out of her bedroom, where she had remained shut since she heard the news of her father's sudden death. They had all left together that morning, Neha and Ria for their respective schools and Mohan for the hospital.

Ria shuffled into the living room in a T-shirt, and jeans through which her hip bones showed. Her eyes wore a vacant look, her shoulders drooped. She didn't talk to anyone or do anything except stand in one corner and stare at her father. She hadn't said a word to Neha yet. No questions about what had happened. Nothing.

When Mohan's body was lifted to be carried away, Neha couldn't hold back her tears. She looked at Mohan's face for one last time. *How could you leave me like this?* she implored of him. *What will I do without you?*

He looked so peaceful and content that she wanted to shake him. His hand had still been warm at her last touch. She couldn't believe he was gone. She broke down, unable to stop calling his name, crying for him to come back, as he was taken out the door. She didn't care about the strong hands that tried to hold her back as she fought to go with him. She didn't care what anybody thought. Mohan didn't deserve to die so young. She didn't deserve a life without him. She cried for their only child. For herself. Cried until she couldn't breathe and there were no more tears left in her.

After returning from the funeral, Neha's father clammed up completely. Neha's mother tried to talk about mundane household things like whether there was enough milk and sugar, would her house help come tomorrow and would Ria like to eat parathas. She asked if Neha and Ria would like to come stay with them for a bit. Neha's parents, Prabhu and Keertana, lived close by, on Sarjapur Road. Ria's school bus would still be able to pick her and drop her off if they moved to their place for a few days, her mother said. But Neha couldn't bear to face her parents day in and day out, especially her father, who was in deep shock over Mohan's death. No, she told her mother. She'd rather stay here with Ria.

Neha called up her school. The principal was understanding. It was obvious that a drama teacher could be afforded a longer leave of absence than, say, a Math teacher. "Take your time getting back," the principal said. "Get back on your feet. Take care of everything at home. We all understand that it's been a shock and could take a few months. Take all the time you need and please let us know if we can do anything to help."

Shweta stocked the refrigerator with some food that her husband, Niru, had brought from his café. Neha gave her house help a few days off. By evening, Neha insisted that her parents and Shweta get back to their homes. She assured them that she would be fine, that she wanted to be left alone. After everyone had gone, the house became quiet again.

Later in the evening, Mrs. Poonam Sharma, an elderly, widowed lady, her seventh-floor neighbour, dropped by with some rotis and palak paneer gravy for dinner. She made herself comfortable on the couch and began her usual rant. "Poor you! Who would have thought?" [In Mrs. Sharma-speak that meant: *Welcome to the widows' club!*]

"Did he have insurance?" [*How are you going to afford anything?*]

"I'm going to miss Dr. Mohan deeply. He always had a patient ear for me." [*Where will I go for free medical consultation?*]

Mrs. Sharma finally left only after she had badgered Neha enough to elicit answers. She was satisfied that Dr. Mohan did have life insurance, which left his family financially stable (*Lucky you!*), Ria and Neha had taken offs from their schools for a couple of weeks (*That's too short!*), Neha was not going to sell or leave this house and go to her parents' (*My parents tried to force me to but I stayed here only*), and that Neha was planning to return to work (*Back in our days we were never taught drama at school*).

At seven o'clock that evening, Neha put the tub of palak paneer gravy in the microwave and set it to heat. Ria had not left her room. She called out to Ria for dinner. There was no answer. Neha went to listen at her door. No sound. She knocked and waited.

This was Mohan's little baby who, at five, wanted to dress up to look like her father. She'd wear an overcoat, carry a toy briefcase like his, walk to the main door and wave goodbye to Neha, like Mohan did every morning.

Knock. Knock. Wait. Then she tried the door handle. It was locked.

Mohan and Neha had wanted a sibling for Ria but three miscarriages had unravelled Neha's knot of desire for a second baby and thrown away Ria's chances of having a sibling, forever.

Knock. Wait. Knock. Knock. Wait. "Ria!" Neha finally called out, when there was no response.

She should have checked on Ria earlier, Neha berated herself. Had she eaten anything? Had she even had a drink of water? What a terrible mother she was!

Bang. Bang. Wait. "Ria! Open up!"

She couldn't even remember a thing about Mohan from that morning at home. Had she noticed the lust in his eyes when he'd glanced at her just out of the shower? Had she squealed when he'd tried to grab her before she could put on any clothes? Or had she simply squirmed and told him off, like most mornings when she was late? Had she even waved goodbye to him when he'd left for work that morning? All she remembered was the heart-wrenching call from the hospital. They'd said that he had complained of a pain in his chest and collapsed, dying on the spot from a massive heart attack.

She jabbed at a falling tear. Mohan had been so busy lately that they hadn't shared a meal together in ages, not seen a movie together in a long time, not gone on a vacation in ten years... And now, poof! Nothing together. Ever. Nada!

Fresh tears started rolling down her cheeks. She couldn't stop the rush of emotions that rose like waves from her belly and thrust at her throat, leaving her gasping for breath. She flung herself at Ria's door and felt her knees buckle. She had no strength left in her arms and legs. Raking the wood with her fingers she slumped to the floor and banged her head on the door. *Ria!* She silently pleaded with her daughter to let her in. To not abandon her. She did not want to be abandoned. She did not—

The lock clicked and the door opened. Neha fell face forward into the room. She couldn't see a thing through the blurry film of tears. Quickly she wiped her eyes and stood up. Ria was back at her desk, her back to the door.

Neha clapped her hand to her mouth as she looked at the mess in Ria's room. Stubs of colour pencils lay everywhere, shaved to the very last bit. The shaving spirals and scraps in every colour were scattered all over the bed, the floor and the desk. Hundreds of A4 sheets were strewn all over the room. Each one had abstract doodles, lines, circles, and squiggly, scratchy, angry renditions of emotions scribbled on every inch of white space.

Ria was working on a fresh piece at her desk. Two sketch pens, red and black, lay open beside her. In her hand was a purple sketch pen. Her hand moved fast. She was not done yet. She did not acknowledge her mother.

Neha left the room silently, shutting the door behind her. She considered bringing Ria's dinner to her room.

Back in the kitchen, surprisingly, the microwave was still on. The glass door was covered with a dark film of vapour. Horrified, she yanked it open. One look at the timer, and she realised that she'd kept the gravy in for ten minutes, instead of one. The oven interior was a gooey, green and white mess. The tub had withered away.

The problem with cleaning up a gooey mess was that it killed one's appetite and she was too tired to do anything now. She didn't want any dinner, and neither did she have the strength to force Ria to eat. Leaving the mess there to be cleaned up in the morning, she dragged herself to her bedroom and passed out on the bed.

3

A few weeks later, feet propped up on a footstool and fingers speed-punching the keys on his laptop, Prithvi was checking out Danby's Heist, the newly launched pirate video game in the market; he'd designed the concept for the game and was excited to see how it had turned out.

As a mechanical engineer, forced to follow in his father's footsteps, it was serendipitous that he had discovered the gaming industry and fallen in love with designing video games instead of engines. And here she was, his latest baby, finally in his possession after months of design and development. And boy, was she smarter than her creator! He chuckled at how he himself had envisioned every difficulty level, and how those were now coming back to destroy him. Oh yeah! It still felt wonderful to have been part of the project although it was now more than six months since he'd resigned from the US firm and returned to India for good.

A crashing sound from the kitchen broke his concentration. He shut his laptop and hurried towards it. Splattered on the floor of the kitchen was a pool of brown curry. His mother had a frozen expression of shock on her face. Daisy was on her knees, apologising profusely, trying to clean up the mess but only making more in the process. "Sorry, really sorry, didn't see that bowl near my elbow," Daisy muttered, as her hands flew all over the place.

"Daisy's here to take care of you, not the kitchen," Prithvi scolded his mother. "Did I not tell you that we should engage a cook and give Daisy some time for herself?"

"Nonsense," his mother said. "She loves being in the kitchen."

"You terrify her in the kitchen!"

It was true. Daisy tried so hard to prove herself around his mother that she was always committing blunders.

Daisy turned around and wiped the sweat off her forehead. "Oh no, Kuttan Sir. This really was an accident. I love to cook. I'm happy to learn under Ma'am."

There was no stopping Daisy, who'd been trying to learn to cook ever since the day she'd come to work for them. Only, her upma tasted like rubber, her rotis were too tough to chew, and all her curries had extra salt. "Ma!" Prithvi looked at his mother, agonised.

His mother ignored him. "Daisy!" she ordered. "Just let everything be! It's almost dinner time. Just get whatever there is, on to the table, now."

Daisy nodded and set about to get the plates and spoons. Prithvi and his mother moved towards the dining room, leaving Daisy to carry on without all the attention to her clumsiness with pots and pans. With her patient, the lady was a gem, so it didn't really matter if elsewhere she floundered.

Out of the kitchen, Vinodini turned to Prithvi. "If you'd married at the right age, I'd have had a daughter-in-law taking care of these things right now."

Oh no, he wasn't getting into that conversation trap again! He was quite happy being single. He'd been with women when he was studying and working in the US but, somehow, he'd never fallen in love. He doubted he even had that gene in him.

His mother turned her wheelchair around. "I don't know how you managed just by yourself all these years!"

"I managed just great. I'm also a good cook, which I'd prove to you if only you'd let me into the kitchen." Before the accident he'd been fine, he thought. Happy and content with his work, and cooking for his friends most weekends. He did not remember spending a single weekend alone. He touched his hip unconsciously.

She noticed immediately. "Does it still hurt?"

"Not much." He took his place at the dining table. "The limp should also go away soon," he added, in case she was wondering about that but was afraid to ask.

His mother frowned. "You're difficult just like your father used to be," she complained, rolling her wheelchair into the empty spot at the head of the table. "You never even told me what happened."

"I'm not like him at all," he was quick to retort. He hated his father so much, he wanted to be nothing like him. If it weren't for his father, he wouldn't have stayed far away from India all those years.

"Your grandfather always said that."

He missed his grandfather. He wished he'd come for his funeral. But that would have meant meeting his father and speaking to him too. That had killed his desire and, for long after the funeral, had fuelled his guilt. He'd been a coward!

She touched his hand. "Your grandfather also wanted to see some great-grandchildren."

"Stop it, Ma!"

"Okay! Okay!" She pursed her lips. "I know, even I may not see them in my lifetime."

"Priyamvada is my baby now. Just get used to it."

"That's a terrible thing to say," she cried. "I curse the day I found your grandfather's letter and sent it to you." She gave him a look before letting out a long sigh. "But at least I got you back because of it. I know I'm right."

She was right about many things. He was not going to marry or have kids in her lifetime, and it was indeed the promise of Priyamvada in his grandfather's letter that had set his mind on returning home to

India. He'd loved visiting Priyamvada Studios as a young boy. Holding on to his grandfather's hand, he'd walk in through the studio doors and gawk at everything around him. Going to the shoots with his grandfather fascinated him, and watching that same movie on the screen, later, awed him. It always amazed him how an ordinary shooting with a mob surrounding the actors transformed into a beautiful work of art in the movies. The lovely background scores, the dubbing studio, the actual reel of print in those days, all held a special place in his heart.

"If only your father had recognised how much you'd wanted to stay," she said with another sigh.

Instead, his father had shamed him and driven him away to pursue a degree in the US. "You want to be a filmmaker, like your grandfather?" he'd roared. "And live on the crumbs of the old man?" Prithvi never understood why his father hated his grandfather so much. Why did he insist that his son not follow his father's legacy? Now, he'd never know. His father had died of a liver ailment a year ago. It was at the same time when Prithvi had been hospitalised in the US, after the bike he'd been riding had been hit and crushed under a truck. He'd been undergoing multiple surgeries for his broken ribs and fractured hip when the news of his father's death came. His mother had found the letter hidden away among his father's belongings and sent it to him. His mother was right—that letter had made him return to India.

Daisy walked in just then with what looked like rice, except that it was one, big white lump.

Vinodini gave her an encouraging smile. "Next time, switch off the gas five minutes earlier, dear," she said. "But at least it's not uncooked like yesterday's."

Daisy beamed. "I'll do better tomorrow."

"The thing is," Vinodini said to Prithvi after Daisy had left to get the rest of the dishes from the kitchen. "In Kochi, that Mariamma wouldn't let Daisy anywhere near the kitchen. The poor girl's quite enjoying herself here."

Whatever! Prithvi rolled his eyes. There was nothing he could do when the two women were hell bent on ruining his meal.

His mother looked at him with a smile. "Come to think of it, I kind of like it here too."

He looked at her, surprised. She was the one who'd complained about the sudden move until a few days ago.

"I mean," she continued, "I knew everyone around back there but nosy neighbours dropping in at all hours was getting a little tiring. Especially, after the…you know what!"

He knew exactly what she was referring to. His debut movie production was only half-finished when the director had hanged himself from a ceiling fan.

"Here, I don't know my neighbours, but it's quiet and peaceful." She chuckled. "I could wear a nightdress all day long and nobody would even know."

Daisy entered with something that looked like pickle and chutney powder. "I'm sorry, there's only this to eat with rice. We lost all the curry."

Prithvi served a little of the white lump on to his plate and ate wordlessly. He was reminded of the days when he'd just started living alone.

"I was thinking we could stay here for a while," he said to his mother, as he got up to wash his hands. In any case, he'd have to wait for the investigation to be completed, and the public memory of the terrible incident to fade, for things to settle down. "I'm going to call on KD soon. See if I can take up another movie in the meantime."

His mother looked pleased. It was she who'd introduced him to KD when Prithvi had returned to India. She'd known KD since he was a young boy and she trusted him. "That would be a good thing. I'm sure he'll do something to help you."

Kalidas, or KD, as he was better known, was a producer and director himself, and there was no one better than him to show Prithvi the ropes of the business. After all, it was KD who had got Prithvi his first movie and had introduced him to the now dead director. After the media commotion over the suicide, it had been KD's idea that Prithvi should move to Bangalore, where he himself lived, until things cooled down.

After bidding his mother goodnight, Prithvi took out his grandfather's letter, still safe with him, and strolled to the adjoining terrace. The feather-shaped leaves of the coconut palms grazed the railing against which he propped his elbows. He could hear Daisy's voice in his mother's room. She was getting her ready for bed. When all was quiet, he picked up the letter and began to re-read it. It was addressed directly to him, written by his grandfather before he had passed away, years ago, when Prithvi was still studying Mechanical Engineering at UCLA.

Even as I'm dying, I have faith in you, his grandfather had written.

The letter had arrived in the US when there was very little hope that Prithvi would survive. But survive, he did. His hand involuntarily moved up to feel the tell-tale scar on his right cheek. The letter was given to him only six months after, when he had recovered from the debilitating accident, and was finally able to walk with support.

I saw the spark in you since you were a young boy. Your father did not have what it takes but you will bring back the fame and riches that he has cast away. I am leaving Priyamvada to you. Today she languishes forgotten and in neglect. It is my dying wish that she be yours and you bring her back to her former glory.

All day, for months as he'd recuperated in his hospital bed, the letter had stared at him. Wasn't this what he had wanted all along?

Well, here he was now—he thought with a laugh—trying to fulfil his grandfather's dying wish. And already his very first movie under the Priyamvada banner had stalled. Here he was, running away from everything—the media, his crew—at the first sign of trouble. He hated the thought that his grandfather had entrusted the reigns of Priyamvada to a coward.

Staring into the dark night that mirrored the darkness that he faced in his life, Prithvi made a silent promise. He'd prove all his detractors wrong even if it meant losing everything.

The lights in his mother's room went out. He slowly headed back to his room. Sleep wouldn't come and he longed for something soothing to do. He remembered the artist's tote he'd brought with him—a parting gift from his friends in New Jersey. He'd always loved to paint. He pulled out the tote made of waterproof nylon with several deep pockets to hold his brushes and palette knives. Inside was a big compartment, divided into three smaller ones that held a dozen jars of paints, more brushes and a long palette tray. He pulled out the materials he needed.

He walked to the living room and switched on the music player to play the soft sound of rain. Standing in front of the little wall above the niche in the corridor, he slowly began to paint whatever came to mind.

4

Mohan's post-funeral rituals were done. The fifth day, and the thirteenth day poojas had been conducted by Shweta and the rest of the family. Neha and Ria had gone through the motions in a daze. Neither knew when night turned to day and back to night again. Now, Neha had insisted she was fine being by herself at home with Ria but she sat like a zombie in front of the TV, its volume muted, while Ria stayed in her room. There was absolutely no evidence of another human in the house. To Neha it felt like the house was coming to bite her. If she lay down, she couldn't wake up, and then she would get no sleep at night. Her back pain had started once again, aggravated by her slipped disc condition, which had been the reason she'd given up teaching yoga some years ago.

"You stink!" Shweta said to Neha, some days later, when she came to visit her. "Have you even had a bath in the past week?"

Neha looked at her blankly. "I don't remember." Her words slurred. The truth was, she wasn't even aware what she was doing these days.

"You should get back to school, Neha," Shweta said. "You can't just while away your life sitting at home like this. It's been over a month since…" her voice trailed away as Neha's eyes filled with tears.

"It's too soon," Neha said. "I'm not ready."

"You will never be ready. You've got to start somewhere."

Neha nodded. She was too tired to do anything.

Shweta tugged at her hand. "Come on. Let's get you a bath."

Neha followed her reluctantly. Shweta filled the tub with warm water. Then gently she washed Neha's hair and dried it for her, leaving her afterwards to finish her bath.

The bath felt good. When she came out of the bathroom, Shweta had set the table and called Ria out from her room. Ria looked like she'd been asked to take a bath too. They sat down at the table to share a simple meal that Shweta had brought from home.

After lunch, when Ria had gone back to her room, Shweta accosted Neha. "What have you two been eating these days? All the food in the fridge is almost as I'd left it a week ago."

Neha looked at her apologetically. "Mrs. Sharma sent over dinner, bread, and some snacks a few days ago. Ria's never hungry, and I didn't want to get something just for myself."

"I think you seriously need something to do," Shweta said, knitting her eyebrows. "For starters, this place needs some sprucing up. Going by the mess, your house help is on extended leave, granted by you, I suppose?"

Neha nodded at her little sister's admonishment. When had Shweta become the older and wiser one?

They started with the family photographs. Shweta felt it was best if they started putting away those that reminded them of Mohan. "He'll always be right here if you want to see him," she said, neatly wrapping up the family pictures and putting them away in a drawer.

After the frames and pictures, they got to Mohan's cupboard and packed up his clothes, to be given away. What were they going to do with the dozen suits, many more shirts, ties and the other items in his cupboard, wondered the sisters.

Ria barged into the room as they were cleaning, and stared at the pile of Mohan's clothes on the bed. "What's all this?"

"I'm giving them away," Neha said, softly.

Ria pounced on the pile and grabbed an old, worn-out T-shirt. It was the one they'd picked up in Sri Lanka some years ago. It had a baby elephant on the front. Mohan had joked that he was so strong that he could carry a baby elephant. "I won't let you give this away," Ria said. "I'm keeping it."

Ria wore her father's shirt over her own, immediately, while Shweta caught Neha's worried glance and gave her a nod. Yes, Neha conveyed in return, through the silent exchange, it was better to let Ria have the keepsake she wanted of her father.

Afterwards, as they were clearing out Mohan's toiletries, a bottle of cologne fell down, breaking into smithereens. Neha slumped to the floor, a tired, weepy mess. "I don't think I can do this anymore," she said, sobbing.

The cleaning came to a halt abruptly, just like it had started, but they were almost done. Shweta finished the rest by herself. The scent was so overpowering that Neha couldn't return to the bedroom. After Shweta left that night, carrying all the things that were to be given away, Neha confined herself to the living room, and slept in the guest room. The living room had spooked her since the day Mohan's body was laid out on the floor. She imagined seeing him there every time she walked by, and to her intense mortification, she found she could not stay in that room after dusk.

The little cleaning exercise had done some good, however. Neha woke up the next morning and decided she wanted to cook. She spent the next few days in a flurry of cooking, sometimes four meals a day, something she had never done before.

Daisy from next door met her at the door when she was bargaining with the fish vendor, one morning. "Hi, I'm Daisy. I'm the nurse for Vinodini Ma'am."

Neha nodded civilly.

"Do you have fish tamarind?"

Neha looked up at her in surprise. She'd never heard of anyone who bought fish when they didn't have any fish tamarind.

"As a matter of fact," Daisy continued, "I just realised I didn't have any left, and there's no one I can ask."

Neha brought the tamarind from her kitchen and offered it to her immediately.

"Also, your cooking smells great," Daisy complimented her. "I'm just learning. Kuttan Sir always complains that I add too much salt or oil."

Neha had so much food sitting in her refrigerator that she had started giving it away to the house help who was now back to work. "Can I offer you some of the fish curry that I'm making today?"

Daisy nodded ecstatically.

Neha's doorbell rang the very next day. Daisy was at the door with a big smile that showed all her protruding teeth.

Neha was surprised to see her. "What happened? Is everything okay?"

"What magic did you do to your cooking?" She spoke enthusiastically. "Kuttan Sir wanted to know where the food was from. I've never seen him lick his fingers like that."

Neha smiled. "I'm happy to hear that."

"Can you teach me too?"

And so began Daisy's training at Neha's house, for a few afternoons. She was a quick learner. A few basic tips and tricks were all she needed, like adding cooked rice to the idli batter to make it soft and to cook fish in an earthen pot to increase its flavour. Also, to use less oil and salt to begin with. Soon she was ready to try out new things in her kitchen with greater confidence.

During some of those days, Neha felt that she could go on and on, and then there were days when her body would refuse to move—she'd be stuck to the living room couch from the moment she woke up.

On one of the days when she was sitting there staring out of the window at the swaying tops of the coconut palms, and sipping her black tea, she heard a voice behind her.

"Ma!"

Ria's voice made Neha jump. They hadn't spoken to each other in days.

"I need money."

Neha looked up at her daughter's forlorn face. "Do you want to buy something?"

"I want more colours and a sketchbook. I've used up everything."

Neha thought of suggesting that they should probably go over to Shweta's house. It'd be a change. But ultimately, she knew it was useless because Ria wouldn't go.

She rose to get the money. "Should I order pizza tonight?" she asked, handing her a hundred-rupee note.

Ria took the money and made for the door. "I don't feel like it." She was gone before Neha could say another word.

5

Prithvi eyed the good-looking secretary sitting outside KD's office, talking to somebody over the phone. She had a cute face, and lush hair that fell to her waist like a waterfall. She put down the phone and walked towards Prithvi. "KD will be with you shortly. He'd like you to make yourself comfortable."

Prithvi nodded.

She sashayed back to her chair, in a business skirt that fell just above her knees, and pencil heels.

KD's office mirrored his personal, classy taste. Cream leather sofas, tan blinds, wooden flooring, glass cubicles and leather swivel chairs around glass-topped tables. A bunch of scriptwriters and production crew now sat there, bent over thick piles of paper.

Prithvi couldn't help but feel a pang of envy at KD's beautiful office overlooking the KGA Golf Course. And the fact that he had so many projects, while Prithvi had none.

One day, Prithvi promised himself, he'd have an office better than KD's.

The secretary peeked around her computer screen and called out to him. "Mr. Prithvi? KD will see you now, Sir."

He'd have someone like her too, Prithvi thought, as he passed her to enter KD's cabin. He choked on the strong scent of jasmine as he pushed open the door to KD's plush, carpeted office. KD was waiting for him, half-reclining, and relaxed in his high-backed, black leather chair behind an elegant, broad, teak table.

KD was a short, bulky man with thick fingers that he waved in Prithvi's direction. He was wearing his trademark safari suit. Prithvi had only met him a couple of times before. "Sit down, young man. I'm sorry about what happened." He was only a few years older than Prithvi but he liked to call him "young man."

Prithvi took a chair opposite KD's desk and looked into the older man's easy-going brown eyes. "The current problem might not be over soon," he said, unable to hide the desperation in his voice. "I was hoping to start something new."

KD straightened in his chair and leaned forward. "You're right. With the police case and all, it would be too much of a legal hassle to get a new director and resume work immediately." He pulled out a few thick, bound sheets from his drawer and handed them over. "Here are some scripts. If you like any of these, you can start now."

"I'll take a look."

KD rose and walked over to Prithvi. "Take it easy, young man," he said, extending a warm handshake. "This too shall pass."

"I'll be in Bangalore for a few months."

"I think that is a fabulous idea," KD said. "It might be easier to work in peace here. Good luck with that!"

Prithvi rose to leave.

"And please convey my regards to your mother," KD called out to him on his way out.

It wasn't much, but at least he had something to work on in his spare time. Also, his fish export business in Kochi had begun demanding his attention lately. That was something else his grandfather had been involved in. Although not as exciting as taking care of Priyamvada, it helped generate extra cash for the movie business. And he had to keep that going.

Back at the apartment building as he was waiting outside the elevator on the ground floor, he saw a tall, spindly girl walking over. She was carrying a shopping bag and had earplugs in her ears. He was sure he'd seen her before. She nodded at Prithvi and then looked away. They were soon joined by a fish vendor with a large, open, smelly basket of fish on her head.

"Ew!" the girl said, pinching her nose.

When the elevator arrived, the fish vendor tried to barge in first but the girl blocked her way. "You wait!" she ordered the harried woman.

"No, I'm going up. You wait!"

There was a brief shoving between the two, but the bulky fish vendor and her basket won. Prithvi was quite amused by the show and he finally found himself wedged between them, going up, with the duo throwing venomous glances at each other.

At the fifth floor, the fish vendor exited first, Prithvi got out next and the girl, who was rummaging in her shopping bag just as the door opened, was the last. The door almost shut before she came out elbowing her way forward.

The door to Prithvi's flat flew open as soon as the fish vendor had set her basket down at the entrance. The fish vendor immediately started to extol the virtues of the variety she'd brought along while Daisy nodded her head, gushing with glee. "Would you like pomfret today, Kuttan Sir?" she asked as Prithvi tried to step over the basket that had turned out to be too wide.

Prithvi was about to tell her to get the basket out of the way when he sensed someone right behind him.

He turned around and was surprised to see that it was the girl from the elevator. She was rooted to the spot and staring into his house, eyes wide. She looked up at him momentarily and put out her hand. "Ria. I live next door." Then she went back to staring inside.

He followed her gaze to the wall above the niche in the corridor, to the painting he'd been working on, nonstop, for the last few days now.

A moment later her face broke into a huge smile. "Incredible!

Who would have thought?"

She was referring to his art, Prithvi realised, as she pointed to the painting and gasped.

"That's the well that Batman fell into, isn't it? And back there is the sky." She stepped into his house, jumping over the basket, much to the fish vendor's annoyance, and leaned closer to the wall. "And they're…they're bats, escaping towards the light." She was squeaking with excitement.

Nobody at home had guessed what it was. Daisy had been going on about how the grey concentric circles of the well were making her feel dizzy. Prithvi beamed with pleasure. "I didn't think anyone could tell."

"From Batman Begins. I've watched the entire trilogy like five times." She looked up from the painting to his face. "And you remind me of Bruce Wayne," she said, pointing to his leg and grinning. "With the limp."

He was amused. In fact, he was quite taken up by her directness. He was tired of people sidestepping to avoid hurting his feelings. The fact was that his limp didn't bother him.

"Back from the dead?" she asked, grinning again.

His face lit up into a smile. This girl was fun! "Dark and scarred."

She pointed to the scar on his cheek. "You mind if I asked how you got that?"

He shrugged. "It was a motorbike accident. A truck ran a red light and rammed into my bike. Tied me to a bed for more than six months."

"Sounds awful! I'm sorry. Must have been terrible." Her gaze returned to the painting. "Where did you learn to do that?" She couldn't seem to take her eyes off it. "It looks so real."

His mother rolled her wheelchair into the living room right then. "Ah, I see we have a young visitor."

Ria spun around to face her. Prithvi made the introductions. "This is my mother. Ma, this is our neighbour, Ria."

"Hi, Aunty," Ria said.

Vinodini beamed. "Oh, what a lovely surprise! I haven't seen neighbours in such a long time." She gave Prithvi a pointed look.

Prithvi laughed. "Well, here's your first."

Vinodini rolled her wheelchair closer. "Looks like my son has found an admirer for his painting. He loves children."

He pursed his lips and gave her another look. Could she stop throwing such obvious hints that she wanted grandchildren so bad?

Ria touched the wall. "The bats look so real." Then she pinched her nose as Daisy walked in with the fish. "And that fish smells terrible."

"My son loves National Geographic," Vinodini interjected. "You can tell by the things he watches and the things he draws. The latest are bats."

"Thanks for being such a showoff, Ma!" Prithvi turned to Ria. "Seen where a real bat lives?"

Ria giggled and shook her head. "Bats! Here?"

"Come on, let me show you." He stepped onto the terrace and pointed to the rooftop, to a dark, structural, square gap right below it. "Do you see that? There are bats in that crevice during the day."

She peered at the dark opening but couldn't make out anything. "How do you know?"

"I've seen a movement there, about dusk." He pointed upwards at the ceiling on his open balcony. "Do you see that hanging light? There are always droppings beneath that in the mornings. I knew there had to be bats around."

"I'll keep an eye out for them. Maybe I can see that crevice from my house too."

"There are pigeons and squirrels too on the balcony," his mother said, wheeling herself around to their side. "The plants that Daisy grows attracts them. She's got a penchant for people, plants and pets."

"So they've become like your pets?" Ria giggled.

It had been a long time since he had actually had fun talking to someone. "Yeah!"

She narrowed her eyes at him. "But do you have real pets?"

He knew she was teasing him. "Ah, smart!" he said, laughing. "Only one golden retriever called Taffy."

Ria's face fell as though she hadn't expected him to have any. "Really?"

"Used to. He's no more."

"Oh!"

"What about you?"

"I'd love a dog."

"Let me guess. You're not allowed to have one?" He grinned.

She pouted. "My mum says our apartment's too small."

"Ah, pets are so much work," Vinodini butted in, rolling her chair closer. "I wouldn't let Daisy keep one even if she wanted to."

Ria smiled sadly. "But they're really nice to have." Suddenly her eyes shot up to the clock on the wall. "Oh my gosh! It's late. Well, see you, Bruce." She shook hands with Prithvi again. "It was nice meeting you!"

Oh, so now I'm Bruce Wayne to you?! He smiled. "Prithvi."

She nodded and turned around, heading towards the door. "See you later. My mum must be waiting."

She shut their door behind her and to her surprise, ran straight into her mother who was standing just outside.

Neha was shocked to see Ria come out of their neighbour's house. "What were you doing there? Do you know how worried I was that you'd been gone so long?"

Ria entered her apartment which was open, followed by her mother.

"I would have thought you had more sense than entering strangers' homes," Neha admonished her, as soon as they had shut their door.

"They're our neighbours, Ma."

"You think I don't know that? But I'd have thought you'd behave more responsibly. You had been gone for so long. Didn't you know I would worry?"

"Could you stop worrying about everything?"

She grabbed Ria's shoulders and shook her. "I worry about everything. That's what moms do. Have you eaten, slept or taken a bath in all these days? Shouldn't I worry about you?"

"You're hurting me, Ma."

"*You* are hurting me. What happened was not my fault. Why don't we talk about what's going on with you?"

"There's nothing to talk about." She wiggled out of her mother's grip.

Neha let out a sob. "You're all I have."

"Is that my fault too?" She pushed Neha away and fled to her room.

"Ria!" Neha called after her but Ria slammed shut the door to her room, and silence reigned over the house once again.

6

In Chengannur, Kerala, squatting on the floor in his double-storied mansion, moneylender Thomachan, or Blade Thomachan, as he was known, was fixing the broken leg on his chair when his thoughts meandered to the Page Three news about the latest movie, *Bangalore Days* that had caught his eye only that morning. Another movie about Bangalore to become such a success, he thought, making a mental note. Now that he had a goal, every bit of related information made him stop whatever he was doing and pay attention.

He was fifty years old, cockeyed and pot-bellied. He knew his shortcomings, but all the wealth he possessed by virtue of whatever his deceased parents had left him—a string of shops lining the commercial street and money in excess to lend and multiply through bleeding interests—made him imagine that he was still very desirable as a groom. But who *he* desired was Indulekha.

This desire had cropped up recently. As recently as last week when Thomachan had gone to collect monthly dues from his shops on MC Road. Indulekha, the daughter of a vegetable vendor at one of his shops, was filling in for her sick father that morning and had asked him to come back the next day. Thomachan had never set eyes on her until then. She was a charming, chubby girl endowed with ample realty to bewitch anyone. In short, Thomachan had fallen in love at first sight but didn't know how to ask for her hand in marriage.

Thomachan had been through hundreds of proposals in his youth but either the girl had rejected him because she was too pretty or his parents had rejected her because she wasn't rich enough. For the last decade, since his parents' demise, Thomachan hadn't too seriously considered finding himself a bride. But lately, the feeling of loneliness had begun to bother him, especially at night, when the empty house and the large single-occupant bed led increasingly to sleeplessness.

"Then, why not choose a lady who's a little older?" his resident housekeeper cum driver, Shambu, had asked. But Thomachan wouldn't have just any woman. If he'd waited this long then she had to be worth every bit of it. She could be less endowed in every other way but beauty she had to have. That was the condition that had delayed his matrimony thus far. Till date he hadn't met anyone as beautiful as young Indulekha. He believed that meeting her was a sign that his life was finally about to change.

Getting her hand in marriage would not be easy, he knew. Indulekha's father, though not well-to-do, would never agree to get his daughter married to a man old enough to be her father. What should he do, he wondered.

As he was returning with the day's collections, his car slowed down in traffic, almost grinding to a halt, and he noticed a commotion next to Indu's vegetable shop. The chicken seller was flailing his arms around, trying to draw attention to the chickens that had somehow escaped from their coop. As Thomachan looked on, he saw a brood of chickens flying out of the shop and scurrying across the road. A tall and heavy boy thundered behind them, bringing the rest of the traffic to a halt. Presently, Indu came out of her shop to watch the show. The chickens scuttled all over the place, and two more boys gave them chase. It took a while for the three boys, with the help of more men on the street, to return all the birds to the coop.

"Who are these fellows?" Thomachan asked Shambu, who'd

been busy watching the couple arguing in the car ahead of them. Ever since the road widening project by the government had begun, the snarling traffic let Shambu enjoy snatches of such fun sights, on occasion.

"Who?" asked Shambu without averting his gaze.

"Those boys. They look familiar."

Shambu turned and peered in the direction of Thomachan's pointed finger. The chicken seller was scolding the trio. "Oh, that tall, fair boy is Manu, that rice trader Raman's son."

Indulekha was now laughing at them, her hands over her mouth.

"The fellow looks kind of handsome. Do you think my Indu fancies him?"

Shambu did a double take. "She's your Indu now?"

Thomachan blanched. "I can call her whatever I like when I'm with you. Just answer my question."

Shambu laughed heartily. "Don't know about that. But he's going to act in a movie, I heard. The short dark one, Aditya, went to some film making school in Chennai and he wants to direct a movie." Shambu snickered. "Bunch of idiots." The traffic eased and the car in front began to move.

"Why did you call them idiots?"

"I heard that Manu is being made the hero in the hopes that Raman will finance the movie but we all know that the miserly Raman will not put in a paisa even if it stars his own son."

"Have they found a producer?"

The car in front of them screeched to a halt and Shambu hit the brakes in frustration. "God knows," he replied, uninterestedly. "As far as I know they haven't found anyone and they probably never will. At least not in Chengannur. We don't even have a decent theatre here. Who has the money to make a movie?"

Thomachan rubbed his belly thoughtfully. The car ahead made a right turn. The road cleared up miraculously, and at that very moment Thomachan had an epiphany. "Shambu," he said, "ask that Aditya fellow to come see me at home."

"Why, Sir?" Shambu laughed. "Are you going to produce his movie now?"

"We shall see about that."

And so, Aditya was called to Thomachan's mansion the very next day. Now as he sat fixing his chair, Thomachan was thinking of how to put forth the very idea that would help his personal cause as well.

Aditya arrived on his battered cycle, puffing down the long, winding driveway flanked by the expansive, manicured lawns. He had never been to Thomachan's house before. He stopped in front of the massive house and gazed around at the impressive property, its compound lined with jackfruit and mango trees. Manu and Bobby arrived on Manu's dilapidated bike that his father wouldn't replace until Manu passed his BSc final exams. The perplexed boys stepped onto the porch and waited for Thomachan. All of last evening, they'd been discussing the matter. "Maybe the chicken guy didn't pay him the rent and he ratted on us," Manu said. "He thinks he can get my father to pay."

"Why would he call Aditya then?" Bobby said. "What if he wants to expand his business to Chennai and he thinks Aditya can help?"

"Nah!" Aditya said. "Maybe he's heard about the movie and wants a role for himself."

"You think he'll pay us for it?" Bobby asked excitedly.

In the end they decided they'd go together, and settle their curiosity once and for all.

Thomachan waddled out, looked at the waiting boys and took a seat on a bamboo lounge chair on the porch. "Sit, sit," he told the boys. "What will you have? Tea?" Without waiting for a reply, he called out, "Shambu, bring tea."

Twiddling his thumbs and shaking his feet, he eyed Aditya. "You want to make a movie, I heard?"

Aditya nodded, assuming the question was directed at him although he wasn't sure where the cockeyed Thomachan was looking.

"Yes, I have a script and I want to make a movie."

"And they are?" he asked, pointing at Manu and Bobby.

"Manu will be the hero. We still need a producer and more actors."

"I have a proposal for you." Thomachan licked his lips and smiled. "I want to produce your movie."

Aditya was stumped for a moment, not expecting a proposal. But he recovered quickly, almost sure that a role request would follow. Meanwhile Shambu arrived with the tea and *kozhukattas,* and lingered.

Thomachan hesitated before asking, "Do you have the heroine too?"

"Heroine?" He'd hardly expected Thomachan to discuss the heroine. "No, we need a lady to play the hero's mother but we don't have her."

"No, no," Thomachan said. "I'm asking about the heroine, you know, the hero's lover."

"No, Sir, it's not exactly a romance."

Thomachan looked surprised. "Romance sells! So why not make it a romance then, eh?"

What exactly was Thomachan getting at?

Thomachan chuckled and rubbed his hands in glee. "And I have just the person to fit the role." He glanced at the other two before he slowly dropped her name. "Indulekha! She can be the perfect heroine." He looked around for approval. "You know the one whose father has the vegetable shop on MC Road?"

Aditya choked on his tea, Bobby gulped down his *kozhukatta* whole, Manu's hand froze on his tea cup. A complete silence followed. It was the same Indulekha whose entire body had jiggled as she cackled nonstop at the boys' distress over the escaping chickens. She had caused so many stares and jeers that the frustrated chicken seller had finally told her off.

"What do you think?" Thomachan's voice boomed.

Aditya found his tongue first. "But she'll look like Manu's older sister. She won't fit the role."

Thomachan narrowed his eyes. "It's either Indu or I won't produce it."

Bobby swallowed a glass of water to wash down the *kozhukatta* stuck in his throat and piped in. "We'll get a better heroine than Indulekha, Sir."

"Yes, Sir," Manu added. "Why do we need Indulekha? We can get someone prettier."

Thomachan rubbed his belly. "You all know that I'm unmarried," he said, after a pause. "I'm convinced that if I offer her a role in my movie, her father will not refuse me her hand." He looked around at the surprised faces, and smiled, pleased at his ingenuity.

Bobby stuttered. "But…But she is a Hindu, Sir."

"A star has no caste," Thomachan retorted. "Doesn't a Christian play a Brahmin? Or a Muslim play a Hindu. If the movie becomes a hit why would her father care that she's a Hindu married to a Christian?"

"I can't ruin this movie, Sir," Aditya said. "With all due respect, we don't want your production."

Thomachan's eyes, pointing in starkly different directions, widened, and his mouth fell open. "What?!"

Bobby rushed to intervene. "Sir, give us a minute to discuss this." He huddled with the other two in a corner, out of earshot. "What's wrong with you?" he hissed at Aditya. "We need a producer. We'll tell Indulekha to go on a diet and we'll give her a tiny role. How does it matter?"

"Bobby, I knew you were dumb," Aditya said. "But I didn't know you were this dumb!" He slapped Bobby's head. "He'll change my script to give her a meatier role. Then he'll ask for a role for himself. For all you know, that's what's coming next. He'll want to be the hero."

Manu started pacing back and forth, raking his hands through his hair.

Bobby took a moment and sidled back to Thomachan. "Isn't it only for the heroine's role, Sir, that you ask?"

"Yes, yes," Thomachan replied, folding his hands across his chest. "That's all I want."

Bobby got back to the huddle. "I say we agree for now. He's only asking for Indulekha."

"I'm not going to do this!" Manu sulked. "I can't act opposite a...a baby *hippo!*"

Aditya groaned. "Oh, for God's sake, you two! Let me think."

Bobby held up his hands. "I may be dumb but I know how to grab an opportunity when I see a shiny one like this. Just say yes. He can't back out once he puts in his money."

It seemed imperative that Aditya agreed. He had had no luck whatsoever with the movie until now. They returned to Thomachan. "Okay," Aditya said reluctantly, and they shook hands.

"One more thing," Thomachan said. "You must do the shooting in Bangalore."

This time Aditya wouldn't stay quiet. "You may be the producer, Sir, but you cannot call all the shots. There is nothing to do with Bangalore in this movie."

Surprisingly, Thomachan's voice mellowed. "At least a few shots of Bangalore then?" he wheedled. "This will benefit us both. The highest grossers last year were movies that were shot in Bangalore or had something to do with Bangalore. I read it in the Movie Magic magazine. It will definitely make our movie a hit."

The words "our movie" calmed Aditya down a little but he still wasn't okay with the idea. However, there was a chance he could milk this opportunity since Thomachan seemed desperate. "I agree to all of the things you ask if I can have a fifteen per cent share of profits."

Thomachan did a double take. "Fif...Fifteen per cent?" His eyes danced wildly as though he was mentally calculating his loss. "I can consider about seven," he said, at length, scratching his jaw.

"Ten!" Aditya countered.

"Seven…seven is the last."

"Okay," Bobby said suddenly, pulling Aditya's hand and leading him away. "See you, Sir," he called over his shoulder to a pleased Thomachan. "Don't worry. Consider this a done deal."

Outside Thomachan's gate, Aditya was hopping mad. "What do you mean this is a done deal? For all this nonsense I'm putting up with, shouldn't I at least be getting a good deal? We have a new character and a shooting in Bangalore that has no place in the script."

"Look, you guys!" Bobby said. "I was just flattering the man. He won't know the difference if we took shots while driving through Bangalore or if we just covered an attraction or two. As of now, he's our only chance."

Manu nodded. "This will be a great chance to visit Bangalore." He raked his hands through his hair. "But I won't have Indulekha as my heroine."

Bobby pushed Manu's chest hard. Manu stumbled backwards. "Suck it up, dude!" Bobby said, glaring at him. "You may be handsome but in this case, it's not your dad coughing up the money for you to show off your dazzling good looks to the audience."

"You!" Manu charged towards Bobby, itching for a fight.

"Hey, cut it out!" Aditya shouted to the two. After all the trouble he'd been through in the last three months since he'd returned from Chennai with stars in his eyes, they weren't likely to find another willing producer. If he turned down Thomachan now, there was hardly a chance they were going to get a producer. "I don't see another way out," he said. "We've got to take this offer."

Bobby beamed. "That's what I was saying." He grabbed Aditya's hand. "And don't forget my commission in this deal."

"Your commission?" both Aditya and Manu yelled together.

"What did you think?" Bobby said. "If I hadn't smooth talked our way into this, Thomachan would have thrown us out a long time ago."

"What do you want now?" Aditya said, grumpily.

"A role. Any small role will do."

Aditya scoffed. "Manu's acted in college shows but you've got no acting talent to speak of. Why do you think I should take you on?"

Bobby pulled him aside and whispered into his ears, "What if I told Manu about your joy rides in his father's car with Priya, huh?"

Aditya felt his face grow hot. Only Bobby knew that Aditya and Priya, Manu's sister, were in love, and that Aditya had been going along in their car to drop Priya at college."

"You won't!" Aditya glared at him. The three had been friends since childhood. Surely Bobby wouldn't rat on him, right?

Wrong!

"Watch me." Bobby turned to tell Manu.

Aditya rushed to stop him. "Okay. Okay."

"Okay?"

"What's going on, you two?" Manu joined their private talk, curious.

"Nothing," Aditya snapped. "I'm giving Bobby a role in the movie for all the help he extended to us back there."

Bobby pumped his hands joyously. Manu looked grumpy.

"Who will I be?" Bobby asked Aditya, excitedly.

"Don't flatter yourself," Aditya said. "Maybe you'll just be…Manu's good-for-nothing friend."

"Yeessss!"

7

"This is our man?" Aditya said, horrified to see Vasu, who ran the local theatre and had promised Thomachan to arrange for the additional cast.

Vasu was a local drunk. Now chugging at his beedi, leaning against the wall of the roadside tea shop, he resembled an emaciated Santa Claus, with his long silver hair, flowing beard and twinkling eyes.

"Don't go by his present state," said Thomachan, who'd got Aditya along to be introduced to Vasu. "He's a brilliant actor himself. Have you seen *Kadal* starring Vasudevan Menon and Ponamma?"

Aditya shook his head.

"He is *that* Vasu," Thomachan said gloriously.

"Don't know him. That movie was probably released before I was even born."

"Exactly!" said Thomachan. "He hasn't acted in years. But I tell you, he's brilliant. Simply brilliant!"

"He can't even stand up." Aditya had never felt more demoralised in his life. First, a chubby thirty-year-old heroine and then, a drunk, casting director.

"He's my biggest hope," Thomachan confided in an undertone. "He runs a theatre group. He's got seasoned actors. When he's working, he never drinks. Anyway, we don't need him, only his group."

Aditya looked at him doubtfully.

"He's a good friend." Thomachan's voice dropped as he leaned in closer. "He's also a good marriage broker." He chuckled. "A good side business I must say. If he takes my proposal to Indu's home, her father can't refuse."

Throwing away the last of his beedi, Vasu crushed it underfoot and made his way towards them. "Don't worry about anything," he called out. "Thomachan has told me all about you. I read your script. It's very good. Top!" He raised his hand, and pinched forefinger and thumb. "You want mother, I got mother. You want sister, I got sister. You want whole village, I got that too. Come with me."

For all his unsteady stance, Vasu had a purposeful stride. He led them down the road. Two houses away was a dilapidated old house with a board hung on its door that read Vatsalya Drama Company.

Inside, was a room with bare walls; a few chairs were lined up against one of them. The single lamp hanging from the ceiling was switched on, swathing the damp and dingy place in pale, yellow light.

"I've called all the actors today," Vasu said, motioning Aditya and Thomachan towards the chairs. "They'll be here soon."

Slowly the actors began trickling in—a middle-aged, matronly-looking woman; a dark, light footed comedian with a thick mop of hair; a smiling, elderly man with grandfatherly looks and a young girl in her twenties with long, knee length hair. Presently the room filled up. There were also lots of onlookers and wannabe stars who had turned up in response to the news of the auditions.

Each aspirant was called to the centre of the room and given a sheet of dialogue to render. Some folks required repeated trials, some were quicker. Karthiani, the matronly woman, was the last for the day.

Standing at the centre of the room, she picked up her dialogue sheet. "Start, Sir?"

Aditya nodded.

Suddenly she started to wail and beat her chest. "Oh, my son! My son!" A few lines later, she began to cry, real tears flowing down rapidly. "I'm a widow," she continued, "and you villagers are like my family." She stopped to blow her nose noisily into the end of her saree and resumed. "You say my son is a criminal...my son...my son..."

"There's only one, 'my son,'" Aditya interrupted.

"Sorry, Sir, I couldn't remember the rest." She looked at the paper and started with the crying again. "You say my son is a criminal?" She pointed to the left side of the crowd. "You, Radha, bought him his first shirt to wear to school." Then she swung her hand to the opposite side. "You, Sarumma, you...you—"

"Let him play with your children," Aditya provided the line she'd forgotten.

She smiled gratefully. "Yes, you think he would rob your homes?" Here, her voice turned into a shriek. "Cheat you?"

Aditya raised his hand. "Okay, that's enough. Thank you, everyone. We're calling it a day. We'll continue tomorrow."

When he stepped outside the house and paused to breathe in the fresh air, Karthiani rushed to him, gushing. "How was my performance, Sir?"

Aditya smiled kindly. "I'll let everyone know as soon as all the auditions are over."

She stepped back, satisfied, and bowed graciously.

"I really need this role, Sir," Aditya heard her entreating Thomachan, who was coming up, behind. "I am a widow and I have two little children to feed."

"It's not up to me. It's the director's call," Thomachan said, sticking his nose up in the air and strutting on.

The next day, Indulekha came for the auditions. Thomachan blushed deeply as he offered her a chair. At her turn to say the dialogues, Indulekha twiddled with the hem of her top and turned extremely shy. She couldn't look up and her voice was barely audible. Aditya gave Thomachan a dark scowl. He returned a pleading look.

Indulekha turned out to be a disaster but Thomachan wouldn't budge from his conviction that Vasu would take care of her rehearsals and her shots could later be improved with editing.

Day two of the audition ended with Aditya still dissatisfied about the mother's role. Karthiani was their only decent option so far. However, not only was she melodramatic and brash but she also did not have the pathos that Aditya was looking for.

"Okay," Thomachan said. "I'm okay if you want time to find somebody else instead of Karthiani. Go ahead. We can give ourselves a month."

But no one turned up for the ads they put out in the local papers.

"Talent here is pretty substandard," Bobby said, mocking.

"Yeah right!" Aditya taunted him back.

While Thomachan and Vasu were scouting around for a house for the shoot, Aditya, Manu and Bobby decided to make the trip to Bangalore. "Yes, let's get that out of the way," Manu said.

8

Neha saw Daisy's Kuttan Sir sometimes, when she went to keep her garbage out or to take in the milk packets. According to Daisy, he was much happier with Daisy's cooking now. Daisy still called in for sugar and cooking tips once in a while. She said Kuttan Sir's behaviour had become more and more erratic, each day, since his movie had gone kaput, and he was painting all day on his walls, like crazy. Neha nodded indifferently, not asking further questions because she didn't feel like inquiring into the details of her neighbour's personal life.

To Neha, he seemed arrogant and unsociable. He did not even acknowledge her with a smile. She didn't offer the first smile either. She felt uncomfortable that he probably thought of her as the sister of the lady who'd scratched his car and then behaved rudely with him.

In one of her short bursts of conversation, Ria, who was still as reticent and grouchy as before, had said that he was a wonderful artist and was fun to talk to. That was hard to believe.

Her other neighbour, Mrs. Sharma, was quite the opposite. By now, her interest in Neha's personal affairs seemed to have waned, which was a relief, given that Neha was never in any presentable state when she called. After all, there was no further need to frequent Neha's house since Dr. Mohan was no more.

Neha felt like she was slipping into a haze again. Day blended into night and night into day, as she lost track of time. After the initial months of trying to get back to some sort of routine, she'd given up altogether. Ria wouldn't leave her room, except when she was leaving for or returning from school, and for her meals, and during these times she rarely made any conversation. All Neha's questions were answered in monosyllables or grunts. Neha didn't even feel like answering her parents' calls about what she was doing. How about, doing *nothing?* Yes, she wasn't doing anything.

The only person she looked forward to talking to was Shweta. Sometimes, to just hear Shweta's voice was enough. This time when Shweta called, Neha wept like a baby. She'd been telling her about Ria and her totally un-communicative behaviour.

"I think it's time you went back to school," Shweta suggested. "It's been almost three months now."

Ria had stayed home for about ten days, then on Shweta's insistence had started going to school—at first, a few days a week, then, full time. But Shweta had been unable to motivate Neha to get back to her old routine. "I don't feel like it," Neha said. "I don't feel like anything."

"Leave all that to me," Shweta said. "I'm coming over."

Later that day, Bhaskar, from Neha's old theatre group, called. "Hi Neha, our play is running at Atta Galatta tomorrow. Would you like to come?"

"Sorry, Bhaskar."

"Sorry to call you so late, Neha. We heard about Mohan."

She felt her throat tighten. "Thanks," she managed.

"Actually, there's also another reason I called," Bhaskar said.

That was surprising. Nobody had had anything to say but condolences for Mohan in recent times. "What's up?"

"We're starting a new play. We were thinking of you for a role."

Neha was stumped by the offer. It was most unexpected.

"Look, this is not a casual offer, Neha," Bhaskar said. "We're really looking for someone."

Neha thought about it for a moment. "Look," she said, finally, "Things are a bit out of whack at home. I don't want to dash your spirits but I don't think I can take it up."

"It's up to you. I didn't say that you had to say yes immediately. Take your time. Let me know by next week."

Neha hung up and checked her face out in the oval mirror that hung right above the chest of drawers. It had been a really long time since she'd acted on stage. Mohan's work timings had become so long and erratic that attending practice sessions in the evenings after work had become a pain. Added to that were Ria's growing up troubles and the fact that she could neither be left alone at home, nor be persuaded to accompany Neha to these sessions. Eventually Neha had fallen out of the group. Other than intermittent calls by Bhaskar, there had been no contact with them.

Could she still act now? Neha pulled her cheeks and made a face at the mirror. Then she raised one eyebrow, her expression like a question mark. If Mohan were here, he'd ask if she could still enact the *nava rasas* or nine emotions. She moved her eyes to mimic each of them—*Shringara* (love), *Hasya* (laughter), *Karuna* (sorrow), *Raudra* (anger), *Veera* (courage), *Bhayanaka* (fear), *Vibhatsa* (disgust), *Adbhuta* (wonder) and *Shanta* (tranquility)—widening, narrowing, rolling and squeezing her eyes into different forms. She laughed that she still remembered. It made her feel alive again, like a human being who was still living and breathing, not the half-dead, sulky woman that she'd been feeling like, lately.

Nah! she thought then, her shoulders slumping. It didn't feel right. Especially with Ria's current state of mind, the idea of going back to theatre looked highly impractical. In fact, silly of her to even consider it, even if Shweta would've badgered her to go, had she known about Bhaskar's call.

Shweta arrived that evening with an armload of new art supplies for Ria and a thick fancy sketchbook.

Ria opened her door to Shweta's call and hugged her ecstatically. Both of them talked for a bit about school and the other art supplies

Ria needed for a project. Neha watched them interact so effortlessly with a little twinge of jealousy. Why wouldn't her daughter open up to her? she wondered idly.

Suddenly, Shweta turned to Neha. "You should get back to school too."

Neha didn't know how to react and instead said, "Dinner's ready. Do you want to eat?"

Over dinner, Neha told Shweta that she had spoken to her school principal earlier. "The principal didn't sound all that excited. She asked if I was up to it, so soon."

Shweta patted Neha's hand. "You're just imagining things. Of course, she only wanted to give you all the time you needed. Plus, drama teachers can afford a longer break. But, now I think you're ready to get back into your routine. If you keep sitting at home, you'll never be able to move on…"

Neha stayed silent because Ria was with them, but her heart was screaming, "Can't you understand? I don't want to move on. I just want Mohan to be back here sitting where you are. I want my old life back." Instead, she sipped on some water and began clearing the table to hide her tears and give her mind something else to focus on.

Ria looked up from her soup. "What about you, Aunt S? Don't you feel like going to work?" She gave her a naughty grin.

Despite being unimaginably sad herself, Neha was truly happy to see the old spark in Ria revive in Shweta's company.

Shweta laughed. "Of course I work, Ria. Just because I'm with my husband at the café all day doesn't mean I'm not working. Our bookstore is doing extremely well and I'm there every day from morning till evening." She winked at Ria. "Niru sends his regards. He wanted to come with me to meet you but couldn't. You know how it is!"

"No, next time, we're coming to the restaurant to see him. I love the fish and chips there."

Shweta beamed. "Sure!"

"Talking of fish," Ria told Shweta, "Our neighbour and I were stuck with a fish vendor the other day, and when we got out, I told him he reminded me of Batman with the limp."

"You did not!" Neha interjected, horrified.

But Shweta was all smiles as Ria told her all about the meeting and the beautiful wall art in his house.

"He reminds me of the grouchy Amitabh Bachchan from *Mili*. You know that nose-up-in-the-air neighbour?" Neha said, when Ria finished talking about him. "Only, Bachchan is more handsome."

"At least, your neighbour is not Yama." Shweta chortled at her own joke.

"After hearing so much about him from Daisy, his mother's nurse, I'm no longer scared of him. For a long time, I thought he was going to make me pay for the damage you did to his car. These days, I'm privately amused whenever I see him."

"Tell me more," Shweta egged her on.

"Well, there's nothing to tell. He seems to be in some sort of trouble over a movie. According to Daisy, he behaves like a sulky child up to no good, and spends his time covering his walls with all kinds of paintings. He drives his mother crazy with paints strewn all over the house. She says she can't have guests over while he's walking around in nothing but paint splattered shorts."

Shweta leaned in. "So, how exactly does he make a living?"

Neha drank up the dregs of her soup. "He also has a fish export business, apparently, and he's often travelling between here and Kochi."

"Oh! Interesting guy," Shweta said, smiling.

"What's interesting? That he's either covered with paint or smelling like fish?"

Shweta mock-frowned. "Don't be so rude. He must be a billionaire with not much to do."

They all burst into laughter, and the mood at the dining table instantly lightened.

After dinner, they settled down to watch *Ever After*, Ria and Shweta's favourite fairy tale adaptation.

Things seemed to be looking up finally. Neha was glad that Shweta had managed to draw Ria out. And for the first time in several months, Neha realised that she was looking forward to school.

9

The Monday she was returning to school started off like most Mondays before the tragedy, three months ago. Lunches were packed. Neha was ready but Ria was still in her bedroom.

Neha knocked on her door. "Ria, have breakfast. It's almost time for school."

There was no reply but faint sounds that sounded like sobs, came from the inside. Neha checked the door. It was unlocked. She opened it and entered the room. Ria, still in her nightclothes, her hair uncombed, lay sprawled on her bed crying her heart out.

"Ria!"

Ria's sobs and hiccups grew louder. Neha patted her back and tried to calm her down. She was at her wit's end. Should she and Ria take an off today? She was on the point of calling Shweta and asking her what to do, when a few minutes later, Ria's sobs subsided and she lifted herself up.

"Ria," Neha said, softly. "Talk to me. Don't you want to go to school?"

To her surprise, Ria flung herself at her chest and hugged her tight. "I miss Papa," she said, amid hiccups.

I miss him so much too, Neha thought. But she had to hold her own tears in check, in front of Ria. She took a deep breath. "That's why we're going to school," she said, smoothing down Ria's hair. "We have to do something. Sitting at home and thinking about Papa will not bring him back."

Ria said nothing.

"If you want to skip school," Neha said at last, "we'll stay at home."

That worked. Ria straightened, shook herself and got off the bed. "I'd rather go to school."

They had missed the school bus by the time Ria got ready, so Neha dropped her off in an auto and proceeded on her way.

The sight of the school gates brought a sense of gladness. Neha was happy to be back.

When she entered her staffroom, the teachers stopped what they were doing and all eyes were on her. She let out a weak smile. Immediately, the teachers gathered around her. Some gave her a hug, some offered condolences, some said meaningless things. Just before class was to begin, she was summoned to the principal's office.

The principal, Mrs. Sulochana, was an impeccably turned out woman, her stiff, starched saree pinned tautly to her blouse, her hair pulled up into a knot.

She offered Neha a seat and steepled her fingers before she began. "I offer you my condolences again, and I understand that your class missed you very much, Ms. Neha." She smiled kindly, but something didn't feel right.

Neha smiled back apprehensively.

"With our annual day coming up it was imperative," Mrs. Sulochana continued, "that we did not neglect the play until the last minute."

Neha nodded. "I hope I'm not too late, Ma'am. I understand it's been three months but we'd finished quite a bit of practice so I'm sure we can catch up fast."

"I hope you understand that we could not take a risk while you were gone." The principal paused. "While we knew you'd come back, we really didn't know when."

Neha felt sweat collect on her upper lip.

"So, we took the liberty of appointing a new drama teacher." She raised her hand as Neha made to interrupt. "Of course, we're not asking you to go. We've made arrangements so that you can assist her until the end of the year and then we'll take it from there."

Neha's chest fell and she felt a slight tremble in her legs. She hadn't thought of this possibility.

The principal's voice fell a pitch lower. "We're sorry we had to make that decision, Ms. Neha. You see, our hands were tied."

Neha nodded as calmly as she could. "Yes, Ma'am." Her insides were churning so violently by then that she barely made it out of the office without bringing on a meltdown right there.

Bracing herself to meet her students, Neha gathered her composure and walked up to the old drama room. Her class was practising Tweedledee and Tweedledum with their new teacher, Ms. Renu, with a bright red lipstick, big red bindi and a Bengal cotton saree bunched carelessly over her heavy bosom. The twins, Harmeet and Sukhmeet, were holding onto each other's shoulders and going round and round in circles to the song Neha had so painstakingly put together and recorded. When they stopped and nodded their heads together, Neha couldn't help the overwhelming sting in her eyes. She had barely stifled her tears when Ms. Renu turned around and saw her.

"You must be Ms. Neha," she said, giving her a toothy smile.

Neha entered. A cacophony erupted when the children saw her. "Miss…Miss," they cried, hovering around her. Soon everyone was clinging to her and smiling from ear to ear.

"I think the play you'd chosen for the Annual Day is alright, Ms. Neha," Ms. Renu said, once the children had settled down. "But I would have chosen Alice in Wonderland instead."

Neha gave her a feeble smile.

"But since so much practice was already done, I thought I'd add more unique characters to the play instead."

She told the children to take a five-minute break and brought the script over to show Neha. She sat down and looked earnestly into Neha's eyes. "Actually, I thought it would be a great idea to bring Gingerbread Man into Wonderland to meet Alice and the entire cast, you know?" She paused. "But then everyone seemed so disappointed at losing their existing roles that I just added a few more roles to make them all happy." She was bubbling with excitement as she spoke. Her eyes twinkled, she clasped her hands together. "Something like, what if Gingerbread Man ran into Mary and her lamb and he followed her to school, you know? Or, what if he rolled down the hill with Jack and Jill too? Don't you think they're wonderful ideas?"

Neha nodded. She had also intended to have Gingerbread Man meet Miss Muffet, Humpty Dumpty, the hare and the tortoise, Tweedledee and Tweedledum, and eventually the fox whom he persuades not to eat him. She would have added more roles herself had she been around all this time. "Yes, the more the merrier," she said, resignedly.

"And not have the fox, perhaps? It would probably scare the children, you know?"

"Then whom will you have?"

"Thought I'd add Little Teapot and make Gingerbread Man fall into it at the end instead."

That sounded ghastly. But it hardly made a difference what she thought, now that things were out of her hands.

"I'm going to need all your assistance," Ms. Renu continued. "I'd like you to be the first to give me feedback and help with all the costumes. I'm so happy you're back." With that, she gave Neha another toothy smile and seated her in the front to watch the entire performance from the beginning.

The children gathered around again in a circle and started over.

Neha called Shweta at the end of the day. "Life is so unfair," she began. "I could tell that the children were so confused to see me there doing practically nothing except clapping for their performances. It was disheartening and…I don't know…humiliating to say the least. I just can't do this."

"We need to talk about this," Shweta said. "Meet me at the mall for coffee?"

"What about Ria? She'll be home soon."

"You'll be back home before she does. Come on?"

There was an hour before Ria got back from her school. Enough time to get a load off her chest, Neha decided.

At the coffee shop in the mall, Shweta put down her cup of coffee and eyed Neha sceptically after she'd heard everything about what had happened at school. "But you've got to have something to do, right?"

Neha shook her head. "I want the dignified thing to do. Not play some second fiddle to another teacher who thinks she's creative just because she added a few roles to my script. I wish I could just chuck the job and shove it up their asses."

Shweta emptied her coffee cup. "Calm down! We'll figure something out."

That is when Neha told her about Bhaskar's offer. She'd meant it as a joke but Shweta picked it up immediately. "Well, there you go! You could go back to theatre for a while."

Neha's mind was thrashing around with that idea when it happened.

There was a loud crash. A young man had fallen down, striking the glass of the café. There was a camera slung around his neck. Blood oozed from his nose and he was writhing in pain. Two of his friends hovered over him, struggling to help.

Without thinking, Neha shot up, swung the door open and ran to the men's aid. Shweta followed.

The trio were new to Bangalore. "Can you please direct us to the nearest hospital?" one of them asked Neha.

"I've brought my car," Shweta said. "I can get us there quickly."

They bundled the injured person into the car and rushed to Sakra

Hospital.

10

The next thing Aditya knew was the feeling of opening his eyes to an expanse of whitewashed wall and the smell of disinfectant. As he focused his eyes, he saw the woman he'd been watching at the café. She was hovering over him, looking at him with deep concern. Moments later, he passed out again.

When Aditya regained consciousness, his friends and two women were staring at him. Aditya recognised her because of her eyes. He couldn't forget those beautiful, kohl-lined, expressive eyes. He'd finally found the person he'd been looking for, for the role. At the mall to capture some casual shots for Thomachan, he'd seen her. The slant of her eyes and the sorrow they held had caught his attention first. She had been in a deep discussion. The gravitas in her face and the heaviness in the slump of her shoulders conveyed a deep sense of loss.

"What is your—" she started to ask him but the doctor walked in and she turned to him.

"Hello, Mrs. Mohan," the doctor said to her. "How are you doing?"

She looked surprised at the doctor's recognition.

"Hi, I'm Dr. Deepankar," the doctor introduced himself. "I

interned under Dr. Mohan. I'm so sorry, Mrs—"

"Thank you, doctor." She gestured to the patient. "Is he going to be okay?"

The doctor walked over to the bed and read the patient's report. "Mr. Aditya Shankaran. Mild concussion and broken nose. Low BP."

He scribbled a prescription and handed it to Bobby. "We'll keep him under observation for twenty-four hours. We'll discharge him as soon as he's fit to leave." He signed another paper for admissions and gave it to Manu. "Please take care of the arrangements."

He checked Aditya's pulse and heart rate and, satisfied, he turned to leave. On the way out, he turned to Neha. "Good to see you again, Ma'am."

After the doctor left, introductions followed and Aditya turned to Neha. "Thank you for bringing me here," he said.

"How did this happen?" Neha asked.

His head hurt and his throat felt dry. He looked at Manu for help to explain.

"We were in the mall to get some casual shots," Manu said. "We're from Kerala. Aditya is a director. We saw him moving towards the café. Next thing, we heard a loud bang and saw him fallen on the floor."

"I...I didn't see the glass," Aditya said. "I was too busy capturing...a face on my camera." Then he gave out a cry, and turned towards his friends. "Is my camera okay?"

"It's safe," both responded in unison.

Soon, leaving him with the two women, Bobby and Manu left to take care of the admission and prescriptions.

Aditya looked at Neha surreptitiously, wondering how to broach the subject he'd been dying to, since he regained consciousness. She was fiddling with her purse. Something seemed to be bothering her. Her forehead still wore the creases from the worried frown he'd noticed earlier at the mall.

He couldn't believe he'd been so lucky to have seen her, and brought here by her, of all people. His intuition had never failed him before. He recognised a good actor when he saw one. He just knew who would look good behind the camera, who could emote, who could make you cry just by looking at you with tear-filled eyes. She was the one. Beautiful. Graceful. Captivating. She was the one he'd been searching for all this time.

"So," Shweta said, trying to joke, "who enthralled you so much that you didn't see the glass?"

Aditya glanced at Neha for a moment before pointing towards her. "Her," he said, feeling nervous.

Neha eyed him curiously. "Me?"

Aditya cleared his throat and felt his face go hot. "I was shooting some casual shots for my film and I ended up noticing you. You have striking eyes. I saw you turning away from the camera so I came closer but I didn't see the glass."

Neha's cheeks turned red.

Shweta laughed. "That's our Neha. She used to be a theatre performer. Her eyes are her biggest assets."

Neha's eyebrows furrowed. "I don't understand what you're saying."

"You fit the person I was looking for to play the mother's role in my movie."

"Mother's role?" Shweta interrupted, grinning. "She's never played that before."

Suddenly, as if she had remembered something, a look of horror crossed Neha's face and she checked her watch. "Sorry, we have to leave," she said anxiously. "See you around, Aditya. Get well soon and please be careful next time."

Aditya put his hand up to stop her. "Ma'am?"

She paused and looked at him. "Neha, please."

He hadn't been able to take his eyes off her face. His heart fluttered as he met her gaze. "Would you consider acting in my movie?"

Neha looked startled. "I—I wasn't expecting this...an offer like this," she said, fumbling for words. "But I'm sorry. I'm not up to it."

Shweta looked at both with her mouth open. She was speechless.

Aditya moved his head and winced. "Sorry, I can't pitch my movie so well in this condition. But if you leave a number, I could get in touch with you." He looked at Neha hopefully.

"I'm sorry this is not a great time. I must leave now," she said softly. Then she grabbed Shweta's hand and hurried out.

"I'll be here until tomorrow if you change your mind," Aditya called out from behind her. But she had left. He wanted to get up and run after her but all he could do was squeeze his eyes shut and groan as he lay immobile on the hospital bed. His head throbbed, his nose hurt, but he didn't care about any of that. His accident was nothing compared to seeing Neha, to finally finding the one who would be perfect for the role. He wished he had more time to show her the script and convince her. But he'd lost his only chance and would probably never see her again. His friends and he were leaving for Kerala as soon as he was discharged. He let out another long groan. She was gone, and he did not have her address or her number. How would he ever find her again?

11

When Neha reached her apartment still thinking about the strange offer from Aditya, she half-expected to see Ria slouching on the staircase, spewing anger because she was half-an-hour late. But to her surprise, Ria was nowhere to be seen. Neha immediately regretted not giving Ria a spare key. She was old enough now to get into the house by herself, but, of course, this was the first time Neha had ever been late.

She didn't know why she thought to check next door but she automatically rang her neighbour's doorbell. Prithvi answered the door. His hair was a mess, the scar on his cheek looked particularly long and scary, and his shorts looked like they'd seen too many Holi festivals. His face was hard like she'd caught him in a foul mood.

"Is my daughter here?" Neha blurted out instead of putting the question across nicely.

Prithvi looked like he could bite off her nose. "No! She isn't here!"

Still the acerbic, angry neighbour. She shook her head. "Sorry!"

He slammed his door shut.

Neha immediately regretted her curt tone. She wished she'd developed better relations with her new neighbours. It would have helped to ask them to keep Ria when she was delayed.

She went down to the ground floor to ask the security guard. But he hadn't seen the bus, he said, and he most certainly hadn't seen Ria.

She called a few of Ria's friends. They'd all seen her leave by the bus after school.

Neha began to panic and called Shweta, then broke down the moment Shweta answered.

"What happened?" Shweta asked.

"Ria hasn't come home."

Shweta told her to calm down and look in a few more, obvious places: the park, the stationery shop, the library down the road, or Mrs. Sharma's house. She said she'd come over immediately.

By the time Shweta arrived, Neha had searched in all those places and returned home, alone. Ria was nowhere to be found.

The doorbell rang. Neha rushed to get it.

Shweta was at the door, her eyes looking troubled. "First, let me make you a cup of tea. We both need one."

Finally with the tea, she sat down next to Neha and cleared her throat. "Ria's with Ma," she said, her voice straining to say the words.

Neha gasped and clamped her mouth. "What? How? When?" She was shocked yet relieved at the same time.

"I called Ma on the way over and she told me. She said she didn't know Ria hadn't told you."

Neha dragged her fingers across her cheeks and let out a deep breath. "Oh my God! She drives me absolutely nuts. Why didn't she tell me?"

"She wants to stay with Ma and Papa for a few days. She took the school bus to Sarjapur Road instead of the usual one. Ma says she's not talking much."

Neha pulled up her knees and buried her head between them. "Why is she punishing me?"

Shweta stroked Neha's head. "She's taken it harder than we imagined. This house is a terrible reminder, perhaps. Maybe staying away will be good for her. Good for both of you."

Neha lifted her head; she wiped her tears and blew her nose. "I want to talk to her."

"It would be better if you didn't speak to her immediately. Ma said to send some of her clothes and uniforms. She can take the school bus from there for a week or two." Shweta squeezed Neha's hand. "She'll be fine if you let her be for a few days."

Neha looked at Shweta through blurry eyes. "Tell me, am I a terrible mother?"

Shweta smiled. "You are a strong, kind and wonderful mother and human being."

After Shweta left, Neha felt a strange kind of emptiness. Three months ago, she had everything. A loving husband, a job she loved, a beautiful home, a sweet, kind, twelve-year-old daughter. Now, all of a sudden, she had nothing. Mohan was no more. Ria was gone. She had no job. No future. What was she to do with herself? If only she could make the pain and emptiness disappear.

That evening, she watched TV, made a bowl of Maggi and ate it in the kitchen. Then, to do some thinking, she headed to her room and began to clean out her closet. After she was finished, she checked her watch. Only two hours had passed.

She switched on the TV again. Her favourite soap was on. The dialogues had been her favourite for years. Funny, weepy, catchy… She repeated them verbatim. It had been a fun pastime of hers in the past. As she spoke, her voice echoed. Suddenly the walls seemed to be closing in on her. It gave her goosebumps to be talking inside an empty house. After a few minutes, she switched off the TV.

The living room fell quiet. Too quiet. She stared at the spot where Mohan had lain on the floor, just two feet from where she was sitting right now. She felt Mohan stare at her from across the room. Her heart began to race wildly. The curtains billowed in the breeze. The trees behind the window cast dark shadows into the night. She should have drawn the curtains at dusk, but to do that now she would have to cross that spot, and her legs froze. Her feet were cold. She shivered slightly.

Her heart beat harder and louder. She was petrified.

Before she lost her mind, she made a run for it, dashing into her bedroom, and locked her door from the inside.

Only once safe inside her room, did she pause to take a breath. Then she realised that her phone was outside and that her throat was parched. She needed a glass of water but was now too scared to step out of her room. She wondered if she would last until morning. She quickly brushed her teeth and changed, got between the covers and squeezed her eyes shut. She said her prayers and tried to sleep with the night lamp on. It took her a long time to calm down and finally drift off to sleep.

The next morning she was crouched into a nervous ball on the couch, and weeping into the phone to Shweta. "I can't do this."

She'd slept badly and her head felt heavy.

"I can't live here alone and I don't want to go stay with Ma." She'd had no luck with talking to Ria that morning either. She'd called her mother but by then Ria had already left for school. "I have no job, my daughter doesn't want me, and I'm shit scared to live alone. Basically, my life is worthless and pitiful."

"You need a break," Shweta said.

"What do you suggest I do? I can't bear the thought of going back to my school again."

"Ria should come back in a few days when she's tired of her grandma. Why don't you look for another job in the meantime and come stay with me for a while?"

Neha groaned. "For how long? And how will it not be the same as living with Ma?"

"Or," Shweta suggested, "How about going on a trip? Haven't you always dreamt of travelling?"

"Travel? With whom? Where? When I want something badly I never get it. By the time I've got it, I don't want it anymore. That's the story of my life!"

There was silence at the other end.

"Shweta, are you still there?"

"Where did those boys say they were from?" Shweta asked.

"Which boys are you talking about? And why are you changing the subject?"

"I'm not changing the subject," Shweta said, sounding hurt. "Back in the day, when Ria was young, you couldn't leave her alone even for theatre practice. Now, a brilliant chance has fallen in your lap and you don't even want to consider it?"

"What brilliant chance? Look, I don't feel like calling Bhaskar."

"I'm talking about the movie. Those young men from the mall."

She snorted. "Aditya? He reminded me of Guru Dutt from *Kaagaz Ke Phool!*"

"And you're like the actress Waheeda Rehman! So?" Shweta sounded miffed. "Shouldn't you give it a try?"

"How can I leave Ria and go?"

"You're forgetting that Ria isn't with you now," Shweta said. "And can't she stay at Ma's a little longer if it's required? I don't understand why you should be so worried for her. She's old enough now. Can't you put yourself first for once?"

"But—"

"Wouldn't Mohan have wanted you to go for it?" Shweta asked, softly.

Neha let out a sigh. "Yes. He would've been thrilled."

"Just what I thought."

Neha could tell that she was smiling.

"Now do something meaningful for yourself," Shweta persisted. "See if there's a chance in there for you. Those fellows will still be at the hospital if you hurry."

By the time Shweta had hung up, Neha was so worked up she didn't know what to do. She could live an aimless life or she could take a chance. Once she'd made up her mind about wanting to do something rather than wasting her life, she pushed away the nagging thoughts and decided to go to the hospital. She didn't want to raise her hopes too high or overthink this. If Aditya was still there, she'd find out about the role. But by then, she had spent so much time fretting about it that she was afraid it was already too late. What if they had left? What if she never saw them again?

Without delaying any further, she dressed and hurried to the hospital.

But when she reached there, she learned that Aditya had already been discharged. She'd lost him.

She returned home, disappointed.

12

As Neha stepped out of the elevator onto the fifth floor, there, to her utter surprise, were the three men standing right by her door. Bobby was helping Daisy with Vinodini's wheelchair and Manu and Aditya were listening to Vinodini with rapt attention. "Oh, you people are making a movie?" Vinodini was saying and smacking her lips. "I used to be an actress once upon a time."

The boys turned around and saw Neha.

Aditya moved too quickly to shake her hand, then stopped and touched his bandaged nose.

"Are you okay? she asked. "How in the world did you find me?"

Aditya smiled sheepishly. "Remember Dr. Deepankar, the duty doctor? We asked him for your address when we were leaving."

"We wanted to thank you personally for helping us," Manu added.

"Oh, no need for thanks," said Neha, blushing. She couldn't believe the boys had found her.

Vinodini carried on, unmindful of the lost attention. "I can still act, you see?"

The men turned to her and nodded.

Shortly, Daisy wheeled Vinodini into her house, while Neha

unlocked her door and invited the men in.

They sat on the couch. Neha sat facing them on the opposite side. Aditya cleared his throat. "We didn't know your husband had passed away. We're very sorry for your loss."

"Thank you. It was very recent," Neha said, with a sad smile.

Aditya rummaged in his bag and came up with a folder. "Actually, the real reason we came was to show you the script." He handed it to Neha. "We thought it might help you come to a decision."

Neha's hands shook slightly as she accepted it.

"This story too is about loss," Aditya said. "We'd be very happy if you read it and told us what you thought."

She nodded.

Aditya rose from the couch. "We'll be back by evening."

By evening? Wasn't that too soon, she wondered. Would she be done reading it by then? But the boys were already at the door, ready to leave. Aditya glanced at her one last time, his eyes full of hope. "Hope we haven't troubled you."

She shut the door after they'd left, then flopped on the couch and began to read the script.

Two hours later, she closed the folder and gave it a pat.

The first thing she did after that was to call Shweta.

"That's so cool," Shweta said, excited, when Neha called her to give her the news of how the men had found her. "And did you read the script? What did you think?"

"I loved the story," Neha said.

"I want to hear it. What's it about?"

"It's about a single mother who hopes her unemployed son will give up his idle ways. The son robs his neighbour's gold to go to the Gulf to find a job. He intends to return the money after he finds a job but fate has other plans for him. Some thieves steal his money and throw him into a river from where he flows into the sea. The movie is part-fantasy where a sea spirit saves him and he returns in an invisible form to avenge his attack and clear his name. He returns the gold and is welcomed back by the villagers for catching the real thieves, finally proving to be a worthy son."

There was a brief silence before Shweta went, "Are you playing the single mother?"

"Yes," Neha said, feeling silly with happiness. "It feels great to have such an important role. The mother and son are the central characters, and it's about having faith, and righting the wrongs."

"It sounds like a great fantasy meets real-life drama," Shweta said.

"Yeah, you know, I think it's going to be an amazing story."

"The only thing I can't understand is," Shweta said, "why couldn't he have gotten someone older to play the mother's role?"

Neha laughed. "I'll be sure to ask him that." Then on a serious note she said, "Now, I only worry about Ria."

"She'll be perfectly alright. Don't worry about her."

When Shweta had hung up, Neha's thoughts went back to the script. The story had struck a chord with her because it was a back-from-the-dead story. She wished Mohan's death were a dream and she didn't have to deal with it alone. His death had jolted her out of her complacence.

Pulling up her knees and resting her chin on them, she wondered what she would have done differently had she known Mohan was to die so soon. Thoughts of Ria came rushing back. What might Ria have wanted to do differently for her father?

Hoping to get some of her worries off her chest, she dialled her mother's number.

Her mother picked up on the first ring as if she'd been waiting for Neha's call. "I know you're missing Ria. It would be good to give her some time."

"Ma, is it okay if Ria stayed with you for longer?"

"Of course, Neha! Prabhu and I love her company."

"Does she talk to you?"

"Not that much, but you know Prabhu." Her mother laughed. "He loves to talk to her. She's warming up slowly."

"I'm glad to hear that."

"Is something the matter? You sound a bit lost."

Her mother had a keen sense for detecting anything out of the ordinary. Neha told her about the movie proposal.

When Neha finally finished telling her how it had all come about, her mother said, "Neha, some chances are meant to be grabbed when they come. Besides, it will take your mind off things that are troubling you."

"But, Ma, it's only been three months since…" Neha's voice caught in her throat. She couldn't bring herself to say, "Mohan's death." Her emotions were too raw.

Her mother surprised her by saying exactly what Shweta had said. "Wouldn't Mohan have wanted you to take the offer? Go for it, Neha," she urged. "Follow your heart."

Aditya, Manu and Bobby were back that evening. Neha could see Bobby hiding something behind his back.

When Bobby saw her eyeing him curiously, he passed that thing from behind his back to Aditya's back.

Neha asked, "What is that?"

Aditya brandished a bouquet and offered it to her sheepishly. "Thanks for everything."

"It's beautiful," Neha said graciously.

"The bouquet was my idea," Bobby said quickly.

Manu pinched his behind. "You were going for teddy bear and chocolates."

"I was not!" Bobby went red in the face. "That was because Aditya couldn't find the florist."

"And I was the one who found one," Manu said.

"And then I said the bouquet was a great idea," Bobby said, sounding pleased with himself.

Manu thwacked him on the head.

"Ouch!"

"Okay guys, enough!" Aditya said, firmly. He looked at Neha

apologetically. "This is from all of us."

Neha raised her eyebrows. "Is this for positive feedback on the script?"

"No, no. No!" they all shouted together.

"Just kidding," Neha said. "Thank you very much."

The boys sat down while she got them tea. "Now I have a confession to make," she said, finally.

The boys looked at each other, worried expressions on their faces.

"I came looking for you at the hospital this morning, coincidentally right after you'd left. I was just lucky that *you* found me."

Aditya, Manu and Bobby looked up together and hope shone in their eyes.

"I have a daughter whom I can't leave alone for very long. I mean she's currently with my mother. But other than that—"

Aditya gave out a whoop. "Does it mean you liked the script?"

Neha nodded. "Actually, I loved it." Her eyes teared up. "But can I ask you why you didn't choose an older woman to play the mother?"

"We think you'd be perfect. A little makeup can go a long way, and we wanted someone who could be an easy prey for the village folk after her son had gone missing. We needed someone graceful and beautiful."

She accepted that with a smile. Aditya sounded like he knew exactly what he wanted and what he was doing.

Aditya leaned forward and rubbed his hands. "So, now that you're comfortable, you don't have to worry about it taking too long to shoot. We're talking about forty days for the entire shooting, and about twenty for your part, at the most. We'll be at a location near Kochi. So it won't be a long stay away from home or too far away."

Shweta was also gung-ho on hearing that things were moving in the right direction and she told Neha exactly the same thing that her mother had. It felt so good to have her family on her side and so concerned about her. All they wanted was for Neha to slowly and steadily move out of mourning and take back the reins of her life. Neha felt much lighter in the chest when she called her mother that evening, to speak to Ria.

This time Ria, herself, answered the phone. "Hi, Ma." Her voice sounded a little subdued.

"Look, dear," Neha said. "I didn't call to scold you for going away to Grandma's without telling me."

"Sorry, Ma."

"Ria, I'm going away to Kochi for a while. Will you be okay with Grandma for a month or so?"

"Is it a new job?"

"Yes."

"I'm happy for you, Ma."

And that was it.

When Neha hung up, she realised with a pang that she had mixed feelings about leaving Ria and going away by herself. Was it too soon? She began feeling guilty about being excited but pushed away her misgivings. She had to start somewhere. Maybe the Almighty was giving her that chance by literally dropping this offer in her lap.

Shweta came over to stay for a few days, while Neha packed her bags for the trip. The house help was given an off. Mrs. Sharma's questions had to be fielded. The lady was a bloody gossip newspaper. Anything she heard, she wanted to know everything about it. She settled on the couch one evening before Neha's departure and shot her mouth off.

"I hear you're going away for a month. Do you have relatives in Kochi?" [In Mrs. Sharma-speak: *I wouldn't be travelling alone if I were you. Wait till my friends hear.*]

"What about Ria?" [*You'll leave her by herself?*]

"And they gave your job to someone else?" [*I didn't know drama teachers were in so much demand.*]

Of course, Neha hadn't told Mrs. Sharma yet that she was going to act in a movie. That could wait.

The day of her trip to Kochi finally arrived. Neha's family thought it was for the best and that was what mattered. Even Mohan would have been proud. Neha knew in her heart, despite the misgivings and the guilt and the pain of not seeing Ria for a month, that she was thankful for the new experience and was looking forward to it. If nothing else, it would give her something to focus on other than the dull constant ache that Mohan's passing had left her with.

13

Somewhere deep down, Prithvi had a vague feeling that things were not right. Industry circles were rife with gossip that he was difficult to work with. The media had only fuelled this negative image. Since the debacle of his half-finished movie, all the directors who'd once wanted to work with him, had backed out. He hadn't been able to start any new projects since then.

"Sit, young man. What brings you here?" KD asked.

Prithvi was in KD's office, sitting across his desk, looking straight into his glinting, brown eyes. "You want to tell me why I'm suddenly out of work?"

KD leaned forward. "Look, all this takes time. We have to win back people's confidence."

Prithvi wiped the sweat off his brow. "People have started taking back their scripts."

"Look, if it's worrying you that much, I'll ask around." He gave him a warm smile. "Rest easy, young man. This business can't be rushed. You need the perfect script and perfect timing. Sometimes, mishaps happen. But you've got to let it go, and move on."

Prithvi nodded, though KD's words didn't give him much hope right now!

KD came around to him and put a hand on his shoulder. "I know you're a little shaken up. Tell you what?" He looked warmly into his eyes. "I've got a new script. It's a new writer but his screenplay is amazing. That's what my team tells me. How about I pass it on to you?"

Prithvi thought about that for a moment. After the first movie had shut down, he wasn't about to bet on new talent. He wanted to take on someone known. Possibly a big name to make up for his current losses.

"I can co-produce if you want someone to back you up, give you more confidence." KD held his gaze as he spoke. "I'm just finishing up one project and I don't want this script to go away to someone else. What do you say?"

"I'll take a look at the script," Prithvi said, finally. "But I need a little time to think this through."

KD laughed. "Up to you, young man! What you need is some relaxing time and a good break. Oliver and I will be at the club this weekend. Join us there. It'll help to get your mind off things." He patted him on his back and saw him out of the office.

At the club that weekend, KD introduced Prithvi to his friend, Oliver Kalra. Oliver had a Christian mother and a Punjabi father, thus the uncommon name. He was a jovial man, dressed in white shirt and slacks. He was around KD's age, but with a shocking mop of white hair that hid his ears. He reminded Prithvi of the renowned filmmaker, Adoor Gopalakrishnan.

Prithvi was towelling off after a brief swim when KD and Oliver joined him after a game of squash, in which KD had lost.

Oliver shook hands with Prithvi. "KD has never introduced me to a friend in the business in all these years. You and KD must be close."

KD scrubbed the back of his neck with a towel. "Yes, I've known Prithvi's family since childhood. His mother, actually."

Prithvi settled on one of the lounge chairs. "I've never heard about how you met her," he said, curious. His mother could talk of no one else but KD nowadays, but Prithvi had not thought of asking her how they'd known each other. "How do you know my mother?"

KD shook his head and laughed. "That's a very old story. Our families used to be neighbours before your mother's marriage. My father and she were childhood friends. When I graduated from film school, I went to Vinodini Bai looking for references for work."

KD called Prithvi's mother "Vinodini Bai," which used to be her screen name. Surprisingly though, Prithvi had never heard about KD when he was younger.

"Vinodini Bai introduced me to her father-in-law," KD continued, wiping his face, then letting the towel hang around his neck. "The well-known Bharathan Nair of the famous Priyamvada Productions. But Bharathan Nair refused to take me."

"That's a shame," said Oliver, mockingly.

But Prithvi was suddenly interested. "I didn't know you knew my grandfather."

"Oh yes, I did," KD said. "He told me he wasn't interested in taking on a newcomer. Or maybe, he didn't like me and didn't want to tell me that, to my face."

Oliver laughed. "His loss, as we all can see."

KD nodded. "I agree."

"And you're helping me now?" Prithvi smirked.

KD shrugged. "Didn't want to hold on to old grudges."

***

At home, Daisy too hadn't been herself lately, Prithvi noticed. Her face was swollen like a ripe tomato.

One day as he was sitting down to breakfast, he heard Daisy in the bathroom, humming a sad, old Malayalam song as she gave Vinodini a bath. She'd left some gooey breakfast for him, which looked like a yellow porridge. He hated porridge and he remembered that he had already made that clear.

"Daisy!" he called out.

In the bathroom the humming continued, intertwined with the sound of mugfuls of water being poured.

Much later, Daisy emerged from the bathroom and took his mother to her room. Several minutes later, after powdering and dressing her up, Daisy returned to check in on Prithvi, her long skirt and top splotched with water.

"Did you call me, Kuttan Sir?"

He pointed to the plate in front of him, which he hadn't touched. "What is this?"

"Pongal, Sir. Our neighbour taught me this. But she's not here these days."

"Haven't I told you I want only egg and toast every morning, please?"

"Yes, Sir!"

"And why haven't you been buying fish lately?"

"The spices have to be bought. Everything is finished."

"You've become very—" He swallowed the derogatory comment and cleared his throat instead. "Are you missing home?"

To his surprise, Daisy began to sniffle. "Sorry, Sir! I'll make something else." She headed towards the kitchen.

Prithvi regretted his harsh tone immediately. Daisy was the only caregiver who'd stuck with them for so long. Although she was a terrible cook, she was very attached to his mother, who adored her too. Prithvi knew that Daisy sent all the extra money to her family back home, to support the education of her younger siblings.

Shortly after, Daisy returned, carrying a steaming plate of fluffy eggs and toast, and a glass of orange juice. Egg was the only decent thing she could make. Though once she'd started going over to Ria's house, she'd started cooking much better. There was no talk of the neighbour recently, however, and Prithvi wondered why.

The TV came on in his mother's room and, in a moment, the laughter in the soap blared through the house. His mother had a hearing problem. In the bigger house in Kerala, Vinodini's room and his were far apart and the noise hadn't bothered him, but inside this small apartment, it was unbearable.

"Has Ma already eaten?" he asked Daisy.

"Yes, she ate before her bath."

"Shut her door, please," he said, and set about to polish off what was on his plate.

"Do you know, Kuttan Sir?" Daisy said, after she'd shut Vinodini's door, "a neighbour I met yesterday said—"

"Haven't I told you not to go talking to neighbours?" He was annoyed that she'd been talking to neighbours, especially after the publicity his last shelved movie had got. He attributed the neighbours' interest in his private life to her gossiping.

"Oh no, she was talking to me. I didn't tell her anything," Daisy said, pleading her innocence.

Prithvi put up his hand to stop her from talking further while he ate.

She stood by watching him eat, which made him terribly uncomfortable but she wouldn't go until he'd wiped his plate clean. She hadn't said anything about missing her family, or even going back for a short vacation, which he assumed she needed, but her mood was better now that he was enjoying his breakfast, and Prithvi decided to let it be.

"Ma'am wanted to speak to you," she said, after he'd finished.

Prithvi opened his mother's door and his hands shot up automatically to cover his ears. The TV's volume was deafening. "Will you lower it?" he yelled over the cacophony.

"What?"

He strode over to the TV and switched it off. "You wanted to talk to me?"

She smacked her lips. "Yes. Sheshadri had called. There are some problems with the labourers at the packaging unit."

"Why did he call you?" Prithvi said. "I've told him a million times not to bother you with trivial things."

"I called him to check on the work and he told me," she said, giving him her usual hard look.

She was assertive and had the ability to get people to move, he had to grant her that. "I'll go to Kochi immediately."

"Also," she said, peering at him, "KD called."

Prithvi waited while she weighed her next few words carefully.

"He told me he has a new script. I think you should take it."

"Why should I take everything he dishes out?" Prithvi lashed out at her. "That director was also sent by him and that man was a debutante and had looked fishy from the start. And you supported KD's choice."

"Nobody could have predicted that he'd hang himself," his mother said, sounding affronted. "You can't blame KD for it."

"All I'm saying is that I don't want to accept anything blindly. Once bitten, twice shy, as they say."

She pursed her lips. "If you weren't as bull-headed as your grandfather, you'd make quick progress."

Which reminded him of his conversation with KD at the club. "KD mentioned that grandfather had refused to take him on board Priyamvada. Do you know why?"

Her eyes shifted. "Your grandfather never gave me any reasons. That's why I want to help KD out now, if I can. He struggled a lot when he started out and there was no one to guide him. I think he's doing a lot for us considering he got nothing from Priyamvada. You should thank him for that."

"Exactly why I'm not so sure about this."

Tears had sprung to his mother's eyes. "I owe him so much," she said, sniffling. "He was the one who helped at your father's funeral since you couldn't come."

She knew how to make him feel guilty and have her way every single time.

"I'll read the script and think about it," he said and walked out of the room.

The moment he'd turned away, the TV came back on, blaring.

"I'm going out," he told Daisy.

Daisy came to see him off at the door. He didn't understand why she needed to mother him so much.

14

Neha landed at Kochi Airport and took a taxi to her accommodation in a village close to Chengannur. It was a house that was one of Thomachan's own properties. It was to serve as the location for the shooting, as well.

She was relieved to see Aditya at the entrance. He was in deep conversation with a man, and pointing in the direction of the building.

He paused when he saw her car roll in, and came over. "Hi, did you have trouble finding the place?"

"No." She got out of the car and gazed in awe at the enormous house in front of her. It was a squat, rectangular structure in the centre of a large courtyard.

"Do you like it?" Aditya smiled.

"It's beautiful," she said, unable to take her eyes off the ancestral Kerala *tharavaadu* house style.

As she stepped into the courtyard, she was taken in by all the equipment, cameras, wires and the lighting. The opening shot was being set up in the courtyard.

The house itself was on a slight elevation. There were half a dozen steps leading up to the long and narrow, red-oxide floored open portico, fringed with a row of red columns. A large mango tree shaded the eastern corner of the house from the sharp morning sun, its long, leafy branches swaying over the old, red, clay-tiled roof. The smell of wood and camphor hung in the air.

"This is where we'll stay," Aditya said as he showed her around. "It has lot of space. We'll only be using the main rooms and the kitchen for the shooting." He led her to one of the rooms where she put down her luggage. "We're starting shooting immediately. I'll send the costume and makeup. Luckily, it's less humid in November, so we won't need to touch up as often."

When he left, she walked around the room, admiring its large, open windows and triangular, high roof.

Shortly, the costume and makeup arrived. Soon, she was wearing a white, crisp, cotton saree peppered with black leaf motifs all over. Her makeup, complete with wisps of grey hair above her ears, made her look at least ten years older. Manu and she were then called for the shoot. Manu, who was playing her son, was dressed in a plain sleeveless *ganji* and *mundu*. His hair looked roughed up and his *mundu* was folded up to his knees.

Aditya waved, and came over to brief them for the shot. He explained the scene, in which Neha was supposed to be having a conversation with Manu about his upcoming job interview. Aditya showed them their seating positions on the steps below the portico. She was to be seated a step above Manu oiling his hair, while he leaned on her lap.

They rehearsed the take. Then Aditya took his place behind the monitor, while Manu and Neha took theirs on the steps. A bowl of water, instead of oil, was placed on the step next to her.

Neha was nervous. During her theatre days, it didn't take her a lot of time to loosen up and get into the part she was playing, but with so many people around her now, her nerves were acting up even before she'd begun.

The camera rolled, the clapper boy gave the clap, and Aditya called "action."

Neha started delivering her dialogues as she was massaging

Manu's scalp. "How is it that you don't care about this interview? Don't you understand how much we need the money?"

"Ma, I'll do well this time. Stop pestering me from a week before." Manu spoke his dialogues with confidence.

But she wasn't feeling that confident. The crowd standing in her line of vision to her right distracted her. Someone in the crowd was jeering and pointing fingers at them. She forgot the next line but remembered in time that she had to smile. The smile came on too consciously. Her upper lip broke into a light sweat as she continued with her lines, "And don't wear that bright colour shirt, the one you wore the last time. Borrow Balu's white pant." She bit her lip at the mistake. She was supposed to say, "white shirt."

"Cut!" Aditya called, and sent an assistant crew to control the crowd.

When things looked satisfactory and the crowd had quietened considerably, Aditya walked up to her and told her to relax. "Just go with the flow and don't pay any attention to the crowd."

Just as they returned to the shot, there was a commotion in the courtyard.

A woman barged in, her salt and pepper hair flying loose from its top knot, the towel covering her bosom slipping away. "You cheat!" she screamed, rushing towards Neha, flailing at her arms, and trying to drag her down the steps. Manu scolded the woman and tried to push her away but she hurled obscenities at both and refused to let go of Neha.

Confused and worried, Neha hobbled down the steps, somehow managing to retain her balance as she was dragged by the woman. She couldn't understand what was going on.

All this happened so quickly that Aditya barely had time to yell "Cut!" and come rushing to her aid.

When she saw Aditya, the woman trained her guns on him. "You! How dare you tell me you'll take me only to replace me?"

Soon, a few more people joined the melee and pulled the woman away even as she lunged for Aditya, grabbing him by the scruff of his neck. Finally, the men from the unit pulled her aside and got her off the set.

Aditya shook himself and straightened his shirt. "Sorry! That was Karthiani, the woman we had considered for the role earlier," he explained. "She's pissed because we told her we didn't want her."

Neha exhaled. "Is she gone?"

"Yup. Good riddance!"

Relieved, Neha got back to the shot. They'd wasted enough time already and she prayed that the shot would go well.

Thankfully, there were no further disruptions. The commotion had caused Neha to forget her acting fears. According to the needs of the scene, she and Manu finished with their lines on the steps, and walked down towards the courtyard where they continued their conversation for the shot. The lines were delivered perfectly, there were no more distractions and everything rolled smoothly.

"Cut!" Aditya gave them a thumbs up from the monitor.

Her first shot was wrapped up with more ease than Neha had expected. She was both ecstatic and relieved.

Aditya started preparations for the next scene. It had Manu having a conversation, across the boundary wall of the house, with Indulekha, who played his girlfriend.

Neha watched as Indulekha walked over to Aditya to rehearse her scene. She was neither young nor pretty enough to play Manu's girlfriend. She even looked much older than Manu.

Neha recognised Vasu, the frail man with the long white beard, who was helping Indulekha out with her lines. Indulekha seemed petrified. Aditya was patient with her, talking to her and explaining the shot. Indulekha nodded her head rapidly but looked nervous nonetheless. Aditya started describing the situation to her in vivid detail and telling her a story to draw out the emotion he needed for the scene. Soon, Indulekha, who was listening with rapt attention to Aditya, seemed to be beginning to feel what Aditya wanted.

Neha watched, in awe of Aditya's skill. He was expert at giving the right cues to evoke emotion from the actor. He knew exactly how he wanted the shot to be taken and had so much clarity for a first-time director. He looked like he had everything under control. Turning away from the shooting and the crowds, Neha strolled to the other end of the house and remained in her room until dinner was called for, from the local *thattukada* shop.

Aditya, Manu and Bobby were staying at the same house as Neha, along with a few others.

In a few days, Aditya and his friends had opened up to her about their lives. Conversation around the dinner table centred around Manu and his upcoming exams. He was doing his final year in BSc Computer Science.

In Kerala, a degree had usually nothing to do with the profession one chose, Neha supposed. Raman, Manu's father, was a rice trader and he wanted his son to help him with the business. But he still wanted Manu to study computers. "He's given me an old bike to use until I pass my exams," Manu said. "He'll buy me a new one only if I pass this year." That seemed to be the biggest motivation for why he had to pass his exams.

From Manu's talk it was clear he'd spent at least two years in each class in the BSc programme. His father didn't know he was acting in Aditya's movie or bunking classes to be here. "As long as I get fifty percent attendance and I pass this exam, my father will be fine," Manu reasoned. He needed to get back to his books directly after dinner, but it was only after a lot of goading that he picked up his study material.

Bobby, on the other hand, was a happy-go-lucky boy. He was apprenticing as a mechanic until he became Manu's family driver. He had many interesting anecdotes to relate to them about the work-related trips he had made with Manu's father. Bobby's dream was to find work in the Gulf. Every Malayalee wanted to go to the Gulf, Neha thought with a laugh. It seemed to be every Malayalee's dream.

Aditya was a topper in his college. He'd graduated in film direction from the Chennai Film School after completing his BA in Malayalam. If not successful at movies, Aditya said, he'd only be able to find a teaching job in a college. Aditya came from a poor family.

His education had been sponsored by Manu's father. Aditya's mother worked as a cook and helper in Manu's house. Aditya's father, who had passed away, used to take care of Raman's accounts. So, Raman had continued to take care of the family, even providing them with a small house on the periphery of his own compound.

Back in her room after dinner every night, Neha liked to settle down in bed with a book, often mulling over their dinner conversations. She had learnt so much about these boys in such a short time. She missed Mohan, and her home and Ria, and yet, in the company of Aditya, Manu and Bobby, she found peace and gladness. Almost every night, Neha would cry herself to sleep, wondering what it might have been if Mohan were still alive, what Ria was doing right then. Was she okay by herself? Did she miss her too? Her mother had promised to call Neha if Ria needed anything at all. Giving up worrying after a few days, Neha finally decided that while she was here, she was going to immerse herself in her work and not think about anything else. Her crying spells became less frequent. And, there were some days, she would be so tired, she'd fall into a deep, dreamless sleep within minutes of hitting the bed.

15

Aditya was deep in conversation with his cinematographer one morning, two weeks after the shooting had begun, when Indulekha's father strode into the set. He quickly pulled Aditya aside. "Indulekha has got a marriage proposal," he said, his eyes wide with excitement.

"That's good," Aditya said. "She should be done with her part pretty soon."

"She's not going to do any part!"

Aditya narrowed his eyes. Suddenly he wasn't sure there was cause for excitement about Indulekha's prospects. "Why?" Did it mean that Thomachan was going to put up another girl for the role?

"Because…" Indulekha's father paused and scratched his nose. "The news of her acting has brought us a proposal that we haven't had in years. The boy works in Oman. He's got only a week left on his vacation. He wants to marry her immediately and take her with him. There is no time to waste. The marriage must be conducted in a day or two."

"You mean Thomachan—"

"I'll tell Thomachan," Indu's father said. "I can't allow my daughter to continue with this, that's all. He can look for somebody else."

Aditya's heart sank as he glanced over to where Thomachan was standing, his legs spread apart, one end of his *mundu* lifted, laughing over something with Vasu. This wouldn't go down well!

Thomachan looked back at the same time and, seeing Indulekha's father, came running across, and folded his hands together in a hitherto unseen gesture of respect. "What, Babu Sir? What are you doing here today? Vasu and I will take care of Indulekha. Don't worry at all."

Babu pushed aside Thomachan's hand. "I've come to take my daughter away. I've fixed her marriage to a boy from Oman. It'll have to take place in the next two days."

Thomachan's eyes darted from Babu to Aditya and back to Babu. "What are you saying? Indulekha is our heroine. You can't get her married!" He looked absolutely shocked. He hailed Vasu and called him over to where they were standing. "Look," he said, turning back to Babu, "Vasu and I were going to come over to your place with a proposal for Indu."

Babu's eyes widened. "What proposal?"

Vasu intervened. "Look, Babu. Let's not rush this. Why send your girl so far away when you can have her right here in a wealthy family?" He paused, beamed at Babu, then lowered his voice. "Thoma here wants to marry your daughter. You're a lucky man!"

Babu spat at the ground, then glared at Vasu, his eyes emitting fire. "You scumbag! You want my daughter to marry this old man. Are you drunk?"

Vasu shrank away from Babu.

Thomachan was outraged. His eyes emitted fire, and he seemed to be looking at both Vasu and Babu at the same time. He grabbed Babu's collar and shouted, "Who the hell are you to call me an old man? Have you seen your daughter? I'm willing to marry her even though she's almost an old maid. The man she's marrying probably wants to take her to Oman and sell her to some Sheikh."

"Let go of me, you jealous pimp," Babu said, breaking free of Thomachan's grip. "Go find someone your own age." He hurried off to find Indulekha and then, sneering at the rest of them, he stalked off with her. "I'm also letting go my shop on MC Road," he spewed over his shoulder on his way out. "I want nothing to do with you anymore."

Thomachan staggered, clutching at his chest. Vasu and Aditya seated him down in the nearest chair. Aditya immediately called for water. Thomachan started hyperventilating and gesturing, but no words came out of his mouth.

"Relax!" Vasu ordered.

Thomachan grabbed the glass of water he was handed, and gulped it down in one go. Then wiping his mouth, he took a deep breath. "I quit!" he declared, breathing heavily. "I was making the movie for her. If she's not in it, I don't want to do it."

"What!" Vasu cried.

Aditya didn't know what to do. "We can't back out now," he pleaded. "You've put in so much money already."

But Thomachan was adamant. He waved his hands at them to stop, and stared at the floor like a defeated man. Sweat was pouring down his face and he was almost on the verge of tears. "Get me Indu and I'll produce this movie," he said, his voice a hoarse whisper. "Otherwise, I'm done here." He rose and staggered towards his car with aid from the unit men.

Even Vasu's pleas didn't help.

Aditya struck the ground with his shoes, kicking up a mountain of dust as he watched the scene unfold in front of his eyes.

Finally, Aditya asked the unit to pack up, and got the crew to start dismantling the equipment. There was nothing else to be done.

Thomachan had been implacable, even though Vasu had literally camped outside his house following his outburst. He was in such deep agony over Indulekha that he shut himself up in his house and wouldn't entertain anyone.

Neha was heartbroken when she heard the news. It wasn't so much for herself but for Aditya that she felt bad. By the next day, the crew had to pack up and vacate the house. She looked back one last time at the magnificent house that she had come to love. It had barely been a fortnight since she'd arrived. She had booked her ticket to Bangalore for that evening.

"We're very near my home," Aditya told Neha, as they were leaving. "I'd really like you to come home for lunch. My mother would love to meet you."

Neha couldn't refuse. The boys and the tales they'd exchanged had brought them all closer. They had all started to feel like family now, in the short span of time that she'd known them.

It was Manu's house that she first saw as they drove in. As they passed through the tall iron gates into the compound surrounded by dense tropical trees, a white washed, two-story house with red Mangalore-tile roof came into view. The thick foliage of the trees rendered the air inside the property cooler than the outside. The house itself had modern architecture with several windows facing the front and two large car porches built on either side of the main entrance.

"This way," said Aditya, leading Neha toward the left side of Manu's house to its back. Several feet away was a smaller cottage enclosed by a picket fence. A little kitchen garden flourished in the tiny space around the cottage.

Aditya's mother ran out to greet them. She looked at Neha admiringly. "Aditya has told me so much about you. It's so good of you to come."

Neha blushed and let Aditya's mother lead her into the house.

The house was dark and cool inside. The linoleum flooring was chipped in places and the ceiling was quite low. They followed Aditya's mother to the dining area adjacent to the kitchen, where against its outside wall, a long table and bench had been placed. Aditya's mother offered Neha a seat at the bench, while she bustled to and fro from the kitchen, bringing the food outside to the table.

As she served the food, Aditya's mother apologised for the meagreness of the meal. "I wish I'd known earlier that you were coming today. I would have cooked some fish for you."

"That's alright," Neha said, looking at the large spread in front of her. "This is great." It was a lot more than she ever made for a meal at home.

"Hold on," Manu said, and disappeared through the back door.

Several minutes later, he returned with a covered bowl. He set it on the table and lifted the cover. A rich, tangy aroma rose from the dish.

Bobby was all smiles. "You managed to bring fish curry from your house?" he shouted with glee.

"Of course, I knew Malathi Amma would have cooked fish at my house today," Manu said beaming, referring to Aditya's mother.

Malathi rolled her eyes. "I cooked it for your family, Manu," she said, in a strict, scolding tone. "Now what will be left when your father comes home?"

Manu frowned. "So? I'm sure a few pieces will not make any difference to his meal."

"You shouldn't have taken the trouble," Neha said to him.

"Nonsense," Aditya said. "Now that the fish is here, let's eat."

Everyone was so hungry that there was no more conversation, and they all began to dig in. Shortly after, Neha noticed a girl standing by the kitchen door. Aditya noticed her too and cleared his throat.

"Priya!" Malathi said, with a smile. "How did you know they had come?"

Priya was a beautiful girl with almond shaped eyes, and long hair tied up in plaits. She looked at Aditya and blushed. "Manu told me. I also wanted to meet Neha."

"This is Priya," Aditya told Neha by way of introduction. "She is Manu's younger sister."

Priya blushed again and stood silently by the door, watching them eat.

From the way Priya smiled at Aditya and gave him the occasional shy glance, Neha guessed there probably was something going on between the two.

They had almost finished lunch, and Aditya rose to wash his hands, when Priya finally broke her silence. "How's the movie coming along?" she asked.

A hush fell over the place. Bobby was the first to recover. "Fine…fine…nothing to worry. Right, Aditya?"

Aditya managed to hide a scowl. Manu came to the rescue, asking Priya to show Neha around. "We have to leave soon," he told her. "Aditya has to drop her at the airport. We don't have much time."

Shortly after, Malathi joined Neha and Priya as they were taking a short walk around the property. She had warm, kind eyes. "Aditya must have told you about us." She held Neha's hands. "This movie means a lot to him. It's his dream and also a way to repay our loans."

Neha smiled sadly. It was apparent that Aditya's mother knew nothing of their predicament. Malathi's eyes reflected hope and worry, Neha noted with a heavy heart, as she gave her hands a gentle squeeze.

Finally it was time for goodbyes. Both Malathi and Priya waved until their car had rolled out of sight. Aditya let out a deep breath. "I'm going to start looking for another producer now," he said, looking at Neha hopefully. "Please hang in there until then."

Neha disguised her worry with a smile. "Sure." She hoped that Aditya would find his producer soon.

16

Back at home, Neha unlocked her apartment and saw the pile of newspapers jammed beneath her door. She'd forgotten to cancel the newspaper subscription, she realised, but was glad now that she hadn't. She kicked the pile aside absentmindedly and stepped inside.

An article from the top of the pile caught her eye.

IS PRIYAMVADA JINXED? its headline read.

The name Priyamvada sounded familiar. She'd read about the company just a month ago. Curious, she picked up the paper and scanned the article.

Priyamvada was first shut down years ago after a fire broke out on its sets. Now, under its new owner, the heir of its founder, the sudden death of a director has caused a stir in the industry. There are no takers for its half-finished movie as new directors are wary of associating with it, after reports that the new producer is difficult to work with. Priyamvada's operations have stopped even before it has had a chance to take off. The wife of the deceased director recently filed a case demanding compensation, the article read.

There was a photo of a young man posted alongside the article.

Neha suddenly remembered the news about Priyamvada from about a month ago. It had been reported that the grandson had restarted the production company, in memory of his dead grandfather, who had been a legend decades ago.

What a pity for the grandson! she thought with a sigh, and laid the paper aside to call her mother and tell her that she was back home.

"You're back?"

While her mother was happy that she was in Bangalore, she sounded curious as to why Neha had returned so soon.

"Ma, is Ria back from school?" Neha asked, irked at her mother's tone, and needing to hear Ria's voice. She and Ria hadn't spoken in days. She hoped Ria would say that she wanted to come home.

"She's out to get something from the store," her mother said.

"Won't she even talk to me?"

"Neha, it's only been a little over a fortnight." Then as if to soften the blow, her mother mellowed down. "She does miss you. Tell me how come you're back?"

Even though she didn't want to talk about the movie, she told her all that had transpired. She wished she could tell her how desperate she was to have Ria back. How desperate she was to have a life!

"Sometimes it's all in your stars," her mother said, in an attempt to console her. "Some things are just not meant to be. Just keep praying that things will turn around."

Neha hated it when her mother attributed all misfortunes to a fault in the stars.

She hung up after a while and plonked down on the couch, while picturing her bleak future, tired from the exertion of talking to her mother. Her eyes once again fell on the newspaper, still lying on the couch. She re-read the "jinxed producer" article and wondered if her life was also the same.

On a whim, she pulled out her laptop and googled Priyamvada. The search results revealed some information about the company, but there were no recent interviews to the media and no news other than what she'd already read. The company had no social media pages either. The grandson and the new owner, Prithvi Nair, seemed to be a recluse.

But Neha kept on with the research. One lead led to another and she spent the whole night clicking page after page, until finally she settled down to watch one of Priyamvada's recent movies.

It was only in the wee hours of the morning that she fell asleep on the couch.

A loud conversation outside the front door woke her up. It was late morning. Daisy was having an animated conversations with the fish vendor. "How can seer fish be so expensive?" she argued. "In Kerala, this is cheaper by two hundred rupees, you know?"

Neha shuffled to the door to catch a glimpse of her friendly neighbour.

At the door, Daisy was sitting on her haunches beside the basket. She looked up and gave Neha one of her broadest smiles. "Didn't see you for many days. Out of town?"

She nodded and gave her a sleepy smile.

"Where did you go?" Daisy's eyes sparkled. "You never even said you were going." She bought the fish as she was talking.

Neha smiled at her sheepishly, feeling guilty about not telling her about the movie either.

"You, Ma'am?" the fish vendor asked her. "No fish today?"

She bought some on a whim. In some ways, it was good to be back in her own home.

"Do you have some fish tamarind?" Daisy asked her, just as she was about to go in.

Neha laughed. Daisy was always out of fish tamarind and yet she bought fish regularly. "Yes," she said, filled with mirth at the silly girl's antics. Sometimes it was good to have neighbours who made you feel better about yourself. At least Neha wasn't as poorly stocked as Daisy.

Neha let Daisy in and went to the kitchen to get the fish tamarind.

Daisy waited in the living room with the bowl of curry cut fish in her hands, and continued her nonstop chatter. "I haven't made fish all week. Kuttan Sir needs it at least three times a week but I didn't have the fish masala. I just bought it yesterday but they didn't have any tamarind. So, I decided I'd make fish without tamarind. So wonderful that you're back."

Neha was still rummaging in the kitchen store for the tamarind when she realised that Daisy had become silent.

A few moments later, Daisy strode into the kitchen, waving the newspaper that was thrown on the couch. "No wonder Kuttan Sir doesn't bring any of these papers home." She looked flustered. "Look at the nonsense they print!"

Neha was surprised to know that Daisy could read English. But, as she immediately learned, Daisy was convent educated.

Neha moved closer to get a look at what Daisy was pointing to. She was talking about the Priyamvada story. Nostrils flared, Daisy snapped, "They've written such rubbish about Kuttan Sir. Jinxed, it seems! My foot!"

Neha's mouth fell open. "This is your Kuttan Sir?" She pulled the newspaper back from Daisy's hand and peered at the photo. The photo in the article was of a younger man, clean-shaven with bright, sparkling eyes.

"This is not Kuttan Sir. It's an old photo of his grandfather, Bharathan Sir."

"What happened to the last movie?"

Here, Daisy hesitated, as if she were revealing something that was meant to be a secret. "You don't know?" she asked in a hushed tone. "Everyone in our neighbourhood in Kochi knew." Daisy's eyes were wide. "Kuttan Sir gets mad when neighbours poke their nose into his affairs." She lowered her voice further. "But I suppose there's no harm in telling you what everybody already knows."

Neha waited with bated breath. She was eager to hear the details.

"Priyamvada, as you know, was started by Kuttan Sir's grandfather," began Daisy. "They had one hit after another. Then one day, a large fire gutted an entire set. Huge losses! This was during his grandfather's time. They had to close down. Bharathan Sir's health was also not okay, and his son, Kuttan Sir's father, wasn't interested in the business. So they shut it down. Then, Kuttan Sir returned from America and took over the business."

Neha nodded, egging her on. She wanted to hear what had

happened next.

"But look at his luck." Here, Daisy tsk-tsked sadly. "The director of his very first movie project committed suicide." Her hand went automatically to cover her mouth. "Kuttan Sir didn't know what to do. The media invaded his house. The neighbours kept talking about it and waylaying him whenever they saw him. Poor Kuttan Sir! Finally, we came here for some peace."

"Has he found a new project here?"

"Where will he find anything?" Daisy sighed. "With news reports like this, nobody will come to him." Suddenly, as if realising something, Daisy clapped her hands to her mouth. "I'm the biggest blabbermouth. Kuttan Sir had warned me not to go talking about it to anyone here. He really wants some peace, you see? And here I am blabbering to you about the story. Please don't tell him I told you anything. He'll be mad at me." She held Neha's hand and looked into her eyes, pleading, till Neha nodded back. Then she pinched the tamarind out of Neha's hand and hastened to leave. "I'm so happy to see you back," she said, as she stepped out. "Kuttan Sir has started complaining about his food again. I'm so happy I can ask you if I run out of anything." With a wide grin, she disappeared.

Neha sat down on the couch and stared at the newspaper by her side. An idea had started spinning around in her head.

17

Neha had several questions running in her mind, over the next few weeks. Would Prithvi consider a proposal for Aditya's movie? Would it work if *she* approached him with it?

She wouldn't know if she could make this work unless she tried.

But, *how*, was the question.

The next time Daisy arrived to borrow something else, Neha engaged her in idle talk about her boss. Where did he work? What time did he leave? She couldn't let on much to Daisy lest the girl started to feel that this was all her fault.

Daisy didn't know much except that his timings were erratic. Some mornings he left at eight but he had no fixed returning time. She didn't know where he went. Sometimes, she said, he was gone for days on end, to Kochi, to take care of his fish business.

Luckily, he was in town now.

A good way to chat him up and ease into a discussion with him, Neha thought, was to casually bump into him in the hallway. That way, she could play it by ear. Throw him a bait. See if he picked it up. But at the same time, she was afraid she might ruin it. She'd probably start to blabber and turn him off. Her mind went off into scary thoughts of unknown outcomes. If he refused her outright, she'd have no more chances. For now, she decided, she'd go easy on the plan and just keep a keen ear for sounds of her neighbour's presence outside her door.

She decided to start the very next day. It was Sunday. It wasn't likely that he'd be getting out, but she listened at her door for the occasional sound anyway. At the first creak, she looked through the peephole to see who it was. It was Daisy dressed in her Sunday best, probably heading to church.

Neha had been idling in her living room for almost another hour before she heard the crunch of a door opening again, followed by the clang of garbage bins being placed outside. Without wasting a moment, she ran into her kitchen, picked up her red and green garbage pails and rushed to open her door. Her neighbour had already kept his bins out, except that they didn't have covers on. He hadn't noticed her, and before she could say anything, he turned around to go back in.

"Excuse me!" she called out.

He looked back, surprised.

A small voice inside her head ordered her to ignore trivialities and focus on the really important talk. But she just couldn't let it go! "You've left the garbage open," she pointed out.

"So?"

She hated that arrogant tone. *So??!!! Did he have no common sense at all?* "So?" she repeated, her hands on her hips. "There are stray cats in the building and one of them could be looking for food in an open bin. Besides, the entire hallway will smell of fish."

He looked like he'd been insulted. He went into his house, brought out two lids and covered the bins. "Happy?"

She could have kicked herself for the timing of her lecture on hygiene. She opened her mouth to apologize but he'd turned his back and shut the door in her face.

Well, so much for trying to strike up a conversation with her neighbour in the hallway! That had turned out to be such a bad idea! And she had no more ideas. She'd just ruined the only one she had.

A week later, as she was browsing at the local library, across the street, Neha got her second chance! She noticed Prithvi walking down the block. Curious, she checked out her book hurriedly, and followed him down the pathway, through the block. At the corner, he turned left. Further down the path was another turn. Worried that she might have lost him, she hastened her steps. He seemed to have disappeared. Suddenly, she noticed a Coffee Day to her left. As she peered in through the glass walls, she spotted him. He was seated inside, engaged in a discussion with someone.

She idled outside for ten minutes. Then, coolly walked into the café, herself. Through the corner of her eye, she could see him listening intently to the man he was with. She quickly headed to the counter, ordered her coffee and grabbed the table next to them. She opened her bag, pulled out her book and pretended to read, hoping he hadn't seen her.

"And in the climax scene—" the man was saying, when Prithvi cut him.

"Stop telling me how the scene will be shot. I'm just interested in the story."

"Of course, sorry, Sir," the man mumbled, and continued. "The villain pushes the hero into a corner and tries to drive the knife into his chest—"

"And miraculously," Prithvi interjected, "The hero turns around, and manages to reverse the situation where now the villain is in the same corner and the knife is about to be plunged into his chest. Right?" His voice boomed.

Neha flinched and her book fell to the floor with a loud thud. Cheeks flaming, she bent down as inconspicuously as possible, picked it up and hid her face behind it, pretending to read.

She did not dare peep out from behind the book to find out the cause of the immediate silence that followed. In a moment, however, Prithvi had picked up the thread of the conversation again, and Neha exhaled, relieved.

"Look," Prithvi said, his feet visible from under Neha's book. "Everyone's looking for a formulaic story but I want something that'll hook the audience from the word go. You tell me such a story next time and I'll be interested."

He pushed his chair back and rose. The rustle of a handshake followed and then Prithvi turned to leave. He was almost at the door. She was about to relax when he turned around and walked back towards her. Her breath caught. He came up to where she sat. There was a sudden tug at her book and it flew out of her hands.

Before she could react, she saw her book in Prithvi's hands. He turned it around and pushed it back into her hands. "You were reading it upside down," he said with a smirk, and strode out of the café.

She banged the book on her forehead, letting out a groan after he was gone.

✶ ✶ ✶

It had been over two hours since Neha had been sitting in Shweta's car, with the driver already snoring in the front. This had been Shweta's brilliant idea.

After following Prithvi right after he'd left the apartment that morning, she was now parked across the street outside an office building near the KGA Golf Course, where Prithvi had entered. She'd given up on the chance to talk to him in the hallway outside their homes. Conversations around garbage bin drops and milk packet pick-ups, or the occasional two-minute door opening-closing routine for which she had to wait hours listening at her door, were out. Maybe, taking the conversation outside the home space might be a better idea, she'd felt. How she was going to actually accomplish that, she did not know. But the plan had been to follow him around for a few days and wait for the right opportunity to bump "casually" into him.

Prithvi had been in there for long. She was pissed with the driver because he'd parked in the worst possible place with not a spot of shade. It was almost lunch time and her stomach rumbled. Hoping for a quick bite before Prithvi exited the building, she made her way to Dosa Corner across the road. She picked a spot where she could have her lunch and also get a good view if her quarry walked out while she ate.

She ordered one of those jumbo-sized dosas and read her library book as she was eating, keeping an eye on the building. A while later, with no sign of Prithvi, she ordered tea. Another hour went by, and there was still no sign of him. The heat outside was so bad that she felt a bit drowsy. As long as the owner didn't mind her taking up a table, she preferred to sit here rather than get back to her car. Slowly as more time went by, her head dropped onto the table and her heavy eyelids closed for a quick nap.

Prithvi had been poring over some scripts that KD had shown him, and he needed a break. Besides, it was way past lunch time and he was hungry. He hated to eat sandwiches for lunch but that was all KD's office boy could bring in from the nearby café. The coffee in this place was ridiculous too. So he decided to go downstairs and buy dosas and tea from the local street shop outside.

As he stepped out into the mid afternoon sun, he spotted a familiar red Maruti parked across the road. He entered Dosa Corner and found himself staring at a woman he thought he recognised. She appeared to be snoozing, her head resting on a table.

He went closer for a better look.

At that moment, she turned her head and, to his disbelief, Prithvi saw that it was *her*. His neighbour!

The one who'd timed her garbage bin disposal with his and then ranted that his open bins made the entire floor smell of fish.

The very one who'd moved in next to his seat surreptitiously, as he was discussing a script in Coffee Day.

Was she following him around?

He tapped his knuckles on the table. "Excuse me!"

She woke up with a jolt and her book fell to the floor. She barely noticed the book; she was horrified enough to see him.

"Are you following me by any chance?" he demanded.

A mix of confusion and regret swirled in her eyes. She rose abruptly and stumbled. Then, she pushed past him and made a run through the exit, leaving him staring at her back, bewildered.

She rushed towards the parked red Maruti and banged on the window to wake up the driver. Then she jumped into the back seat and ordered him to leave. In a minute, the car revved to life and made a swift turn, and she was gone.

Prithvi bent to pick up the book from the floor and made his way to the counter to get his lunch.

While eating, a thousand thoughts ran through his head. What was she doing here? What did she want? Why was she following him? Had the media caught up to him again?

By the time he had returned to KD's office after lunch, he was determined to find out what this was all about.

Shit! Shit! Shit! Neha raved as her car sped away. Now, she'd blown it completely. How was she going to explain running away like a mad woman at the sight of him?

And then, to her horror, she realised, she had lost her library book, but hell if she was going back to get it. She'd just have to hope not to run into him anywhere for a while. Until the matter was forgotten.

Her heart beat harder against her rib cage until her breathing became ragged and difficult. Maybe, she should have taken Daisy's help. All this would have been so much easier. But no, she realized at the same time, that things might have been worse.

18

It was one of those days when Neha just felt like crying her heart out. It had been five months since Mohan's untimely passing. And, not a day went by when she didn't miss him with every fibre of her being. Yes, she had distracted herself with the hopes of the movie, and then again the hopes of convincing Prithvi to invest in it. There were times when she felt like her old self—full of joie-de-vivre and hope. And, then there were days like today, when she missed her husband terribly. She missed her daughter. Why couldn't she just turn back the clock? She'd woken up with a terrible dream that Mohan had found Ria and they were both never coming back. She bawled into her morning tea while making her breakfast, and left both untouched. She sprawled on the couch, her hair undone, still in her night clothes. Every little thought brought on fresh tears. Nothing could make her stop crying since morning.

Prithvi left home at the usual time. Daisy at the door, waving to him like she was his wife or sweetheart, made him groan.

He stepped into the elevator and went down to the ground floor. He waited there for ten minutes. Then he called for the elevator again, and rode back up to the fifth, fingers crossed that Daisy had closed the door and gone back inside.

When the elevator door opened with a ping, Prithvi peered out, and breathed in relief. The floor was empty.

He walked up to his neighbour's house at 502 and rang her doorbell.

After a few moments he heard a muffled shuffling of feet. When the door opened, there stood his mysterious neighbour, her face blotched with tears, and her nose red and puffy. She had a handkerchief in one hand, into which she proceeded to blow her nose.

"*Beda*! Don't want," she said, without looking up. Blowing her nose again, she was about to close the door when she stopped and looked up at his face. "You?"

Prithvi got his foot in, before she could slam the door shut.

"What do you want?" she yelled, her voice hoarse.

He glared at her. "What do *you* want?"

"Peace," she said, her eyes wet. "Get out!" She sniffled.

Oh no, you're not outing me like that!

"Why?" he asked. "So that you can get me on your terms?"

She pulled her handkerchief away and blinked at him. "What the hell do you mean?"

"You tell me," he said, noticing the fresh puddle in her eyes. "Why the hell have you been following me? Are you from the media?"

"I'm not up to talking right now," she said, trying to push him out. "I'm down with allergies."

"I'm not giving your book back unless we talk now."

She stared at the library book he was holding and looked up at him uncertainly. Then she stepped aside. "Can we talk inside?"

He stepped in. The house looked lived in, but clean. The living room had two large, olive green couches, an orange, shell conch that made for an interesting, centre show piece, and brass artefacts in all shapes and sizes taking up most of the floor space. There was a large oval mirror framed with tiny shells in the corridor, and books, magazines and CDs everywhere. The whole place smelled of incense and he couldn't help remembering the first time he'd stood outside her door. His feet, now that he'd taken off his shoes, felt cool to the touch of the marble floor.

She sat across him. "I'm Neha," she began hesitantly.

He waited while she pulled out her handkerchief and blew her nose again. "Let's begin," he said, "by you telling me whether you're trying to hound me about the debacle my company is facing."

She shook her head. "No, not at all."

"Then why have you been following me?"

She rose and pulled out a folder out of a desk drawer. "Please take a look at this."

"What is it?" He opened the folder. It looked like a script.

She sniffled again. "One moment. I'll be right back."

He knew it was none of his business but it looked plainly like she'd been crying, even if she liked to call it "allergies." When she was gone, he scanned the folder and read a few pages before she was back again.

"Whose script is this?" he asked.

Her chest heaved. "We need a producer," she said without preamble. Her words caught him off-guard. He'd met a lot of script writers and people in the movie business in the past few months, but none with red, puffy eyes and an attitude.

"Is this why you were following me?"

She nodded and blew her nose again. She looked like she was going to burst into tears one more time.

He had a feeling it was Daisy who had told her about him. But she hadn't asked Daisy for help. Smart woman! He was curious now. "Why couldn't you have given it to me directly?"

"For one—" she started, almost as if she had a litany of complaints against him, but then, just as quickly, she shut up. "I just didn't know how," she managed, followed by a hiccup.

It didn't look like she was up to much talking. He'd also rather let the script talk to him instead. He rose to leave. "I'll give it a read."

She nodded but remained seated, staring at her hands folded on her knees while he let himself out.

That night, he nursed an Old Monk as he read the script. By the end of his second drink, he had finished reading. He shut the folder, let it rest against his chest and leaned back in his chair. He knew what he wanted to do next.

At eight the next morning, he was back at Neha's door, after the same up-and-down elevator routine, to throw Daisy off.

Neha was dressed better today and obviously hadn't been crying. She looked apprehensive as he entered and sat on the couch.

"May I ask whose script this is?" he asked, returning the folder.

She gave him the entire account of the script's journey from the start until then.

"Everyone on this project is a newcomer?" He couldn't take any more chances unfortunately. "It's risky," he said.

"All the actors have some theatre experience, including me."

"I'm talking about the director."

"He studied film making at the Chennai Film Institute. He's made short films. This, of course, will be his first full-length film." She inhaled and narrowed her eyes at him. "Will you take this on?"

Once again, her directness took him by surprise. She probably didn't know how the industry worked. You either had references or credentials. "I don't take newcomers," he said, stressing each word. "It's just too big a risk."

He sounded pathetic even to himself. He could have said that he didn't like the script. But he couldn't, because the truth was he rather liked it.

"Then I will not waste your time," she said, rising immediately, forcing him to rise too.

But she was far from done. "Before you leave," she said, her eyes blazing, "I'd like to let you know that I spent a lot of time researching Priyamvada and the movies it made. Your grandfather stood for talent and humility. A lot of talented newcomers walked through Priyamvada's doors all those years ago, and so many later rose to fame. It's a shame you don't share your grandfather's ideals. Since that's the case, I want nothing to do with either Priyamvada or you."

Prithvi was pissed as hell at her sudden change of tone. How dare she insult him like that? "I want nothing to do with you either," he yelled, barely able to contain his anger. "And stop following me around!"

She glared at him, her eyes continuing to smoulder with golden specks of fire.

He turned and stalked out without another word.

When Prithvi barged into KD's office an hour later, he was in an extremely bad mood. "What the hell does that new director you sent, mean when he says he doesn't want to work with me?"

"Calm down," KD said, coming around his desk. "I told you it's going to take some time."

Prithvi paced the floor, scowling.

"I sent one scriptwriter to you, didn't I? But you turned him down. Look, young man, one cannot be too choosy when the chips are down. One successful movie and you can start calling the shots. But until then, you've got to be patient."

This was the movie KD had been willing to co-produce. Prithvi had come down to accepting even that. But that opportunity too was lost when the new director had been told that the movie was for Priyamvada. "Patient?" Prithvi raged, his head exploding. "I've been more than patient and I can't take it anymore."

"Then do you have an alternative?"

"No!"

"Then may I suggest you go home and wait this out?"

Prithvi walked out of KD's office in under a minute.

Instead of returning straight home, he went over to Neha's door and rang the bell.

She was surprised to see him. "You?"

"I've changed my mind," he said, wanting to make it short and snappy. "I'd like to meet the director of the script that you showed me."

She scowled at him, arms akimbo. "Why?" She looked neither happy nor surprised.

"Because I need to meet him, dammit!" Frustration swept

through his veins. "Will you bring him to see me tomorrow or have you changed your mind about the movie?"

19

In Chengannur, all work on Aditya's movie had stopped. He couldn't find another producer. Thomachan had been going around collecting his rent from the shops on MC Road, and he'd totally given up on the movie. Bobby and Vasu tried to persuade him not to, but that had proved to be unsuccessful. Aditya was at his wits' end. All the actors he'd hired, still had to be paid; some had moved on and that left Aditya hard pressed to find alternatives.

That morning, while watering the plants around his house, Aditya found a note from Priya hidden under a stone, behind the hibiscus plant. She wanted to meet him at their usual meeting place in the evening. At the temple near their house.

Aditya and Priya didn't enter or leave the temple together, but that is where they met when they wanted to talk. There was hardly another suitable place where he could meet Priya in peace. Aditya had inadvertently turned into a "temple Romeo."

"Haven't seen you in a while," the old priest said, giving Aditya a knowing look when he entered the shrine. He'd possibly guessed that he was there to meet Priya. It was hard to escape people's eyes in small towns.

"Was busy," Aditya mumbled.

"Mmm," the priest said, before entering the inner chamber to light the lamps.

After three rounds around the shrine, Aditya joined his palms in prayer and waited for the priest to emerge from the sanctum, carrying one of the the lighted lamps. Aditya's hands hovered over the lamp, and then he touched them to his eyes in veneration. After smearing the customary sandalwood paste offering from the priest on his forehead, he headed to the stone slab seating next to the compound wall, to wait for Priya.

Aditya's mother had cautioned him against dating Priya. She was a rich man's daughter after all, and that too, from a family on whose mercy Aditya and his mother depended, to continue to live in the outhouse. "It would be foolish to think that her family would accept you," his mother had always warned him.

But there was no one else he'd rather have. He'd been in love with Priya since childhood. As neighbours, Manu, Priya and he used to play together, climb trees and spend hours with one other, until Priya grew up and was restricted from hanging out with grown-up boys. But his love for her had never faded. In time he hoped that he could ask for her hand in marriage, but before that he needed his career to take off.

Presently, he saw Priya enter the compound and walk up to pray at the shrine. When she'd finished, she came out and joined him, taking care to sit a few feet away.

"Any news?" she asked, concerned.

"I'm going to Chennai to see if I can sell my screenplay. That's my last hope."

"Papa has started getting proposals for me," she said, her eyes filling up all of a sudden. "In the next few months my exams will be over and they'll marry me off."

She looked so vulnerable that his chest tightened. He fought the urge to pull her towards him and kiss away her tears.

"I'll do something soon," he said, hoping to calm her down. "Don't worry. Just hold them off as much as you can."

"Is there no way you can take up a job until something works out?"

"I'm doing the best I can, my dear," he said, softly. "Bobby thinks if he and Vasu can find another girl for Thomachan, he may take on the movie again."

"That's a silly thing to hope for."

"I agree." He smiled weakly, trying to hide his despair.

The evening prayer bell chimed, telling them it was six already. It was time for the evening worship. The temple would soon be thronging with more devotees, perhaps even Priya's mother. It was time for Aditya to leave without calling attention to himself and Priya.

He gazed at Priya lovingly and nodded a quick goodbye, leaving her to wait until he'd left.

"Manu's father was looking for you," Aditya's mother said as soon as he came home.

"What for?" he asked. Had he or any of his associates seen Priya and him at the temple earlier?

"He was saying he's lined up some job for you."

If only he'd offer money to produce the movie instead, Aditya thought. Reluctantly, he went up to the big house.

Manu's father, Raman, was playing his violin when Aditya entered.

"You know what *raga* I'm playing?" Raman asked, looking up from his instrument.

"No, Sir."

"This is called *Raga Amruthavarshini*, the harbinger of rain. Sit down."

Aditya took a seat.

"What did you graduate in?"

"Malayalam BA Arts, Sir."

"And are you going to sit on your butt and do nothing?" Putting down his violin, Raman peered at Aditya. "If Shankaran were alive, would he have been proud of his son?"

"I've been trying, Sir."

"What have you been trying?" Raman's voice rose a notch. "Where is the money I gave you for Chennai? And, mind you, it was only because your mother begged me. You can easily work as a college lecturer. Why not do that? Movie business is risky."

"But this is my passion, Sir."

Raman sniffed. "Passion or not! Is it true that you've roped in Manu as an actor?"

Aditya grew silent, wondering how he'd come to know. He looked down, instead of at Raman's face.

"Let me make this very clear. My son will join my business after he passes college. If there is anything standing in the way of that, I will personally destroy it."

"I understand, Sir."

"And I hope you do understand that he is not to hear anything about our conversation." Here he paused. "And neither is Priya."

"Yes, Sir."

"I had promised Shankaran I would take care of you. But it will not be at the cost of my family. If you have something to prove, prove it, or you and your mother can vacate the premises and be off. I think I've done more than enough for you."

Aditya rose to leave but could barely stand, his knees feeling wobbly. "I will return your loan soon, Sir."

"Here," Raman said, handing him an envelope. "It's for a lecturer's job at Bharatmata College. It's the last favour I'm going to do for you."

Aditya accepted it and managed to make his way out of the house. Never before had he felt so admonished and insulted. While Raman had only hinted at Aditya's association with both his kids, the message was loud and clear. Get a job or get out.

Out of the blue, he got a call from Neha that night.

"I've found a producer," she said, unable to contain the excitement in her voice.

Aditya had heard about Priyamvada but thought it was closed down decades ago. He didn't know the grandson was now running it.

"They've run into some problems," Neha said. "But that's not our concern. The main thing is they're looking to start a new movie and, as luck would have it, the grandson turned out to be my next-door neighbour."

Aditya was excited thinking about the prospects of meeting Prithvi and re-starting the movie. He hoped things would move faster so that he could pull in the other actors before they'd gone on to work on something else.

"Can you be in Bangalore tomorrow?" Neha asked.

"Manu has exams," he told her. "But Bobby and I will be there."

Neha was excited to hear this. "Let's meet at my house. Dinner will be on me."

Aditya had just enough time to call Bobby, book the bus tickets and send a note to Priya that he was going to Bangalore and that things were probably going to look up.

Bobby and he set out for Bangalore the very next day.

20

Ria called Neha unexpectedly the next morning. She seemed to be in a bright mood. "I've been selected for the painting competition," she said.

Neha was ecstatic to hear that. "That's wonderful news! And are you keeping yourself busy at Grandma's?"

"Nothing much. Just homework and the usual."

It was at moments like these that Neha wished she'd had another child. Ria would have been much happier if she'd had company. She sighed at the useless thought. For a moment she considered telling Ria that today was a big day for her too.

But it was too late. Ria had already hung up after a quick goodbye.

Neha spent the morning in a tizzy over what to cook for dinner. She sent a message to Prithvi for the dinner meeting, through Daisy.

Daisy was surprised that Neha had kept this from her for so long. "Why didn't you tell me before?" she said. "I would have arranged for you to meet Kuttan Sir."

"But Kuttan Sir wouldn't have met me at all if I had asked you!" Neha retorted with a laugh.

Daisy nodded, looking cheerful. "When I go to church I'll pray that this movie goes well. I'll be the happiest to see Kuttan Sir starting another project soon."

When Shweta heard the news, she was over the moon.

"It's too early to say anything yet," Neha warned.

"Oh, I'd say not!" Shweta said with a laugh. "I think the billionaire got tired of waiting for something to do."

Back in her kitchen, Neha looked around, flustered, for she hadn't prepared for a dinner party in years. Just thinking about it gave her the jitters. She made a shopping list and spent the afternoon at the grocery store picking up the things she needed. After much deliberation, she decided to make rice *idiappams* and a Malabar chicken curry.

Daisy called in to say that Prithvi would come by seven. The boys were expected to arrive around the same time too, straight from the bus stop.

Precisely at seven, her doorbell rang. Her heart lurched to see Prithvi at the door. She hadn't expected him to arrive first. He looked dapper in a blue shirt and tie, and also too formal, she thought, smiling inwardly. But the thought of having to strike a conversation with him made her nervous again.

Prithvi hesitated at the door when he realised that no one else had arrived yet. He wondered if he should go home and come back later, but as an afterthought, he accepted her gesture to come in, and took a seat on one of the couches.

"Is Ria here?" he asked.

"She's at my mother's place."

"I thought I could talk to her. She's a smart girl. She seems very interested in art."

"Yes, she is. She's learning oil pastels now." Neha smiled, setting off the dimples in her cheeks, which he now noticed for the first time. "She was admiring your wall art," she continued. "Did you learn to paint?"

Prithvi laughed. "Oh, no! I was self-taught. When I used to work long hours, it was a stress buster."

She offered to make him some iced-tea but he declined. An air of discomfort hung between the two. Neha made an excuse and ducked into the kitchen. He heard the clinking of glass as she got busy in there, getting something for him.

Hands on his knees and eyes to the ceiling, Prithvi just sat there and stared. For the first time in his life, he found himself feeling awkward and as nervous as a teenager on his first date. He'd tried to dress up with a little more effort, hoping it would make up for the times in the past that he'd frightened her. But he could sense that she was uncomfortable around him.

He was thinking of what to say to her when she came out of the kitchen, when suddenly he heard a loud crash of shattering glass. A second later, Neha screamed, "Owwww!"

He rushed into the kitchen. Shards of glass littered the entire stretch of the floor from the door to where Neha stood, hopping on one foot, the other foot raised. She was in such pain that tears were streaming down her face.

"Hold on. Stay where you are." He looked around for something to move the shards out of the way. "Do you have a broom?"

She pointed to the left corner near the door.

Sweeping the shards away while she stood there helpless, he came towards her. "Are you hurt?"

She raised her foot a little more. He could see that her sole was bleeding. Some pieces of glass might have got in there. "Can you hop over to the living room?" he asked. "So, I can help you?"

She nodded hesitantly and tried, but it was hopeless. After a couple of hops, she stopped. "I can't!" she cried.

There was no way she could get there by herself without help. "Is it okay if I hold you?" he asked.

She nodded meekly, her face twisted in pain.

He stood next to her, holding her by her waist. "Put one hand up on my shoulder," he instructed.

She hesitated.

"Come on," he insisted, and waited until she did. They got to the living room that way, she, hopping with one arm on his shoulder, and he, lending her support. He let her rest on the couch, then got a stool to place in front of her so that he could take a look at her injury.

She closed her eyes as she lifted her foot, as if she were afraid to even look at it. There were at least two thin shards that he could see.

"I'm glad you weren't alone tonight," he said, wondering what might have happened if she'd had no one to help. "Do you have a tweezer?"

"No."

"Okay, gimme a moment." He headed to the fridge in the kitchen and found what he was looking for.

Back to her, he lifted her foot up again and rested it on his knee. Then, as carefully as he could, he rolled the cool ball of dough slowly under her foot.

She winced.

"I'm sorry. But I promise it won't hurt too much." After the two big pieces were out, he took another ball of dough and ran it thoroughly under the foot again, looking for smaller pieces he might have missed. Finally, satisfied, he gave her foot a good look. "Do you feel any more pain?"

"No, I'm good."

"One more thing," he said, lifting her up by the shoulders.

"Where are you taking me?" she asked, surprised.

"To the bathroom. We need to give this a good wash." He helped her carefully to the bathroom, washed her foot with soap and water, put on some antiseptic and then brought her back to the living room couch. "Feel better?" he asked.

She let out a sigh of relief. "Yes, thanks!"

He worried if he was prying too much into her life. It was none of his business. But, he couldn't help asking. "Was that your husband the other day when I barged into your home?" He pointed to the floor where he'd seen the body lie.

She nodded. "He was a cardiologist at Sakra." Then, with an apologetic look, she added, "Sorry about your car. I meant to apologise before. My sister—"

"Don't mention it," he said, feeling like a jerk for the way he'd behaved that day. "I got the paint touched up." His hand was still holding her ankle. His eyes went to the silver anklet with dangling stars. She noticed his gaze, and squirmed. Suddenly, he let go and she pulled back her foot. "Sorry. I think we should put on a band-aid," he said.

She tried to get up and get it herself but lost her balance and fell back on the couch, her cheeks going red.

"Tell me where it is. You stay put."

She gestured to the drawer and he went looking. He found two and brought them to her. He didn't remember using a band-aid for the last twenty years at least. He reached for her foot, and resting it back on his knee, he stuck the band-aid on the cuts.

There was another awkward silence

"You said, long hours?" she asked, a few moments later.

It took him a minute to understand what she meant. "Oh, about my previous job? Yes, that was before I came back to India. I was a games designer and a full-time video game junkie." He laughed and it made her smile.

"What about you?" he asked her.

"What about me?"

"Were you always into theatre?"

It was funny he remembered what she had told him the other day. "That was a long time ago. Until last month I taught drama at a school."

He smiled. "Let me guess. You gave that up for a career in acting."

"Nope, they pushed me out because I was off for almost three months after Mohan…"

"I'm sorry to hear that."

"Don't be. I didn't know drama teachers were so much in demand until—"

The doorbell rang. He ordered her not to move and got up to get the door.

It was Aditya and Bobby. The introductions were made, and they shook hands. The two boys were full of concern to see Neha on the couch. "He was my saviour and doctor for the night," Neha said, pointing to Prithvi, and told them what had happened. They laughed about it and it spurred Neha on to tell them how she'd met Prithvi, all thanks to her sister scratching his car. Prithvi, in turn, found himself joking about having Neha as his neighbourhood hygiene police. It broke the ice quickly. Soon, the boys and Neha were telling Prithvi about how their movie had stalled under Thomachan's production.

Prithvi's interest was suddenly piqued at the mention of Chengannur, Aditya's home town, and their old producer. "Is he the same Thomachan who owns the acres on the hills?" he asked.

Aditya and Bobby were surprised that he knew the area.

"I've visited that town when I was a young boy," Prithvi said. "My grandfather knew an old friend there. His name was Vasu."

All three of them were stumped now.

"It's such a small world," Neha said.

It was Prithvi's turn to be surprised. "Is he still there now?"

"Very much so," Bobby said.

"He runs a theatre company and we got most of our actors through him," Aditya said.

While they kept talking, Neha tried to rise from the couch to start laying out dinner, but Prithvi put out his hand to stop her. "I think you should give yourself a break tonight."

But she insisted on hobbling up to the kitchen to show him where everything was. With her directing him, Prithvi set up four places. Aditya and Bobby also pitched in.

Soon everyone moved to the dining table.

The aroma wafting from the dishes put the three men in a very good mood.

Bobby raved about the soft *idiappams*. Even Aditya couldn't stop making approving noises while eating. Neha blushed at their obvious appreciation.

Although Prithvi didn't say much to her, the food had put him in really good spirits. The chicken curry was spicy and delicious. He felt happy and light-hearted. He couldn't help but note what a wonderful cook she was.

"What inspired you to write that story?" he asked Aditya, directing the conversation back to the script.

And that set off another animated discussion about stories that were about journeys rather than destinations.

The story was inspired by his own life, Aditya said, where his mother, a penniless widow, wanted him to be successful.

Prithvi took a second helping of the chicken curry. "And what about the fantasy element?" That was what set this script apart from the scores of others he'd read.

"That's a metaphor for faith," Aditya said, starting off another discussion on the topic of faith.

"As in faith in God?" Prithvi questioned. He'd never visited a temple or a place of religious worship. To him, faith was a belief in a higher power.

Aditya broke another piece of *idiappam* before replying. "Whatever you want to call it. God or higher power. Creating our own answers. That's faith to me. Sleeping peacefully at night, content, knowing that there is nothing to fear."

"So, to you, is faith about peace?" Prithvi asked.

"Faith is about prayer and belief," Neha threw in, as she refilled their glasses of water. "That someone up there will bring you to the shore when you're being pushed against the tide and drowning."

Prithvi became silent for a moment, surprised to find that her words moved him. God, how desperately he'd prayed to be saved from drowning and not giving up on his dreams. Her felt her words touch him somewhere deep within, reassuring him; it was as if she was speaking to his soul. And he felt a pang for the way he'd misread her and had been arrogant towards her, in the past. Here she was, trying to help people she barely knew and trying to be a good hostess, despite her pain. She deserved an answer to her prayers, whatever they were. She deserved to regain the love she had lost in her own life and was trying to give others.

The discussion moved on to neutral topics, along with the obvious relishing of the food by the group. Time flew, and the party moved from the dining table back to the living room couch. Conversation flowed amid servings of dessert, and coffee, which Prithvi insisted on preparing, himself.

Sometime towards late evening, the decision to sign the contract in a couple of days was reached. They made a consensus to start work within the fortnight.

Aditya and Bobby had to leave to catch the late night bus back home. They thanked Neha profusely for the dinner.

Prithvi was the last to leave. He turned to Neha at the door. "Please tell Ria I would love to meet her some time."

"Will do," Neha said, smiling, her dimples showing again.

"Thank you for the dinner," he said, feeling an unexpected lurch in his heart, now that the beautiful evening had come to an end. "You've also been a great help with Daisy. I'd reached the end of my patience with her cooking," he said, for nothing better to say as they shook hands. At the door, he turned to her one last time. "Thanks for introducing me to the boys. I'm glad I didn't pass up this opportunity. Good night."

Neha smiled again after she'd shut the door. It had been a while since she'd truly had such a good time. Smiling again, enjoying others' company, felt good! And Prithvi! She'd changed her mind about him, she realised, unable to believe that this was the man she'd earlier disliked. No longer was she scared of his dark skin and the scar. In fact, she'd barely even noticed it today. What she'd noticed, instead, was how warmly he laughed, tossing his head back. He had a full blown, mirthful guffaw that was so infectious, it made her smile even now as she thought of it. And today, she'd seen his softer side as well. He made her feel comfortable and safe. Like a friend.

It was almost ten P.M. when Neha wound up work in her kitchen. Her foot felt much better. She switched off the lights, went to her bedroom, and shut herself in, which was what she'd been doing since the past few weeks without Ria.

Just as she settled into bed, relieved that it had all worked out well, her phone chimed.

It was her mother.

"Come quickly! Ria needs you," was all she said.

21

Neha rushed to her parents' house within half an hour of her mother's call. Ria had severe stomach cramps and had to be taken to the hospital.

Her father drove them over to Sakra, and they rushed to the emergency ward as soon as they reached.

Ria was writhing in pain, but there seemed to be no other symptom to indicate what the problem could be. They waited for the reports for what seemed like forever. When the reports arrived, they were all normal except that Ria was heavily constipated. Neha breathed a sigh of relief.

They were sent home with prescription laxatives for Ria.

Neha spent the night with Ria at her parents' house.

In the morning, Ria was feeling much better. At breakfast, she nibbled on a little toast and tea.

Neha was concerned about her. "Would you like me to stay here or would you rather come home?" she asked Ria.

"I'm okay, Ma. I should have paid attention to it earlier."

Neha wasn't convinced and decided to spend a few days with her even if it meant going to the shooting location a week or more later than she'd promised Aditya, who'd called earlier. Work was to begin early next week and they'd be waiting for her to join them.

Shweta came to visit a little later in the day. "Oh, you had us all very frightened," she told Ria, ruffling her hair.

"I'm fine now, Aunt S. Nothing to worry."

"I have no worries for a smart cookie like you."

They moved to the porch and Ria settled down on the swing.

"I quite like it here," Ria said, swinging her legs.

"Do you now?" Shweta teased her.

Neha remembered that she hadn't told them about the previous night. "By the way, we had visitors last night."

Shweta and Ria couldn't wait to hear the details.

She told them all about the dinner.

Ria made a face. "I wish you would have told me, Ma. I would have come home yesterday if I knew Prithvi was invited."

"Aha, so we'll only go home to see Prithvi, is it?" Shweta teased her again.

"He did ask about you," Neha told Ria.

Ria kicked her legs out to propel the swing higher. "I'd love to paint like him."

"I'm not sure I should leave you here and go to Kochi, Ria," Neha said, now that her thoughts were on the movie.

"You shouldn't worry about me, Ma. I'll be fine."

After Ria went to sleep that night, Neha sat with her mother, out on the porch. It was perfectly silent except for the fireflies buzzing in the darkness and the sound of the leaves of the mango tree swaying in the cool December breeze.

Neha touched her mother's hand. "Ma, I'm not sure about this. I don't know if I should let Ria stay without me."

"She's not a baby, Neha. Besides, you won't be that far away. We're here to take care of emergencies." She looked deep into Neha's eyes. "It's going to be six months now, my child. You need to start thinking about yourself too. You must pull yourself together, so that both you and Ria can find peace and eventually, happiness. Besides, Shweta, too, is just a phone call away. So, you should just go ahead and not worry about all this."

Neha squeezed her mother's hand and they sat there in silence a little longer, until her father came to call them in. "You're going to catch a cold, Keertana."

"I'm not a baby," her mother replied, and laughing, Neha and she rose to go back inside.

Neha lay awake in Ria's room for a long time that night. She couldn't help wondering if she was doing the right thing leaving Ria with her parents. She pondered over what Mohan might have advised in such a situation.

Of course, he'd have been over the moon about her starting the movie again. Of course, he'd have said that Ria would be fine without her. She could feel her tears fall on to the pillow as she thought of him. She could have been lying next to him now, snuggling into his chest. He'd be stroking her hair and laughing about the strange circumstances that had made her an actress. A small laugh escaped her at the thought, before a deeper sadness followed. How much she missed him right now. I wish you were here, Mohan, she heard herself whisper into the night. You would have been so proud!

* * *

Prithvi spent a good week, putting the finishing touches on a new wall painting at home, and making plans for the upcoming movie. It was a productive week spent in planning publicity, meeting distributors and coordinating with his production team about accommodation, budget and travel for the actors.

Prithvi was in a wonderful mood when he met KD and Oliver at the club for a drink that weekend.

They finished a game of squash at the club, and headed over to where Prithvi was seated at the table, waiting for them. KD had a towel around his neck. "I'm going to beat you next week," he said to Oliver, laughing.

"Not before I give you a run for your money," Oliver shot back.

They sat down at the table and ordered chilled beers.

"Haven't seen you in a while, buddy," Oliver said to Prithvi.

KD put up his feet and lit a cigarette. "Ah, he's having movie troubles." He took a long puff and exhaled. "I'm having trouble too. The dashing young Lal had promised to give me dates for my next film but I just don't have the right story to interest him."

"Lucky you to have got Lal at last," Oliver said, slapping him on the back. "This is fantastic news."

"Which Lal is this?" Prithvi asked uninterestedly.

"Who else but the one-movie-a-year guy. Asif Lal," Oliver said. "Am I right?"

KD blew out the next puff upwards. "Yeah, if my screenwriters were more efficient I'd have churned out a story by now."

"Relax, man."

"This guy is very choosy about the story," KD told Prithvi. "Somebody else is going to snap him up if I don't conjure up an interesting story in time."

"Well, then tell your boys to read a Russian novel. You'll find a gem of a story in the blink of an eye." Oliver laughed, dabbing at the fresh sweat collecting on his forehead.

Prithvi leaned forward to put down his empty beer bottle, and wiped his mouth. This was the perfect moment to tell them the news. "*I* have a new story." He paused for a moment to let the announcement sink in. "I'm starting work on it next week."

Oliver thunked his bottle on the table in surprise. "While we're just talking about a movie, here's a young man who's already out there in action."

KD's bottle paused inches from his lips. He lowered it, his eyes wide. "Well, that's great news, young man! Who's the screenwriter?"

"It's a new director and screenwriter."

"Oh!" KD sounded surprised but he collected himself quickly. "Let me read it then. And if it's fantastic, as you say it is, we can offer it to Asif Lal. What do you think, Oliver?"

"It's a fabulous idea," Oliver said. "But ask our man Prithvi here."

"There's nothing to ask. He's our man of the hour. Right, young man?" KD rubbed his hands together. "This is good news!"

"The casting is done," Prithvi said in an even tone. "I've already signed the contract."

KD's face fell. "We could have discussed it before you signed. That was pretty quick."

Oliver laughed. "Now, that's a true businessman. One who doesn't waste any time." He turned to KD. "Too late! But there will always be another time."

"It's not as simple as it sounds, Oliver."

"I guess not!" Oliver said, amused.

"There's nothing to worry about," Prithvi said. "These boys are an enthusiastic bunch."

"Boys? Young man, are you out of your mind?" KD blurted. "If the script is good, you can make a killing out of this movie. It could be your comeback. Let me direct this. Let me handle it for you. We'll get Lal and—"

"I've already accepted the proposal," Prithvi said, maintaining his cool. "I liked the story and I met some of the team. We struck a great rapport."

KD fiddled with the large diamond ring on his thick middle finger. "Well, of course, your call, young man. I guess I was jumping the gun, and besides Lal has to like the story too. I just wanted you to be safe, that's all."

"I appreciate the gesture, KD. But I think I got this."

"That's all well and good then," KD said finally. "Do you have a team that is ready to go?"

"There's a local team."

"Oh, you've made contacts pretty quickly in the business." It didn't sound like a compliment.

"It's a new re-acquaintance," Prithvi said, wishing he hadn't finished his drink so quickly. "It was someone my grandfather knew."

KD leaned forward. "May I suggest someone capable for you? It's the least I can do. I'll send Ramu to work with you. He's been my trusted production exec for years. He'll manage everything. It'll take a huge load off your shoulders."

"That won't be necessary."

KD waved his hand dismissively. "I insist. You'll thank me later. When do you start?"

"As soon as possible."

"All good then, young man. I'd like to take a look at the screenplay, if you don't mind."

"Actually, I want to go with my gut on this."

KD looked startled at the reply. "Fine!" he said, shrugging his shoulders. "Suit yourself. You always have me if you need me." He held out his stubby hand and they shook hands. "Congratulations!"

"Congrats!" Oliver joined him.

"Thank you!" Prithvi said, and called for another round of cold beer to celebrate.

* * *

"Have you discussed this with KD?" Vinodini asked when she heard about Prithvi going away to Kochi to start his latest movie.

Prithvi was having dinner with his mother at home. Daisy was feeding her.

Prithvi narrowed his eyes at his mother. "I'm not a little boy, Ma. I don't need KD's advice on everything. Though I did tell him about it."

"He's been like an older brother to you since you started out. You mustn't forget that."

"I'm not forgetting anything!"

His mother looked upset at his outburst. Then she straightened herself. "What about the nuisance from the media?"

"I'm hoping it'll be a while before the media catches wind of this."

"Kuttan Sir, have you made sure about the family background of the director?" Daisy's eyes held a look of concern. "Hope we won't have another suicide or something like that."

"Stupid girl!" his mother admonished. "Talk of something good."

"Don't worry, Daisy," Prithvi said. "Take care of Ma for me while I'm gone." He turned to his mother. "There's some trouble brewing at our packaging plant again. I'll make a short trip there first. In the meantime, KD has assigned us a new executive producer. A fellow called Ramu. I'm meeting him tomorrow."

"KD is a good boy," his mother said, her eyes welling up. "I'm glad he's there for you."

"Don't get pulled in by his charm, Ma. KD is a shrewd businessman."

A tinge of sadness crossed her face. "He wouldn't be helping you now if he didn't want to." She sighed. "He was the only one around to perform the last rites after your father died. I owe a lot to him. He helped you get started, advised you to move here when you got into trouble. I'm obliged to him now, more than ever."

It was pointless to argue with his mother when she became overly sentimental like this. Besides, she looked tired and unwell. This didn't seem like the right time to bring up questions like why would KD insist on sending his man out there, or want to read his script. He had a vague feeling that KD was being overly possessive. Either that, or he didn't trust Prithvi to make his own decisions. But instead of telling this to his mother, he held her hand. "Good night, Ma," he said softly. "I'll be fine."

Prithvi made a visit to KD's office the next morning to meet Ramu, before leaving for Kochi.

Ramu rose from his seat when Prithvi was ushered into the spare office room.

The strong smell of *attar* assailed Prithvi's nostrils, the moment he stepped inside. Ramu was a man with a short bulbous nose and a shaved head. He was dressed in a garish coloured shirt.

"Hello, Sir!" Ramu stuck out his hand. "I'm Ramu." His smile revealed a row of crooked, yellow teeth.

Ramu was a smooth talker; he smiled a lot and bragged about his ability to handle all types of situations. Prithvi pegged him as eager to please.

As Ramu spoke about his experience of working for KD for many years, Prithvi couldn't help wondering why KD was sending this man over to him. If Ramu was so crucial to KD's business, shouldn't he be keeping him?

As they discussed the movie's upcoming schedule and plans, Prithvi had the nagging feeling that something didn't feel right. Was it because of the recent problems he'd been getting into, or was he being uncharacteristically suspicious? Or was it something about Ramu that he couldn't quite put a finger on?

Ultimately, he gave up trying to figure out the reasons for his doubts, and settled for trusting KD's suggestion to hire Ramu. Ramu was all set to take on as the new executive producer and leave for Kochi immediately.

Prithvi had never felt more ready to take on the responsibilities of running his business.

22

When Prithvi arrived at the site a few days into the shooting, Aditya and his crew were setting up the cameras by the side of a river. A large crowd had gathered to witness the annual boat race that had already begun kilometres away, upstream. The team had already gotten the permissions required for shooting on the river bank, and had planned and arranged the shots for the next few days. Today, they were going to shoot during the live boat race.

Ramu walked over towards Prithvi with a jaunty stride, his overwhelming *attar* smell preceding him. "Hello, Sir!"

Prithvi's hand almost went up to his nose before he shook the proffered hand.

Ramu's eyes shone. "How do you like the arrangements, Sir?" He pointed at the crew and people milling around.

"Aditya told me you suggested this venue?"

Ramu puffed up his chest. "When I saw the boat race scene in the script I suggested we shoot during the Pulinkunnu boat race, Sir. It will give us the perfect backdrop for our casual shots." He led Prithvi to the edge of the river and pointed upstream. "The race will start from kilometres away, upstream, pass this spot and continue onward to its destination quite some distance away, downstream."

"Right," Prithvi said.

"If I hadn't thought of this idea, we might have had to book the boats and hire the boatmen and the costumes. It would have cost us a lot of money," Ramu said, looking proud of his idea.

Prithvi nodded. There was no doubt Ramu was a resourceful man.

Aditya walked over. "We have the cameras in place. We're going to capture the live boat race and village crowds. Then we'll shoot with our own men within the backdrop to make it look more realistic. Ramu's plan turned out to be a great idea."

"I think he's living up to the reputation my friend KD claimed," Prithvi said, and Ramu beamed.

Manu's fight scenes were also getting set up against the background of the boat race.

A little away and closer to the river, a team was helping Manu rehearse his scene. Prithvi watched the rehearsal from a distance.

Manu was looking up the riverside. A few minutes later, a few hooligans came running towards him and tried to snatch his bag. A fight ensued. The AD explained the ending of the shot where one of the hooligans would push Manu into the river and escape with his bag. According to the script, Manu would struggle and drown because he didn't know how to swim.

Manu sat down on a nearby chair to take a break while the crew readied the cameras and lights.

Bobby arrived just then.

"That's my shirt," Manu yelled suddenly, pointing at Bobby.

"Too bad. It was hanging in the vanity van and I thought it was mine," Bobby exclaimed.

A scuffle started. Manu made a growling sound in his throat and lunged at Bobby's collar. "Give it back. I need it for the next shot."

In a blink, Ramu ran up to the two and separated them. "Hey, cut it, you two!"

Manu's face went red. "He's wearing my shirt."

"Nobody told me it was his." Bobby scowled.

"Okay, here's the deal," Ramu said sternly. "Bobby, remove that shirt and give it back to Manu."

"But I'm already wearing it!"

"Then take it off. We're getting ready for his shot."

Reluctantly Bobby removed his shirt, but instead of handing it to Manu, he flung it on the ground, getting it muddy and dirty.

"I don't want it," Manu said, smarting. "He was always jealous!"

Bobby scoffed at him, and walked away while Ramu sent someone to bring the spare shirt.

The boats were now visible as dots, far away in the distance. The shots had to be taken soon and as perfectly as possible.

The ADs rushed to their positions. Manu put on the fresh shirt and went to his spot to start the shooting.

The shot needed a few takes before Manu got it right. Just as the boats glided downstream, Manu was pushed into the water. After thrashing his hands around for a few minutes, he went down.

"Cut!" Aditya called.

Manu rose, drenched, and came up to the shore. While he was towelling himself, Prithvi walked up to him and held out his hand. "I'm Prithvi. I saw the rushes. They're looking good."

Manu blushed. "Thank you, Sir!"

A boy soon brought Manu a dry shirt, and then they went to check up how the shot had come out.

Shortly after, Prithvi left and headed back to his car.

It had been days since he'd rested well. But if he hadn't been to his Kochi plant on time, a massive fight would have erupted among his workers. He'd had to settle a dispute over wages and increments between some older workers and the newer bunch that had just arrived from Bengal. And then he had had to sort out the issue of a minor theft.

He drove to the lodgings where the movie crew had been put up. That was a two hour drive. It was the nearest motel they could find in the area close to where the rest of the shooting would take place. It was near Cherai town but it was a sleepy village. The motel was at the end of a long stretch of a near-empty road that ran along a narrow strip of the Cherai beach. As the beach was not a popular one, there were no signs of any people around, apart from a few tourist cars parked in some shady spots. Prithvi's car drove through the gates of the motel into an open courtyard, lush with low hanging fruit trees, and stopped under the pergola entrance of the motel. Prithvi smelled an overpowering flowery fragrance in the air.

He decided to go on a tour around the premises before checking in. Although a small property, it was peppered with green, shady patches created by large trees. Benches and hammocks were put up at several spots. A water fountain in the centre of a small, manicured lawn offered respite from the scorching sun.

From a distance, he saw her in a hammock, sheltered by the shade of a large Champa tree, bursting with white flowers. She was relaxing, reading a book. He wondered if it was alright to walk up to her, when she suddenly looked up and saw him.

"Hello. You're here?" he called out and started walking towards her.

Neha shut her book and turned to face him. "Yes, I arrived a few days ago."

"How's your foot?" he asked.

She blushed. The breeze blew her hair across her face and he found himself staring at the star-shaped nose pin that a lock of her hair had caught on. He wanted to reach out and free her hair but she moved.

"It's okay now," she said, and tried to sit up but wobbled before she could get her foot on the ground.

He lunged forward to steady her, and gripped her arm, catching the faint whiff of her perfume. She smelled like flowers too. Sweet. Refreshing.

"I'm okay." She laughed, and he slowly let go. Her gaze flickered in his direction for a moment. She was blushing again.

"I was at the shooting site," he said, not wanting it to get awkwardly silent between them. "Thought I'd spend a couple of days here before heading back to Bangalore."

They spoke of mundane things for a bit. She laughed easily. She enquired about his mother and Daisy. She'd heard his mother wasn't keeping too well.

He could see why Daisy was so fond of her. There was a softness in her eyes, a genuineness that ran deep. He could feel the raw vulnerability in her gaze as she looked up at him. And yet there was a poise and strength that held her together.

Daisy had told him that she lived alone, now that Ria had gone to stay with her grandparents. He wondered if she felt lonely. Like him. If she needed a friend, someone to talk to. Like he did. He hadn't been able to stop thinking about her since dinner that night. He found that he couldn't stop gazing at the dimples in her cheeks when she smiled. He could see her eyes shining even though she had her hand raised to shield them from the sun. To his utter consternation, he found himself staring, hopelessly; he hadn't felt like this around a woman in years. The moment stretched until she spoke again.

"I hope Daisy is taking good care of her and cooking up a storm even without me." Her eyes twinkled. "Please do tell her I miss her."

He found himself giving her an awkward nod and taking his leave.

As he headed to his room, he was still thinking about her. He pondered over her troubled face, the way her eyes became clouded with sadness in her unguarded moments, even though she laughed while she spoke about Ria. He wished he could take away her troubles, ease her sadness, be the shoulder she could lean on. He wanted to help her. Yet he had no idea how.

* * *

At the dining hall that evening, Prithvi saw Ramu engaged in conversation with Aditya. From the excitement in their talk it was obvious that the shooting had gone well and that they'd got all the shots they'd wanted.

He headed towards their table. "It looks like things went to your satisfaction?"

"Yes," Aditya said, excitedly. "The fighting scene with Manu was a little tricky but we managed to get even that done well with the way the cameras were set up. We shot from two different locations so that we didn't miss the backdrop of the boat race during the shot."

"Very good!"

Aditya's phone rang right then and he left the table. Prithvi turned to Ramu. "Obviously KD was right when he said you were great with production."

Ramu's eyes shone. "I've been with him for five years now. He trusts me completely."

It was obvious that he loved to brag about his closeness to KD.

"There was one time that we had to blackmail an actor to do a role as promised. I tried to persuade him nicely at first, but he wouldn't agree. Then KD made me take some compromising pictures of his and show it to him. The poor dude was so shocked." He laughed a belly shaking laugh.

He reeked of alcohol and seemed to be having a ball.

"I know KD Sir so well," he continued, obviously enjoying Prithvi's complete attention. "KD Sir had a crush on a director's wife once. That poor man did not know what he had coming." The laughter and stories continued. Ramu had just then begun talking about how they shot in public parks without permission when Aditya returned to the table.

Prithvi waved to him. "Join us. We were just talking about the time when Ramu got into trouble when shooting in a public park without obtaining police permission."

But Aditya's face looked grave. It was as if he was lost in serious thought.

"What happened?"

"The extra lights we had ordered are going to be delayed. They won't be here tomorrow. Without them we won't be able to shoot as planned."

"I'll take care of it," Ramu said immediately. "I'll make sure it'll be here by the day after."

Aditya seemed somewhat relieved.

At the next table, Bobby and Manu still seemed to be angry with each other over the shirt incident. Although they were sitting together, they weren't talking. Neha, who was sitting in between the two, was trying to pacify them both.

Prithvi went over to them.

"When Ria was a little girl," Neha was telling them, "she always fought with her best friend. They'd be playing together all day, and then suddenly one of them would get upset and stop playing. Then, for days, they'd stop talking or going over to the other's house. I would constantly be trying to pacify them but they would only look the other way and refuse to be the first to give in." She laughed. "You both remind me of Ria and her friend now." She looked up as Prithvi walked over, and stopped.

"Please continue," he said. "Let me not stop this discussion."

Neha smiled. "I was just trying to tell them how childlike they seem when they fight."

Prithvi pulled up a chair.

"He's always sulking these days," Manu said. "He's taking my things without asking and causing trouble just because he has a very small role."

Bobby crossed his arms around his chest. "I am not sulking. In fact, you're the one who wants to act superior as if just by becoming the hero you can get whatever you want."

Prithvi looked at the two and laughed. "I don't think this is going to get resolved all that soon. I thought you guys were close friends."

Manu sulked. "Not that I care."

"I don't care either," Bobby rejoined.

"That's too bad," Prithvi said, grinning. "I thought we'd all go out tomorrow for a treat. Aditya has a delay with some equipment and we cannot shoot tomorrow." He looked at both of them. "But if you'd rather stay here and squabble, we could forget about going."

"Depends on where we're going," Manu said, immediately curious.

"Uh...I was thinking of Veegaland Water Park."

Bobby's eyes gleamed. "The whole day?"

"That would be the idea, yes." Not only did an outing to a water park seem to be a good opportunity to get to know the people he was working with, but it was also probably the best way to make use of a free day.

The two smiled instantly. "That's been our favourite place to hang out since school," Bobby said.

"It's settled then. What do you say, Neha?" He gave her a look that begged her to play along.

And she did. "Yes. If these two promise to behave, then, yes, it sounds like a good idea."

Bobby and Manu whooped.

When they left the table together in an open display of renewed camaraderie, Prithvi laughed and looked at Neha. The beautiful dimples were back as she smiled. "I hope we have a great day tomorrow."

She nodded with relief. "Thank you. I had almost failed at getting those two to quit getting at each other's throats. And, yes, I'm looking forward to tomorrow."

And I'm looking forward to it too, he thought to himself.

23

At Veegaland Water Park, Neha was the only one who did not do the water rides. When she'd said that she was looking forward to it, she'd meant to have a quiet day off, not in the water but lazing outside in the sun. She hated getting into the water.

There was a bookstore nearby for people just like her and she went in there to browse. Several minutes later, she exited, armed with a romance paperback and made her way to find a table outside a café. She picked a seat right below an awning facing the giant water slides, from where she could watch the rest screaming with delight as they dove in and kept coming back for more.

She ordered a cup of cold coffee and entertained herself by trying to read amid the din, in the crowded park where hundreds of people were loitering around in their swimming trunks, their bodies glimmering with a mix of sweat and water trickling down. At the far end of the giant pool, Prithvi sportively allowed himself to be dunked by a group of boys, and rose back to the top of the pool. He looked years younger, and happier than when she'd first met him.

She sat there for a couple of hours, swatting flies, and deeply engrossed in her book. Then, it began to feel hotter once that the mid-afternoon sun was higher up, and she moved further inside the café looking for a table where it was cooler.

"Still here?" The voice behind her startled her.

She turned around and saw Prithvi in nothing but swimming trunks, a towel hanging over his bare torso. "You look like you had a great time in the sun," she said, noticing his tanned face.

"Do you mind if I join you?"

She shrugged. "You're done already?"

"I'd catch a cold if I stayed in the water too long. It gets pretty cold in December." He began towelling himself. "I thought I'd order a cup of hot coffee. Can I get you anything?"

"No, thanks. I've had two cups of coffee already."

As he went to get his coffee her gaze was drawn to the scar on his right calf that was longer than the one on his face. He'd stopped using his walking stick and his limp was barely perceptible. He couldn't be very old, she thought, as he returned with his coffee.

He placed the cup down and took a seat opposite her. Instantly, the sun was off her face and she felt much cooler. "Did you get bored by yourself?" he asked.

"I was having a good time watching all of you," she said, smiling. "I don't like getting wet, that's all."

"I haven't seen anyone who doesn't love water."

"Well, now you have."

He laughed at that, with his head thrown back again. It made her giggle.

A plate of brownies arrived at their table. She looked at it and then at him, surprised.

He grinned at her sheepishly. "I have a soft corner for brownies. They're so perfect with coffee. Have some?"

She shook her head and gazed outside while he dug in. "This place is so perfect for families," she said, catching a glimpse of a family of four by the sidewalk, holding hands, and their little girl laughing with glee. "Have you been here before?"

"I'd say any company is fun at a place like this though I haven't been here before."

"For lack of company?" she teased.

He smiled. "You could say that. Even though I'm in Kochi quite often."

"Do you have family here?" she asked, and then thought it was too personal.

"None that you haven't met already. Only Ma and I. And Daisy."

That's not what she'd meant but she had her answer: He was a bachelor, and she wondered why, and then she told herself that it was none of her business. "Daisy told me you run a fish export business," she said, to change the subject.

"Someday, I could give you a tour of how we process fish for export, if you like."

"Ria would love it too." She glanced at his face surreptitiously while he sipped his coffee. She was happy to see him excited about his new movie now. The usual frown, a permanent fixture on his face, had disappeared. He appeared more confident and relaxed. Happier. Younger. Like years had fallen off his face. A day's break had been a great idea.

He looked up just then and caught her staring at him. "Are we getting late?" he asked.

"No, no. I was just thinking of going over to the store and buying something for Manu and Bobby."

"Still playing peacemaker?" Mirth shone in his eyes.

"I've kind of got used to that role, being the oldest sibling. I was always solving disputes between my younger brother and sister."

He was interested in hearing more about her family and she didn't mind telling him all about her siblings. He, in turn, told her all about his early life, his accident, and the reason he'd come back.

"How do you know Aditya?" he asked out of the blue.

She told him how they'd met. "He's become like family now."

"Your family must be worried about you being here alone." His eyebrows were raised, a look of concern lining his face.

"It did feel strange that I ended up coming here alone for the movie. But I'm not alone, especially with all of you."

It was like a cloud of worry had lifted off his face when he smiled again. She liked to see him that way.

"I had never considered acting, for anything in the whole world. My father would have chased me with a stick if I'd told him that I wanted to be an actress," she said, sure it would make him laugh, and she was right.

He chuckled. "What does he think of it now?"

She squinted at him. "You know, you're very inquisitive."

He gave her a sheepish grin. "I know I am but you're evading a very simple question."

"He's softened, I suspect, after my tragedy..." She was suddenly aware that she was thinking about Mohan again and her mood dipped. Every day was a struggle, trying to shake off the debilitating thoughts of his death. She rose. "I'd better get to the store before it's time to leave."

"Carry on," he said, albeit a little regretfully. Then, on a sudden whim, he added. "Wait, I'm coming too."

She made her way around the corner to the exit, tensely aware that he was walking with her. Once inside the air-conditioned store next door, however, she lost herself in the colourful display of shirts, swimwear and other knick knacks.

Prithvi could have kicked himself for having reminded her of her tragic past. He hated seeing the sadness shrouding her eyes. If it were up to him, he'd always keep her happy. He walked around the store with her, tried on some hats she wanted to buy for Bobby and Manu, and let her click pictures of him in funny poses. She laughed at his antics, and when she did, he felt as if a weight had been lifted off his chest. After the shopping was done, they went in search of Bobby and Manu.

When she showed Bobby and Manu what she'd got them, they were surprised. Bobby was openly excited as he tried on his new wide-brimmed hat. Manu put his on too. "You shouldn't have," he said, affectionately.

"That's alright." She patted their hats by turn. "You both remind me so much of Ria."

She'd got Ria a hand-painted cloth bag to hold her art supplies.

After lunch and a few more water rides, it was almost time to leave.

The Volvo bus ride back to their motel in Cherai was raucous, with singing and dancing.

For the next few hours till they reached the motel, Neha loosened up, getting into the spirit of the moment, clapping and singing along with the group.

* * *

Back at the motel, Prithvi stepped out on the terrace after dinner, for a breath of fresh air. He lit a cigarette and took a long puff, looking up at the black, night sky, with not a star in sight. He hoped, among other things, that this movie, unlike the first one, would go through without any problems.

A shadow by the gate suddenly caught his eye. The light from the veranda below was dim, and he could barely make out the gate of the motel from the second floor where he was standing. He couldn't see who it was at first, but soon another figure walked out of the motel towards the gate. As the figure passed under the dim lamp, the form revealed a man with a shaved head, wearing a bright orange shirt. It was undoubtedly Ramu. He'd stayed back at the motel instead of going with them to Veegaland. It was to make sure the equipment arrived safely, he'd said. Prithvi looked on curiously.

The shadow at the gate moved forward. Now Prithvi could see that it was another man. Ramu and the man briefly engaged in conversation, and then Ramu pulled out something from the knot at the top of his *mundu* and handed it to the man. The man counted what looked like a bundle of notes.

Prithvi extinguished his cigarette and returned to the dining hall. A few minutes later, Ramu entered through the door, went straight for his dessert and was back at his table, engaging in desultory chit-chat with the others.

Prithvi dismissed the exchange he had just witnessed; Ramu must have met someone he had to pay for work. He had nothing else on Ramu since the strange feeling at their first meeting, and he wasn't about to start another round of probing now.

It had been a long, exhausting day. He scrambled into bed immediately after dinner. He felt finally at peace about this movie and his new team. He couldn't have been happier at how things were going. Thoughts of the afternoon spent with Neha drifted into his mind. Talking to her had been a refreshing change. After months, he had enjoyed lighter moments, without emptiness and loneliness devouring him. As his eyelids began to droop, he wondered what it would be like to bring back the smile on Neha's face as she'd brought one to his, to be there for her, to make sure everything was going to be okay.

24

Manu was burning the midnight oil. His preliminary exams were in January, just a few weeks away. His days were fully occupied and the final board exams were just two months away, scheduled for the beginning of March. He knew he couldn't afford to fail.

One night, he knocked at Neha's door. She was surprised to see him holding his textbook and reading outside her room.

"What are you doing here?" she asked, rubbing her eyes.

"Is it okay if I disturb you? I need someone to sit beside me when I study."

She let him in. "Sure."

"I'm in no mood to study by myself. But the only way my dad will get me a new bike is if I pass."

"So you must!" Neha laughed and ruffled his hair.

He sat up with her, studying until the wee hours of the morning.

Manu reminded her of Ria in so many little ways. Ria, her little baby, who always wanted her Bournvita milk at night before her sleep, who wanted to leave the night lamp on. Even grown-ups were like that, she thought. When they were nervous, they too needed a comforting presence.

For the next few days, Manu was a frequent night visitor. Then, he took a couple of days off to attend his practical exams. Prithvi too had left for Bangalore.

The shooting had been going on uninterrupted, for the last few weeks. Ramu initiated a plan for a bonfire one night.

The evening promised to be lively and relaxing. Food and booze were on the menu. An outdoor barbecue was set up and one of the chefs from the motel had been entrusted with the job of cooking some spicy, grilled, chicken kebabs and fish.

In the backyard, logs were stacked up for the bonfire, and lit. Soon, there was a large fire roaring. The meat was grilled and passed around, straight from the barbecue. Bottles of beer were opened.

By late evening, the party was in full swing, and the whole crew was around the bonfire, singing and dancing. Ramu asked for Aditya. Someone said they had seen him in his room, working on his script. Ramu and Bobby went to get him.

The scent of Ramu's *attar* reached Aditya's nose much before Ramu knocked on his door. "Aren't you coming?" Ramu asked, peering in. "The barbecue is getting cold. Come on!"

"Yes," Bobby chimed in. "The most hardworking man in the group needs to loosen up and take a break."

Aditya looked up from his desk and stretched his arms above his shoulders. "You guys carry on! I'll be out in a few more minutes."

He was exhausted, but so close to a perfect ending this time, that he didn't want to stop.

Ramu walked in, followed by Bobby. "What's the matter? Is there any way I can help?"

"I was just re-writing the last few scenes. The previous ending wasn't working."

Ramu leaned in to take a look, his breath smelling of alcohol. "When will we get a copy of this?"

Aditya rubbed his eyes. "Very soon. I'm nearly done. Can't believe I didn't think of doing the scene this way, before."

Bobby pulled his notes off the table to take a look. "What's so exciting about the new ending now?"

Aditya grabbed his sheets back. "Stay away from this copy. I'll share it when I'm ready."

Bobby mimicked him. "I'll share it when I'm ready." He crossed his arms and scowled. "Like it's so precious, we can't even have a look."

"Well, you can't unless I say so," Aditya snapped before he could stop himself.

Ramu waved his hands trying to diffuse the situation. "Well, come now, both of you. The barbecue is waiting." He tapped Aditya's shoulder. "And you do look like a little diversion could be good for you. You can look at that in the morning with your batteries recharged."

"I'm getting back," Bobby said, turning to go. "I'd ordered some prawns. They should be coming up soon."

Ramu tugged at Aditya's hand. "Now put that away and come along. Enough of work. Let's enjoy tonight."

There was very little left to do and Ramu was right, he could use a break tonight. Aditya stuffed the folder and a sheaf of papers into the drawer beneath his desk and they left together, closing the door behind them.

It was a beautiful night with the orange glow of the fire casting a small circle of light in the centre of the dark backyard. Several people were already seated in chairs around the fire. Someone was singing a song and others around him were clapping and swaying to the beat. The wood crackled and sparks from the burning embers were scattered into the air. As he neared the fire, Aditya felt its warmth, and the stress eased from his body.

Determined to enjoy this well-deserved break he joined the boisterous party, seeking Bobby in the crowd. As a sort of apology for snapping at him, Aditya thumped Bobby's back and grabbed the empty chair next to him. Bobby seemed to have forgotten the episode; he was cheerfully digging into the prawns and offered some to Aditya. Ramu pulled up another chair right next to them.

In time, the singing and dancing ended. The crowd dispersed

slowly, people going off to their rooms to crash after the hearty meal and drinks, while a few remained, talking among themselves. Bobby and Ramu were drunk. Aditya was on a pleasant high. The conversation veered towards production jokes. Since Ramu had been on several movie projects, Bobby pressed him to relate some funny stories.

Ramu lit a cigarette, crossed one foot over his thigh and began, "One time we needed a mouse for an actor inside a jail."

Bobby leaned forward and rubbed his hands. "Ok!"

"The shooting had to be completed that day and we couldn't find a stray mouse, so we managed to get a pet mouse and brush it with black tooth powder." Ramu's body shook with laughter as he said this, and he had to stop to wipe the tears flowing from his eyes.

The image of the pet mouse squirming, as hands held it down and covered it with black tooth powder seemed hilarious to Bobby, and even Aditya, found himself grinning.

Ramu aimed his fork at the plate of barbecued chicken, failing a couple of times before spearing a piece and popping it into his mouth. "It was hard but they did it! Then, they kept a plate of food beside the actor, and released the black mouse so that he would run across and sniff at the plate."

Ramu wiped his mouth after another gulp of his drink. "The mouse was made to run across the same three by three cell again and again, until they got the shot right. And then, bam! He suddenly vanished!"

Bobby jolted forward and clapped his knee. "Vanished?"

"Yeah! They couldn't find him. Everyone began searching. Until they found him hidden inside a drain pipe and he wouldn't come out. Then, one guy got so frustrated that he threw a bucket of water into the pipe."

He took a large swig before he went on. "Hell of chaos that mouse created holding up the entire unit that night but finally, they got him. Shooting with animals is frustrating as hell." He waved his glass at Bobby. "Taking your shots was much easier than that, Bobby!"

he said, his eyes dancing with mirth.

Hooting laughter broke through the group. Bobby took the joke like a sport, laughing and nodding his head animatedly. "Yes, I am a much better actor."

More food and drinks were brought to them as the night wore on. One story led to another and pretty soon Bobby was so drunk that he started rambling on about his hard luck. How his father had a chance to go to the Gulf but couldn't because he got into an accident, and how he himself had to then become Manu's family driver.

Aditya said he was tired and rose to leave but Bobby pulled him back to his seat by force. "You know this movie was the biggest break for me. All because of you and a few days off from Manu's father, so that I could come here."

Ramu put a hand on Bobby's shoulder. "Don't worry, you'll get a lucky break in your job too."

Aditya sat down again. "You'll be fine, my friend."

The bonfire had been extinguished by now. Everyone else had left the yard. Dinner had been wound up, long back. It was past eleven at night. Aditya gulped down the last of his drink and decided to call it a night. He could feel his legs wobble and he was tired, but he was also feeling light and happy.

Bobby was onto the next sad story of his life, hiccupping as he poured out his woes. "You won't be working for Manu's father all your life," Ramu said to Bobby, trying to calm him down.

Aditya left them and went to his room even as Ramu continued to pacify Bobby. He collapsed on the bed without bothering to change and was out like a light.

25

Over the next few weeks, Ramu spent most of his time getting locations, equipment, cameras and props organised, making sure the unit had meals on time and basically ensuring that the shooting ran smoothly. He also spent a lot of time with Bobby.

Bobby had taken a special liking to Ramu, especially since the barbecue night and, although his scenes were completed, he stuck around Ramu whenever he could, learning from him or driving him around, while also travelling to Chengannur intermittently on work at Manu's home.

A few evenings later, Bobby and Ramu were at dinner when the conversation veered towards Bobby's Gulf dreams again.

"Haven't you ever thought of going abroad?" Bobby asked Ramu as he eyed the plate of pakodas at the buffet table.

Ramu delved into his pocket and took out his wallet. Inside was a photo that he removed and showed to Bobby.

It was a photo of a young man holding the hand of a little boy, their backs to the sun and laughing at the camera. They were in front of a huge building.

"Is that you?"

"That's me with my father," Ramu said. "We were in Muscat

when I was a child and I was there for many years."

"Haven't you wanted to go back?"

"I lived there until I was around twenty. But dreams of Bollywood and the movie industry pulled me to India. This is where I wanted to be. Five years after I came back, I met KD and shifted base to the South. So here I am and there's nowhere else I'd rather be."

"I've always wanted to go to the Gulf," Bobby said. "If I could be a driver there, I'd earn so much more. I almost got a call for a visa once, but I contracted chicken pox right before the interview and couldn't go. I wanted to try again but it didn't click."

"I have some people I know who can help you. You make some arrangements for the money. I'll let you know soon."

Bobby's eyes lit up, but their conversation ended abruptly as Manu joined their table. Ramu left to take care of other things and Bobby turned to Manu. "Will you lend me some money?"

"What for?"

"Ramu has promised to set me up with a Gulf employment agent."

Manu laughed. He didn't have any money to lend but he couldn't help rubbing it in. "Why? So you can cancel at the last minute and lose all the money like you and your father did the last time?"

"Don't be such a prick!" Bobby shouted. "I had chicken pox and my father couldn't go because of the accident. It's not because he failed the interview like you failed your exams. Look at you!" He sniggered. "You were stuck in the same class for so many years."

Manu was touchy about the subject of his exams, just as Bobby was, about going to the Gulf.

"At least I got close to graduation," he said, fuming. "I did not remain an eighth grade fail like you, you fool!"

Bobby lost his head. He picked up the nearest object on the table, which happened to be a steel ashtray, and hurled it across the table at Manu. Manu didn't see it coming. It clanged against his head and went flying across the room.

"Ow!" Manu yelped, his hand cupping his forehead. Aditya looked up from where he was sitting a few tables away. But before he could intervene, the two had locked horns. Manu pushed his chair back and lunged towards Bobby for a fight. But he was no match for a guy like Bobby who was built like a mountain and had huge arms. Bobby landed a punch across Manu's jaw. "Take that for being such a jerk," he growled.

Aditya tried to disentangle the two, who by then had grabbed each other's collars and were raining blows on each other.

"Stop it, you two!" Aditya shouted. He grabbed Manu and pulled him aside. Meanwhile, a few people sitting at the other tables grabbed Bobby's arms and held him back.

"What is it with you two?" Aditya yelled at both.

Bobby pointed at Manu and yelled back. "This scum was insulting me."

"Bloody illiterate driver!" Manu retorted, eyes glaring.

"Stop calling each other names," Aditya said, pushing them apart as they came towards each other again.

Manu's anger spilled over, as he turned to Aditya. "Do you know how jealous he is?"

Bobby spat at him. "Jealous? You're jealous because you still live on your father's money whereas I earn an honest living. You can't find that kind of work even if you want to."

"Oh yeah?" Manu replied, "Isn't what I'm doing here, honest work? At least I got this on my merit and not because I had to beg for a role like you."

"So what?!" Bobby bellowed. "Aditya is my friend too and I've already proven that I can act."

"Act, my foot! You're nothing but a leech!"

Bobby glowered at him. "You think you're a hero just because you bagged a lead role. We'll see about that!"

Aditya glared at Bobby. "Get out!" he growled softly, hating that it had come to blows between his two, best friends. "We don't need to create trouble around here. Don't you have something useful to do rather than hang around the sets?"

"Don't bother with empty threats!" Manu blurted out to Bobby, pulling his hands free. "Show me what you got!"

Bobby looked from Manu to Aditya, his eyes smarting. "You're on Manu's side now? I expected fairness from you."

"I'm on nobody's side. I'm just trying to get this movie completed. If you're hell bent on disfiguring the lead actor, I'm going to have to order you to go."

"Yes, we can complete this movie only without fools like you!" Manu shouted at the top of his voice.

"Let's see you complete this movie," Bobby threatened. Then he turned to Aditya, eyes flashing. "Are you threatening *me*? Me? Who lets you ride with Priya to her college every day?"

Aditya was shocked to hear Priya's name dragged into this. "Don't bring up her name, you fool! This has nothing to do with her."

Manu shook his head in disbelief. "Why are you talking about my sister? What has she got to do with this?"

"Cut it out, you two!" Ramu was back.

Bobby got back to the table in a huff and Manu left for his room. Aditya turned to go back to his dinner. "Everyone, please get back to dinner," he said to the gathered folks. "The drama is over."

"Will you take Manu home tomorrow?" Aditya asked Bobby, later that night, hoping the misgivings between the two hadn't been too serious.

Manu had another exam that week and Aditya wanted him to go and return the same day.

"Why should it be me?" Bobby asked, still angry.

"Do you have something else to do?"

"Ramu asked me to stay. He has some work for me here. I can't go."

"But this is more important. Manu has to be back by tomorrow or we'll lag in our schedule."

"Can't he book a taxi?" Bobby said. "Or am I the only driver?"

"A taxi won't wait there to get him back. I'll have to pay to and fro fare for two taxis."

"Surely the producer can arrange transport for him?"

"Sometimes, you're simply impossible, Bobby!"

"He's your star actor and your problem, not mine," Bobby said and strode off.

By that night, Manu had a purple bruise on his jaw the size of Bobby's fist. And a lot of pain to boot. There was no way he wanted to return the same day, and hell no, he didn't want to go with Bobby. He ended up leaving for Chengannur by himself.

26

Aditya woke up in good spirits the next morning. Almost three-fourths of the shooting was complete. There were a couple more scenes with Neha, and some other scenes that he hoped he could complete before Manu was back.

He went to get his script right after breakfast, except it wasn't in the drawer. At first he thought he might have misplaced it. He pulled out everything and searched the whole room but the folder was missing and he just couldn't find it. To his exasperation, he realised it wasn't anywhere in his room. It had disappeared.

He called Ramu to ask if he'd seen his copy by any chance.

"No," Ramu shrugged. "Have you looked in all the usual places? Where did you see it last?"

"I was reading it in my room until dinner. It was the only copy with the recent scene changes I was working on. I had put it away in the drawer and then I didn't look for it again until this morning."

"By the way, did Bobby tell you I'd arranged a Gulf employment interview for him?" Ramu asked. "He's gone. His room is empty."

Aditya scowled. "That's so unlike Bobby to not say anything before leaving."

"I should have watched Bobby," Ramu said, sighing. "KD had

told me to keep an eye on things. Or something here was likely to go wrong."

Aditya looked at him, surprised. "Go wrong? How? What do you mean?"

Ramu's eyes darted across the room as if he was uncomfortable talking about it. "I shouldn't be talking about this. I thought everyone knew."

"About what?"

"Why do you think Prithvi accepted your script?" He paused to let the question sink in. "He wasn't getting any work. His company is jinxed, that's what it is. Nobody wanted to work with him after what happened to his last director."

"What happened to his last director?"

"Committed suicide," Ramu said gravely.

"What's that got to do with this?"

"His movies are said to be jinxed," Ramu said. "Bad things have been happening since his grandfather's time."

"This has probably nothing to do with the problems with Prithvi's company," Aditya said, dialling Bobby's number but it was unreachable.

Aditya called Prithvi, who went ballistic when he heard about the missing script copy. "You should have known not to leave it lying around," Prithvi barked into the phone.

"It was in my room!" Aditya said, equally peeved. "How could I have known somebody would take it?"

"Have you looked for it?"

He hated to tell him that Bobby had left without a word too.

"You should have been more careful," Prithvi said, sounding angrier by the moment.

Aditya couldn't take it anymore. "If I'd known about Priyamvada, I would have been careful!"

"What does that mean?"

"Tell me," he snapped, "Why did you accept my script? Was it because you had nothing else going for you?"

For a minute, Prithvi was stumped. Then he cut the call.

Aditya put on his sneakers and left for his usual morning jog, and he couldn't help thinking about Bobby. He didn't think Bobby had anything to do with the missing copy yet the thought that this could have been one of Bobby's childish acts gnawed at him. That he would have to work on those scenes again was annoying. Yet he wished Bobby had told him that he was leaving or that he was applying for a job. He would have been the happiest for his friend. There was no need for him to disturb the efforts of the entire team in the name of revenge against Manu.

Neha was on the second round of her morning walk when she saw Aditya jogging towards her from the opposite direction. He slowed down when he came closer.

"Please don't let me slow you down," Neha told him.

"I've already finished my five kilometre quota for the day."

She fell in step with him and noticed the troubled look in his eyes. It was obvious that something was bothering him. "What's happened?"

Aditya cleared his throat. "Is it true that Priyamvada seems to be jinxed and Prithvi was out of work? Did you know about it?"

"I had told you the company had been in trouble but I never believed the jinx story. Why?"

Aditya raked his hands through his hair and told her what Ramu had said. "Now my copy of the reworked scenes is missing. And Bobby's gone."

She was painfully aware of how that sounded.

"He's missing and my copy's disappeared, since the morning, and he and Manu had an argument last night. So either he left with the script to spite Manu, or something else isn't right."

"If it is Bobby, then maybe he is just playing a joke on you," she said, thoughtfully. "He'll come back with it in a few days, just you watch. Maybe he thought it was fun to irritate you."

"I never thought Bobby would do such a thing. Bobby, Manu and I are friends since childhood. Best friends!" Then he stopped. "I'm going to go back now. I need a shower."

Neha nodded and continued on her way.

It was still dawn, and to her left, she could see the orange sun making a slow ascent on the horizon. The waves whooshed against the tall rocks, which blocked a full view of the narrow strip of brown, sandy beach. She enjoyed her early morning walks, before the unit was up and getting ready for the day. She would have loved to walk barefoot on the sand, but the beach was littered with broken glass pieces and trash. Instead, as always, she took the roadside stretch beside the low wall bordering the beach, which was a short distance from the hotel. There was still an hour to breakfast.

The sound of the ocean usually had a calming effect on her, but today, after talking to Aditya, her mind was restless. She shuddered a bit, feeling a chill in the weather, and wished she'd brought a shawl along. A lone tea stall loomed in the distance. She usually walked up to the block after the tea stall, before turning back.

Somewhere behind her she heard the clink of a stone. It startled her. The loneliness of the stretch dawned on her, making her uneasy. She turned around, hoping to see Aditya, but he was at the hotel's gates by now, and nowhere in sight. Instead, far behind, was a man, his face partially hidden by a cloth tied around his head. The road was otherwise deserted, except for the man following her, his head bent. Her heart thudded. It could be one of the locals on his way to work, she told herself. She hoped to get to the tea stall not far ahead, quickly. She hastened her steps, her breath quickening.

Then, her ears picked up a distant sound behind her. A low hum at first, it sounded like an engine but as she hurried on, the sound drew closer. A motorbike.

Something didn't feel quite right. Her heart was thudding; she didn't dare look back again. She broke into a run instead to make it to the tea stall. A few moments later, the bike came close. It seemed as if the biker was about to zoom by, and she almost let out a breath of relief that it hadn't stopped when suddenly, she heard a crack in the air, then a whoosh and then something hit her leg hard. A sharp pain shot through it. Crying out, she buckled down in pain and fell to the ground, instantly losing consciousness.

27

Aditya had showered, and had just entered the hall for breakfast, when he heard the news of Neha's accident. Somebody had recognised her as belonging to the movie team staying at the motel and rushed to call him.

Aditya hurried to the site and called for help to take the still unconscious Neha to the hospital.

There was further bad news. Her right knee had taken the brunt of her fall and needed surgery, the doctor told him.

For the moment all his anger and concerns were forgotten, and he called Prithvi to tell him about Neha's injury. Prithvi was quiet for a while, before he regained his voice and said that he would be there as soon as possible.

Aditya got so busy with Neha and the hospital visits after that, that he'd had no time to think about Bobby. He'd also gone to the police station to file a complaint about the attack on her but nothing had come out of that either.

Then, he got a call from an unknown number, and was flabbergasted when he recognised the voice.

"Where the heck did you go?" he asked. It was Bobby.

"I'm sorry there was no time to let you know," Bobby said.

"Did you take my script copy?" Aditya asked him without any preamble.

"No!" There was shock in his voice. "I don't know anything about that."

Aditya believed him because he knew that no matter what, Bobby would have owned up to it if he had really taken it.

He was in Oman, he said, working as a driver for a Sheikh's family. "How's the movie coming along? Is that idiot Manu better?"

When Aditya told him about Neha's accident, he was shocked. They spoke for a while and then hung up. Aditya let out a breath of relief. At least he didn't have to suspect his own friend anymore.

But then, who? Why?

"What did I tell you about Priyamvada being jinxed," Ramu said, when he told him about Bobby's call. The missing copy had not yet been found. Neha was still at the hospital. "Now can you see the signs?"

"What signs?"

"Look at it yourself, Aditya. Priyamvada has been in trouble for a long time. His grandfather had to close down because a huge fire gutted the entire set, causing crores' worth of losses. After Prithvi took over, his director commits suicide, and, as for this movie, the shooting gets stalled for various reasons. First, the equipment delay, then the misunderstandings within the team, the lead actor gets bruised in a fist fight, an important script copy disappears, and now the actress has an accident. I'm not saying we have to think negatively. I mean, accidents and delays happen all the time. But too many of these, and they cannot all be called coincidences."

Aditya had nothing to say. He was baffled, even as Ramu left him alone with his troubled thoughts.

* * *

Neha was groggy after the surgery, and resting in her room. Prithvi was the first to visit her that evening.

She'd never seen him look so worried before, standing at the entrance to the room, looking like a lost puppy. He could hardly bear to look at her. "I'll call the nurse," he said when she moaned, as the effects of the painkillers wore off.

"No, I'm fine."

"I'll be back," he said. "I want to speak to the doctor." And he was gone in a flash.

"Someone out there is very concerned about you," Shweta said, as she entered Neha's room a few minutes later and embraced her in a hug. Neha had told Aditya to inform only her sister about the accident.

"What do you mean?" Neha asked.

"Billionaire boy was busy asking the doctors outside all sorts of questions about you and the surgery and your recovery. He was so terribly sweet I just couldn't take it anymore," she said, teasing.

"Did you tell Ma about this?"

"I told nobody, but Ma wanted to know why I was making a sudden trip, and I told her I wanted to spend some time with you.

Neha smiled weakly.

"Hi...sorry!" Prithvi barged into the room and then stopped short when he saw Shweta. "I can come back later."

"Oh, no, no," Shweta said. "Please stay. I was just going to get something to eat at the canteen. I got here straight from the airport. I haven't had anything since morning."

Shweta left, and Prithvi approached Neha's bed.

His face looked ashen. "I'm sorry," he said, looking sadly into her eyes. He seemed to be at a loss for further words.

She was groggy and in pain but, she realised for the first time, she could not bear to see the look of worry and regret written on his face. An inexplicable feeling of heaviness settled in the pit of her stomach. A desire to hold his hand and wipe the creases off his brow swept through her, catching her off-guard.

She squirmed as he helped her pull up her sheet over herself, and brushed some stray hair off her face.

"Thank you," she said, blushing, and suddenly conscious of his closeness. He smelled of coffee; she could do with some herself. She hadn't eaten for hours and was thirsty too, but the nurses wouldn't let her drink anything for a few more hours at least.

His eyes were full of concern. "Did you see the person on the bike?"

"No. He came suddenly…" Speech seemed such an effort. "And he was wearing a helmet…" She felt her words beginning to slur and trail off, as her eyelids drooped. The medication was so strong. She felt his hand cover hers as she eased into sleep.

Prithvi looked at her small oval face and the tiny mole on her upper lip, wondering how he hadn't noticed it before. Something squeezed in his heart as he watched this frail and beautiful woman lying in front of him. His heart beat wildly and the urge to envelop her in a hug wreaked havoc in his brain. For the first time, a feeling that he'd never experienced before swept over him. He had fallen in love. Even if the feeling was new, something that had never happened to him before, he knew what it was. He was in love. The intensity of that truth startled him, jolted him out of his comfort zone.

Then came the pain. A vast sweeping pain that tore at his heart. The remorse over what had happened to her. The realisation that it was all his fault, when it hit him, was too much to bear. It was almost as if he had caused her to risk her life for his movie. None of this would have happened had he stayed back at the motel with the unit, he chided himself. As he looked at her face, at the long, dark lashes that formed beautiful crescents beneath her closed eyes, he made a promise to himself that he'd do whatever it took to protect her.

Casting one last glance at her, and closing the door softly behind him, he stepped out into the corridor. He headed to the canteen to talk to Shweta, and found her seated at a table in the far corner.

She smiled as he approached her. "Thanks for letting me know."

"Thanks for coming."

A tinge of embarrassment crossed her face. "I never got to say how sorry I was about your car."

Prithvi waved his hand. "Please, that's all in the past."

Assuring her that everything would be fine and that she could stay at the motel until Neha was better, he headed there himself to look for Aditya.

A few hours later, Prithvi found Aditya still cooped up in his room, pacing the floor. "Why don't we take a short drive?" he asked Aditya, sensing that he was tense.

Shortly after, they were out of the motel gates and cruising towards town to find a decent place where they could talk and have lunch.

Along the way, Prithvi wondered what Aditya was thinking. He was looking straight ahead and hadn't spoken a word since the call to tell him about the missing script and then, of Neha's accident.

"I went to see Neha on my way here," Prithvi said. "Did she say anything else about the accident?"

Aditya continued to stare ahead, and sighed. "It looks like it wasn't an accident. The bike came close and hit her. She thinks it was deliberate."

Prithvi's grip on the wheel tightened. "Deliberate? But why?"

Aditya clamped up again. Prithvi found it difficult to concentrate on the road, as well as get him to talk.

"What are your plans for the shooting now?" Prithvi asked in an attempt to draw him out.

"Some of Neha's scenes are still left. I have some others I can complete in the meantime. Some village scenes, some money lender issues and a local brawl."

"That sounds good. At least we can go on and keep Neha's scenes for after she recovers."

They arrived at the city centre soon. They parked outside a busy pub with hard-to-find parking, and entered the dimly lit space to occupy a couple of barstools at the counter. A few drinks and a meal seemed to calm Aditya's nerves to some extent.

"We have to keep going despite all of this," Prithvi said earnestly. "And no," he clarified, "I didn't take you on because I had nothing else. I believed in the script then and I still do."

"I want to know whether what I've heard about Priyamvada is true," Aditya said, and went on to tell Prithvi what Ramu had told him about the past and current problems.

"I honestly don't believe that Priyamvada is jinxed," Prithvi said, feeling a bit unnerved by Aditya's rant. "I think it was, and still is, a sabotage."

"But why would someone go after Priyamvada?"

"Beats me! All I want to do is to find out who's behind this and finish him off."

Aditya sipped the last of his drink. "I just hope we're not in any more trouble. But I do feel better after talking to you."

"I do too," Prithvi said, sighing. He paid, and they drove back to the motel.

28

The day Neha was getting discharged, Prithvi drove over to the hospital to pick her up. Shweta had been there all morning, signing the discharge forms and making the payment.

When it was time to go, Neha dressed herself in a long, flared skirt to cover the braces on her knee. The attender came to her bedside to help her into the wheelchair but Prithvi gestured for him to step aside. Before Neha realised what he was doing, he had pushed one hand beneath her knees and lifted her up with his other, rounding her shoulders.

"It's okay. I can drag myself into that," she protested.

But he'd already got her off the bed in a single heave. He walked the short distance to the wheelchair and set her down gently.

His thin linen shirt grazed her face and almost blinded her as he bent over her.

"You look like a pro," Shweta teased him.

"Right!" he said, as he helped Neha set her feet on the rests. "I am a pro by now. I've done this for my mother a million times." His Adam's apple bobbed in his throat. His voice was so thick and reverberating up close, Neha got goosebumps. She turned her face away only to find that his face had moved closer, trying to adjust the cushion behind her back and that she was nuzzling his neck. His beard felt fuzzy and tickled her face. Her cheeks burned.

Finally, he straightened up to appraise his handiwork. "All set?" he asked her. There was a twinkle in his eyes as if he was trying to be cheerful just to make her feel better.

She nodded and swallowed, telling herself she was blessed to have such a good friend, and feeling a tinge of sadness overcome her she avoided his eyes after that. He cared. God, was she ever so thankful for having such a friend! He probably even felt guilty over her predicament. But he didn't need to. She'd give anything to make him believe that she had nothing against him, no ill feelings whatsoever. Whatever had happened to her hadn't been his fault.

Shweta offered to push the wheelchair. She bent and whispered into Neha's ears, "This looks like what Amitabh Bachchan did for Mili, no?"

"Does this look like some soppy movie scene to you?' Neha hissed back. Luckily Prithvi didn't hear.

* * *

They reached the motel and Prithvi scooped Neha up again. Strangely, it felt like he'd held her in his arms for a lifetime. She was so shy she wouldn't look at his face even if he was talking to her, muttering all kinds of nonsense into her ears so that she didn't have to worry about how heavy she was or how much of a trouble she was for him, which was what she'd been agonizing over, all the way from the hospital.

Her skin smelled of candy floss and the soothing scent of lemon grass. The hem of her skirt grazed her ankles and revealed her silver anklets. She looked so delicate and trusting that he wanted to hold her close in his arms forever, and never let her go.

"Please, you're going to break your back. Put me down," she pleaded, as he carried her all the way to her room.

"I got this."

She winced as he laid her down gently on the bed, in her room.

He supported her feet and moved a pillow under them, then straightened her skirt that had ridden up to her calves. He looked up at her and their gazes held for a brief moment. He brushed a stray lock of hair off her face.

"Thank you." Her voice sounded hoarse, and she winced again as she moved her leg.

His breath caught in his throat.

She looked so beautiful, his heart ached to hold her in his arms and kiss her. Something inside him urged him to tell her how he felt about her but he fought that urge down. He'd wait for her to recover before he bared his heart to her.

Neha was left alone with Shweta when Prithvi left the room.

"What was that all about?" Shweta said when Prithvi was out of earshot.

"What?"

"He likes you!"

Neha shifted and winced again. "You and your silly imagination!"

"Didn't you see how he wouldn't let anyone else take care of you?"

"Is that why you timed your entry late? To give us time alone?" Knowing Shweta and her antics, this was just what she might have done.

"What!" Shweta said, rolling her eyes in mock-surprise. "Prithvi needed time to settle you in. I thought it would be better if I left you two alone."

"He's a good friend," she warned, knowing Shweta's penchant for going crazy over mushy love stories.

"I think he's devoted to you," Shweta said, with a toothy grin.

"Yeah, right!"

Though she scolded Shweta, she was secretly thankful she'd left them alone. She couldn't have taken another embarrassing glance from Shweta.

Neha moved her knee and the pain shot through her leg once again. A tear escaped her eye.

"Hey!" Shweta had a questioning look on her face.

"Nothing." She turned her head away, trying not to show her how overwhelmed she was. How much she was missing home and Mohan and Ria, and a normal life.

* * *

Shweta returned to Bangalore, in January, after spending a couple of weeks making sure Neha was on the mend. Prithvi stayed back at the motel and kept a hawk's eye on Neha and the rest of his team. He would stay with the team until the completion of the movie, he decided.

Neha's knee still hurt but she was much better. She was also worried about her remaining scenes. How would they finish the shooting on time if she couldn't walk?

Manu had returned after his preliminary exams. Aditya suggested that they take the rest of Neha's shots, mostly while she was seated. Or, he suggested, he'd add a scene where she actually fell and hurt her knee so that she could limp if she had to.

They managed to finish Neha's part of the shooting somehow, Manu helping as much as he could to adjust to the time it took for her to get ready for the shots and, sometimes, to keep the expression on her face cued in to the demands of the scene, despite the fact that she couldn't bear the pain.

* * *

"What do you mean it sounds the same?" Prithvi looked at his mother, flabbergasted. He'd come to Bangalore on an urgent message from his mother and here she was telling him that his story was the same as the one KD was working on.

"I'm telling you because KD told me his story, just like you did, and it sounded the same to me," his mother said.

"That can't be possible! My movie started more than a month

ago. We should have been done by now if it had not been for all the delays."

"Isn't your movie about a poor boy who's robbed and then becomes invisible in order to teach the thieves a lesson?"

Prithvi nodded in surprise.

"See, I did think it sounded familiar."

Without waiting for a moment longer, Prithvi grabbed his car keys and headed for the door.

"Don't tell me you're going to see KD *now*?"

He was.

A quarter of an hour later, he was at the club where he thought he'd find KD playing his usual squash match with Oliver.

"To what do I owe this surprise?" KD said, walking up to him after the match, holding out his hand.

"Are you working on a new movie?" Prithvi asked without preamble.

"Didn't I tell you I had a new screenwriter? I just happened to show the script to Lal and he loved it. We're quarter of a way through it. Why do you ask?"

"The same guy who came to me? That's not the script he showed me!"

"Relax, young man. What is this sudden spurt of inquiry about? He must have had another script. Anyway, the point is, Lal took one look at it and okayed it. So we started shooting for it."

"Is it about a poor boy who is robbed, meets underwater spirits, becomes invisible and takes revenge on the thieves?"

KD looked shocked. "How do you know that?"

"Because that's what I've been working on!"

"Look young man, this is Lal's movie we're talking about. My whole business would go kaput if Lal came to know that he was working on a script that has been stolen."

Prithvi felt his neck grow hot. "Stolen? Who says it was stolen? My director wrote it."

"But we don't have any proof, do we?" KD said smoothly. "Your fellow could have written it with somebody else, and maybe that somebody else showed the script to somebody else. Whatever it is, I've had the script for a while now. Besides, a Lal-starrer will attract a bigger audience than a movie with no known stars. So it would be better if you drop your script like a bag of hot potatoes, or your movie will flop anyway."

"Drop it? We're almost done with it already."

"Young man, I'd hate to go the legal route but Lal would force me to go for it, to clear his name."

Prithvi buried his head in his hands. "But I have a registered copy of the script."

"So do I!" KD shouted. "If you want me to take legal recourse to prove that my script is original, I will. So…sorry to say this but I think you must drop your movie."

Prithvi paced the floor. The air inside the club was stifling.

"There is one more option," KD continued. Prithvi stopped and turned around. "Ask your fellow to change the story so it looks nothing like the original. A few clever tweaks should do the trick. If he indeed wrote such a brilliant script, that should be no problem for him, right?"

* * *

It was late when Prithvi returned home. He was so shocked by KD's blatant accusation that the script that he had could have been stolen, that he'd walked out from the club without any more discussion, not knowing what to do. While the script in Prithvi's possession had also been registered with the Film Writers Association, how could it have been possible that KD had registered the same script, and that too before him? If he filed a lawsuit and disputed KD's first claim to the script, would he win, or did he risk losing everything he'd worked so hard for?

His mother was still waiting up for him when he unlocked the door to his apartment. But he was in no mood to discuss anything right then. He poured himself a glass of whiskey and was about to go to his room, but she rolled her wheelchair towards him.

"What did KD say?" she asked.

Prithvi sighed. For once he wished Daisy had made his mother go to bed earlier, instead of herself going to sleep. "Ma, can we talk about this in the morning?"

"No, I want to talk about it now."

He turned to face her. "Okay, yes, the script is the same."

She nodded. "I thought so. So one of you is going to have to give it up."

He was silent.

"What are you going to do?"

"I don't know." Prithvi tightened his grip on the whiskey glass. "I don't know what to do."

"KD has helped us more than I can repay him for," his mother said, turning her wheelchair around. "I will not stand for jeopardising his future just because it's my son's movie. I owe him that much at least, until I die." Those were her final words before she wheeled herself out of the room.

Prithvi was struck by the irony of the situation. His mother's wishes were the polar opposite of his dead grandfather's. What were the options left to him? What should he do?

He downed his drink in one gulp and poured out another. Then another, and another, until his brain felt numb and he could barely think or feel anymore.

29

A few days later, Prithvi drove back to the Cherai motel. Thinking about the current dilemma had brought no solution whatsoever. He was still deep in shit. His mother refused to hear him out when he tried to tell her that he was sure his script had been stolen.

"KD has been in this business for so long," she had reasoned. "He doesn't need to compete with you for work." That left nothing for Prithvi to say for himself.

He knew he was taking a coward's way out, but there was a bleak chance that they could still wriggle out of this messy situation. And there was only one man who could help him.

Aditya.

Prithvi went in search of Aditya and found him in his room. When he told Aditya what had happened and suggested changing the script, Aditya was furious.

"This is my script and it is original. I'd registered it. I've never discussed it with anyone and neither did I show it to anyone except you."

This was the part even he didn't get. "Then how is it that KD has the same script?"

"I should have known that working with you would jinx my

movie too. I should have known," Aditya burst out in anger.

Prithvi pulled out a sheaf of papers from his bag. "Look, this is just a big mistake. I've put down some possibilities for this script. If we can change it in some way, we can still salvage this movie."

"I don't want to change a thing." Aditya's voice cracked. "This movie will be made as I'd written it or I don't want to be a part of it."

From the corner of his eye, Prithvi noticed a slight movement outside Aditya's room.

Was it really someone moving or was he imagining it?

Aditya was pacing about, fuming, unaware of the turn Prithvi's thoughts had taken. The door to the room had been left ajar, and Prithvi was sure whoever was outside could hear what was being said inside the room.

The things happening to his projects suddenly didn't feel like coincidences. He knew in his gut that someone was deliberately trying to sabotage him. But who and why?

Like a jigsaw puzzle, the pieces of this mystery were forming a pattern and he had to get to the bottom of it.

Without saying another word, Prithvi laid the sheets on Aditya's desk. "Take a look at it when you get some time."

"I don't want to be a part of this sham anymore." Aditya didn't even bother to look at Prithvi's proposal and stalked out of the room in a huff.

Whoever was listening in at the door had disappeared. Prithvi left the papers conspicuously on Aditya's desk and walked out of the room himself, leaving the door ajar. If someone had been spying outside, he would surely make a move now.

Prithvi walked a few steps to the left of the hallway, rounded the corner and returned a minute later.

Sure enough, there was someone in Aditya's room, peering through the papers that Prithvi had left behind on the desk on purpose. The man, his back to the door, was wearing an unmistakably familiar attar.

Ramu.

Prithvi entered the room and bolted the door from the inside.

When Ramu heard the bolt, he spun around. He had the sheaf of papers in one hand and his phone in the other.

"What were you doing?" Prithvi growled.

He put the papers down on the desk. "Nothing," he said, nonchalantly. "Just passing by and I saw these papers flying off the desk, so I came to put them back."

Prithvi nodded but wasn't going to accept the explanation so easily. He hadn't expected Ramu's smooth comeback. And although he knew that he had no solid proof that Ramu was indeed trying to get his hands on the changed script, he was sure that he was.

It didn't take too much to guess what had happened.

Ramu had overheard his conversation with Aditya and realised that they were discussing the changes in the script. He'd wanted to take pictures of the changes to send it to someone. Someone who had been sabotaging Prithvi's movie. Who could that be?

"I guess I picked the wrong time to walk by," Ramu said, with a laugh.

And that was when it struck him.

His first meeting with Ramu had felt odd. Now he knew why. Ramu had the air of a man who couldn't be trusted. He was the cheat who was working for KD.

It became easier to connect the dots now. KD was the man who'd sent Ramu here in the first place. And KD was the only person who had the exact same script.

Did that mean that KD was behind the sabotage?

Prithvi staggered at the realisation that he may have hit upon a vital clue. Although he had no proof to link KD to Priyamvada's misfortunes. Not yet. But he had a feeling that he was close to finding out the truth.

It was all coming together now.

As Ramu turned to leave, stepping out with the confidence of a free man, Prithvi called out to his back. "You were talking about KD dating a director's wife once. What happened to her? I'm curious."

Ramu turned around and scratched his head. "Oh that!" he said. "She was one among many for KD. Only she didn't know that, and took it bad. Her husband, the director, couldn't take it either, and he ended up taking his own life."

Why hadn't he guessed?

Ramu laughed. "I heard that he pulled strings to hush up the investigation into the wife's infidelity angle in the suicide case."

Of course, that was it! That was why the wife had been trying to put the blame on Prithvi. She needed a way to clear herself of the blame. Probably she'd been advised to.

KD's affair with his director's wife and its consequences had worked in KD's favour. It must have been a long shot but it had ruined Prithvi's first movie. Then he'd sent Ramu here to mess with Prithvi's next movie so that he could get hold of the script. Realising that it was good, KD had started shooting with the stolen script. Then all he had to do was to make it look like Bobby had disappeared with it, and then spin a legal angle on the whole thing.

The pieces of the puzzle began to fall into place.

Ramu, who had been with KD for so long, had been sent to work on Prithvi's project. Now, all of it—the delays in the shooting, the fact that Ramu had stayed back when the whole team had gone to Veegaland, the missing script copy and Neha's accident—made sense. All minor diversions while KD was busy getting Lal signed on and starting off a movie with Prithvi's script.

His conversation with KD at the club came back to Prithvi. How, many years ago, Prithvi's grandfather had rebuked the young KD and denied him a chance.

Another piece of the puzzle clicked into place and KD's motives suddenly became crystal clear.

Could it be that the fire at his grandfather's set hadn't been an accident at all? Had it been KD who had ruined his grandfather's business all those years ago? And now, wanted Priyamvada closed down forever?

That was it, wasn't it?

Why else would KD go out of his way to harm Prithvi's projects and put him out of business?

Prithvi looked at Ramu's retreating back. He could frame Ramu right now, beat him up and make him cough up the truth but that would only alert KD. But he wouldn't have anything on KD. And he didn't want that. Not quite…

One burning question still remained, confusing the heck out of him.

How the hell had KD managed to register the script earlier than Aditya?

*****

When Aditya heard of what had happened in his room after he'd left, he couldn't believe it. "So Bobby was framed?"

"I think Ramu thought that we'd never hear from Bobby and we'd never be able to get in touch with him to know the truth."

Aditya was hopping mad and would have strangled Ramu if he could lay his hands on him right then. But Prithvi calmed him down. They still had no proof.

The only thing left to do, Prithvi told Aditya, was to see if the script could be reworked to make it look different. "The only way to beat KD is to complete the movie despite the challenges," he stressed.

But Aditya would have none of it. "Why don't you file a lawsuit against them? Let it be proved that both registered scripts are the same and KD's date-stamp is earlier than mine."

Prithvi tried everything he could to convince Aditya that it was risky to go to court. It would delay the movie and the negative publicity could kill Priyamvada forever.

"This has cost me my life's work and you're concerned about the publicity?" Aditya yelled.

"It's too late to stop the shooting now," Prithvi pleaded. "The only thing we can do is to change the script."

"Changing this story is not possible," Aditya said with finality. "In fact, working with you is not possible."

"Look, Aditya! Think of how far we've come," Prithvi tried to reason. "Trust me! We can make this work."

"Trust you? You cheated me!" Aditya yelled, his voice loaded with contempt.

It felt like a slap on Prithvi's face.

"My story was stolen by a person sent by you," Aditya said bitterly. "It is you who cannot be trusted."

Prithvi's voice was hoarse. "Isn't it foolish to give up now?" It was his last attempt to save his movie. But it was futile.

"It may sound foolish to you and may cost you money. But this has ruined my career." Aditya laid his suitcase on the bed and began packing. "This movie has been my undoing and I wish I'd never accepted it even if I had had to beg on the streets. My mother had such high hopes for me and I have let her down."

Prithvi watched on helplessly as Aditya finished his packing, shut the suitcase and stormed out of the room. "Please don't look for me or try to reach me ever," he said. "I hope our paths never cross again."

Prithvi stared mutely at Aditya's retreating back.

What was he to do now?

He was still staring at the door, wondering what to do when Neha barged into the room. "What do you mean this movie can't be completed? I just saw Aditya outside and he told me he was leaving."

He looked at her angry face and wished that at least she'd understand what he was going through. "It wasn't my decision," he said, the words bringing fresh pain.

"If everybody knows it was Ramu, then why not!" she said, exasperated. "Why can't you file a case and get back what belongs rightfully to you?"

"There's no right or wrong," Prithvi said, trying to make her see the point, trying to tell her that risking a lawsuit would only prove to be a dumb mistake.

She flared up. "Oh no, that's not the whole truth. You're trying to protect the man who's involved. Let me guess! He's your friend in the business? Someone you can't stand up against?"

"Stop it, Neha," he shouted, shaking her by the arm. "You don't know what you're saying."

She shrugged herself free. "Oh yes, I do," she said, her eyes spitting fire. "You're running away again, just like you ran away when your first movie was in trouble."

She'd hit him where it hurt the most. "That's not true!"

Her eyes dared him. "If only you'd face up to the truth. If only you'd stop believing that you can't change what's happening. If only you'd think of the lives you're playing with."

He looked at her, praying that she'd believe him. "I'm not playing. This is serious. I can't point fingers until I can prove something. If Aditya supported me, I could have turned the tables on my enemy, but he has abandoned me when I need him the most."

"Too bad that the people you trust don't trust you back," she said, turning on her heels. "I took you for a tough man and a friend, Prithvi. But you've let me down too." And without further ado, she stormed out of the room.

His confidence and self worth crumbling, he watched her go. There was nothing he could do to stop her.

Her words seemed to reverberate in the room even after she'd left. The one woman he'd come to love and respect had left with nothing but regret in her eyes. He'd let her down. He'd destroyed the trust she'd had in him. For the first time in his life, he felt ashamed of himself. And experienced a deep rage that he couldn't handle. Looking around wildly, he grabbed a chair and flung it across the room. Its legs cracked and broke. It lay there in the corner, limp and shattered. He slumped on the bed and buried his face in his hands. He was not only a failure but also a spurned man.

30

Neha ran into her room and flung herself on her bed. She knew how it felt when people you needed the most, abandoned you. She'd believed and trusted in Prithvi. The thought brought tears to her eyes.

Her phone rang suddenly. It was her mother. Her heart plummeted when she heard her mother sob and ask her to come back immediately.

Ria had fainted in school.

It was all Neha could do to forget everything else and just rush straight back to her mother's house by taking the first possible flight.

Ria was still asleep in her room when Neha peeped in through the partly open door.

Ria stirred a little as Neha entered the room. Tiptoeing, she went to sit by her bed. Her eyes misted as she gazed at her darling daughter.

Ria's eyes fluttered open and she smiled weakly at Neha.

Neha held her hands, her heart brimming with concern. "Have you not been eating anything, Ria?"

Ria turned her head away.

"Talk to me," Neha said. "Please, tell me why you won't talk to me."

Silence.

"Did you also want to leave me Ria?" Neha asked, her voice choking.

Ria turned her head back to Neha. "Do you miss Papa?" she asked.

"Every day."

"Then why did you have so many fights?"

Neha hadn't expected that question. Had it been weighing on her child's mind all these months? "We had arguments," she said, choosing her words wisely yet not wanting to hide the truth. "They're not the same as fights. Sometimes the only way I could get him to talk to me was by provoking him. I had to force him to listen to me, spend some time with me. He was too busy."

Ria was listening to her with rapt attention.

"Sometimes loving someone causes one to want more attention," Neha said, sighing wistfully. She now wished both Mohan and she hadn't always been so busy that they hadn't found enough time for each other, and that they hadn't argued so much.

"Do you think Papa was happy?"

She ruffled Ria's hair and smiled. "I think he was very happy to have us both. He knew we'd always be there for him when he came back from saving the world." She patted Ria's hand and let her think about that. Then, she added softly, "Is it okay if I ask you something now?"

Ria nodded.

"Do you know what Papa wanted most for you?"

Ria shook her head. "No."

"He said his little girl was a princess and he would buy her the whole of Terabithia."

"Terabithia?" Ria couldn't help but grin a little. "Ma, I'm not a five-year-old."

Neha pinched her cheeks gently. "Who said you were? Your dad would have bought you Terrabithia, or close." She laughed, thinking about Mohan joking about it once. Her eyes welled up. "If he'd been here he would have wanted you to be happy and well, Ria. He'd want you and me…to be together and happy. We couldn't help what happened. It wasn't in our hands but what we do now will determine what happens to our family, to us."

She paused to wipe the tears streaming down her cheeks and gave Ria's shoulder a comforting pat. "So, be happy for Papa's sake."

Ria got up and threw herself into her mother's arms and squeezed her in a hug. "Ma, I—"

"And don't ever scare me like that again, okay?" Neha said, and tickled her, making her laugh.

Neha's phone rang. She gestured to Ria to lie down and left her room.

It was Aditya. His voice was clipped, disappointment oozing from it. When he told her he was dropping out of the movie, it broke her heart. She wished there was something, anything, she could do. But this time, things were truly out of her hands.

"What are you going to do now?"

"I'm trying to find a job," he said. "That's the only way I can marry Priya."

She knew what he meant. Manu's father would never give his daughter's hand to a jobless guy.

When she hung up, she was feeling restless and disjointed with her own life too.

Later, she called Shweta and told her about the end to the movie.

"What! I can't believe this!" Shweta said, shocked. "So the stories about the jinx were true?"

"Don't be silly, Shweta! Is there any such thing that can't be explained by logic?"

"Then, how come?"

She told her what she'd heard about Ramu and his treachery, and Prithvi's inability to set things right.

"Poor dude! If only someone could understand what he's going through. After all, he has suffered the most." She tut-tutted. "What are you going to do?"

"I don't know what to do. I can't just stay at home and do nothing."

"It'll be better now if you just stay at Ma's until things settle down."

Neha had been thinking about that herself. There seemed to be no other way out other than staying at her parents'. If Ria wasn't ready to go home, the last thing she wanted to do was to drag the poor, unwilling child there to deal with painful memories all over again. "But I can't manage in this uncertainty, Shweta!" she cried. "If Ria refuses to come home, how long do you think I can stay with Ma and Papa?"

"Do you want me to talk to her? Ma told me she fainted at school."

"I think there's more to that fainting than she'll have us believe. I think she needs to get out of this rut too. I want to help her but—"

"Take it one day at a time," Shweta urged, gently. "Things will get sorted out slowly."

As the days wore on, Neha thought it was better to stay at her parents' for a while. Ria was eating better now and looking more cheerful. For herself, she knew that she wanted to pursue something meaningful but she didn't yet know what. Shweta visited from time to time and she was the only person who brought smiles to Ria's face.

* * *

"Go right, there," Neha had to yell at the driver to make herself heard above the blaring of his radio. She was in an auto, travelling from her mother's place to her own, to get her house cleaned. She'd also called her house help over to meet her at the apartment.

The auto driver stopped. "No right turn there. There's digging going on."

"Okay, go straight ahead and take the next right."

The driver zoomed ahead and stopped at a narrower street,

further up. "Here?"

"Yes."

She hadn't come through this street before, but she guessed that the streets would converge sooner or later. This one would take her home too. The area had fewer buildings and more green cover. The auto shook and rumbled, going slowly over the humps and swerving to the right to avoid a drain.

Ahead of her, stuck to a post right by the side of the road, a flyer flapping in the wind caught her eye.

TO LET.

In smaller letters on top was the name of the establishment, more than half of which was hidden by the fallen branches of a tree dangling over it. She barely managed to read the last words.

DRAMA.

"Stop! Stop!" she called out to the auto driver.

He screeched to a halt.

She paid him and walked up to the post. Her hand couldn't reach up and grab the flyer, and she couldn't make out much from where she stood.

She approached a corner tea stall just at the bend. "What's that about?" she asked the fellow who was busy mixing the tea, literally throwing the tea from one glass to another. He made it frothy and handed it to his customer. Then he turned to her. "The drama studio is closing."

"Where is it?"

He pointed to a building down a side lane and went back to stirring the next batch of tea.

She took a walk down that lane, keeping her eyes open for any signs. At the end of the road was a pretty bungalow with blue striped awnings and a bold red door.

She went up and knocked. It swung open effortlessly. She stepped in to what was a bare room with a few things strewn around, which probably belonged to the previous owner. Beautiful things. Poufs, blocks, a tall wooden rack, art magazines.

"Hello," she called. "Anybody here?"

A woman hollered from somewhere within, "Coming!"

She waited and took in the wooden flooring, the tall bay windows, the yellow walls...

An older woman appeared in the doorway. "Are you looking to rent?"

Neha found herself nodding.

The woman beamed. "Come, let me show you this place." She gestured around. "We have two rooms, this is the main lounge space and next-door is the performance area."

Neha followed her into the next room. It was gorgeous! Sunlight filtered through and there was lots more woodwork and a platform that resembled a stage.

"What's that?" Neha asked.

"We had it specially made," the woman said proudly. "For Laila's Drama Group."

"Laila." The name rolled smoothly off her tongue. "What happened to Laila?"

"She moved to the States. She was amazing." With a hint of disappointment, she added, "She's not coming back."

"She did up this place?"

The woman nodded.

Laila seemed to have taste. There was an eclectic feel to the room. The modern mixed in with the traditional. Armchairs and brass lamps. Electronic sound system and mics holding up against paper lanterns in the place of bulbs. Wow!

She couldn't take her eyes off the sight even for a moment. "How much to rent this place?"

"Five thousand a month."

That sounded like an awful lot!

"It includes everything you see," the woman persisted with a smile. "The customer before you liked it, and will come back to pay. If you pay first, it's yours."

There wasn't much to consider. It was now or never.

She wasn't sure she was carrying that much cash or a cheque book. "Credit card?"

"No, sorry!"

She dug into the recesses of her purse, rummaging for cash hidden away inside the pockets. Rounding up everything she had, she counted exactly five thousand and one rupees. It felt like serendipity.

She handed it to the woman.

The woman gave her a key. "This place is yours. One for the main door. You get these two rooms. Rest of the house is detached."

Neha felt the heft of the key in her hand. It was minuscule. Hardly weighed anything. Yet she'd never possessed a more precious thing in her life.

In her heart, a major dance was happening. She couldn't believe she'd paid for this place. She couldn't believe she was going to start a studio of her own.

NEHA'S SCHOOL OF DRAMA.

The name popped into her head and stuck.

That's what she'd decided to call it.

31

Prithvi was back home, battered and defeated. His plans had failed. His mother still believed in KD. Prithvi had had enough.

As he was getting his things, his mother entered the room. "KD called me."

Prithvi just stared at her.

"He says he doesn't want you to suffer."

"I've suffered enough!" he growled.

"He's offered to make you partner in the movie with Lal."

Should he serve his own interest by letting down his own team? *Is that what he ought to do?*

"You can work with KD," his mother continued. "He's promised me that he won't let you down."

"He's already done the worst. What I don't understand is why the drama? What's in it for KD now?"

"Don't say such stupid things. If he didn't care so much about us, he wouldn't have suggested a way to help you tide over your present troubles."

"Help me?" he asked vehemently. "KD is the reason Priyamvada is in trouble. Why does he want to jeopardise my company?"

She clicked her teeth. "What do you mean? He has no such

intentions. Or he wouldn't have suggested that you join him. He's willing to share his profits in Lal's movie."

Prithvi had had enough. "Why is he so interested in helping me all of a sudden? Did he tell you how he masterminded Priyamvada's ruin by making Ramu steal the script, and forcing me to abandon my project? And now he wants to show you that he's doing us a favour!"

"That is not true!" his mother yelled. "I don't believe a word of it. KD only wants the best for you."

"What he wants," Prithvi yelled back, "is to turn me against the people who trusted me and to close Priyamvada for good."

And, for that, he would have to find another scapegoat!

"Where are you going?"

He was gathering a few of his things into a travel bag. He'd not even unpacked fully since he'd arrived at Bangalore. A few clothes in and that should last him well. What he needed was a few days/weeks/months until he could sort things out in his head. Get over the humiliation and figure out what to do. Anything but stay here and wallow in self pity. The last thing he wanted was to explain his sudden departure to his mother.

"Where are you going?" his mother asked again, when he picked up the keys to his car.

"Where I can be alone," he said defiantly.

And then he was gone before she could say another word.

"Take care, Kuttan Sir," Daisy said, rushing to the door to see him off, tears rolling down her face. He was happy to see that she cared for him, probably as much as his mother did. But the woman he'd wanted to love him and care for him was probably beyond caring any more.

* * *

"Eleven-Nine! I win!" KD yelled and threw his racket to the ground and got down on his knees to celebrate a tiring but well-deserved victory against Oliver.

"What's up today?" Oliver said, laughing. "You seem very happy about something. It's got to be something other than this match." He smiled knowingly.

He was joking, of course, but KD did have reason to be happy. Ecstatic, in fact. He grabbed a towel and collapsed into the nearest chair. He had executed his enemy's downfall so well, he had every bloody right to be extra happy.

He thought of how Vinodini Bai had cried into the phone. "KD, please take care of Prithvi. Please help him." She had literally begged.

He scrubbed his sweaty face until it hurt and then threw the towel to the ground. Legs spread wide open, he rested his head back against the chair, thinking.

Had Bharathan Nair thought twice before shutting the door in his face all those years ago? Why should he grant the dead man even a little happiness through his grandson? Bharathan Nair's Priyamvada had spawned many a sensational actor and director, but to KD its doors had been shut. After all, what had been KD's fault? Only that he was a poor, struggling twenty-four-year-old son of a struggling actor?

Now Vinodini Bai had wept over the phone, saying that the fool, her son, Prithvi, didn't want to be associated with Lal's project.

Instead, the fool had gone back to his cave, with his tail between his legs, never to come back. And that was what had been worth celebrating.

KD sat up, his throat feeling parched. He lifted a bottle and guzzled some ice-cold water, letting stray drops seep through his sweaty shirt. He felt good. Vindicated. Like a conqueror.

Priyamvada had been vanquished at last. Gone! Poof!

Vinodini Bai had wept some more, and that weighed on him briefly. A twinge of guilt passed through his conscience as he put the water bottle down. He had let her down, and then he'd said, "Don't cry, Vinodini Bai. Bharathan Nair would have expected his daughter-in-law to keep her chin up and brave the storm."

He felt a pang for saying that now. He'd adored her as a young boy pining for his non-existent mother. His father had told him that his mother had died at childbirth but every time he'd seen the beautiful and kind Vinodini Bai, he'd wished she were his mother. She'd been kind and loving, and given him gifts the few times they'd met. They'd been precious at the time. A wooden play horse, cash, a watch. His father could never have afforded a watch. And then there had been that joy in her face every time she saw him. A glistening in her eyes, a special warmth to her embrace. He'd adored her. Then. As a boy and later, as a young man.

Pity he hated her father-in-law and everything to do with Priyamvada! Including, now, her son!

"So what's the other score?" Oliver asked, bringing him back to the present.

He turned to Oliver, laughing. "I've kicked my archenemy in the balls. This score dates back to years ago when I was a young man in search of a job in this big bad world. Isn't it an irony that that very producer and I have switched positions? What they had, has now become mine. Forever."

Oliver didn't ask too many questions. "Every dog has his day!" he said, nodding. He knew and understood KD's vengeful tone.

"I convinced Lal to do it," KD said, rubbing his hands with glee. "It was like magic when he said that he loved it. A brilliant story indeed."

32

As Prithvi drove to his ancestral home in Kochi, he knew he'd screwed up his chances. Pretty much. This movie had been his last chance. With this loss, he'd never be able to make a come-back. Priyamvada was as good as finished. But come what may, he'd been certain, he would not join KD and let down his own team of people who'd trusted him.

He entered his house and rounded up the caretakers of the mansion—his house help, the cook and the driver. They were very pleased to see him back and asked if his mother was fine.

He had no patience for trivialities. Although these were the people who'd known him all his life, he wasn't the man they'd known, anymore. "No visitors are to be allowed in the study," he ordered. "No one. No phone calls, no visitors, not even my mother can speak to me. No one must know I'm here," he warned them.

They nodded their heads in unison, pledging total allegiance to his wishes.

He made his way to his study, which was to the western corner, and away from the main living areas.

They followed.

"Place all meals outside the study," he said. "None of you need enter it for any reason."

They nodded again.

He entered the study and bolted the door in their faces. He heard the patter of feet as they disappeared to their assigned stations.

Only then did he let out a sigh and turn around. The huge wall on the opposite end was staring at him. He hadn't entered this place in ages, he realised, and yet it was exactly as he remembered it. His grandfather's old gramophone sat on the left, next to the armchair and the tall bookshelf. A large mahogany desk and chair occupied the centre, facing the tall bay windows. A wide cushioned bench below it doubled as a bed. It was his father's place to rest if he wanted to spend the night in the study while working on his electrical installation project designs. It was where, as a young boy, he'd lie down when no-one was around and stare up at the sky.

The study also had a small back door that opened out to a walled-in patch of yard. A few mango trees that he'd hidden on top of, as a young boy, were out there.

As he threw open the door now, he stood facing an overgrown patch filled with shrubs, fallen branches and leaves. He couldn't believe how much this place had changed. It hadn't been maintained as well as the rest of the house. His favourite place to sit hidden, among the thick branches of the mango trees, or just play make-believe games in the yard, was now covered with rotten leaves and wild, unkempt grass. It was true, he'd forgotten all about the study after he'd returned to India.

He came back in and shut the door. Settling on the window seat, he stared out at the clear blue sky, envying it its peace and clarity. If only his own life were that pellucid.

* * *

Several hours had gone by when Prithvi woke up. The sky outside had turned purple and grey. He was hungry, he realised, for he hadn't eaten anything all day. He opened his door, and kept outside was a covered tray of food, a jug of water, a flask of tea and a cup, on a service table on wheels. He pulled the table inside and began to eat ravenously. When he'd finally polished off the entire meal, he pushed the table back outside, and closed his door again.

He paced the room until he was tired, then went back to the bench and curled up on it. And stayed there, alternately watching the sky that rose over his head beyond the window, and the blank walls that seemed to be mocking the broken man that he was. Here he was, back in his hiding hole. There wasn't a more broken, aimless and helpless man he'd ever known, than himself.

For days on end, all he did was curl up on the bench. He felt like he was going crazy. He'd never felt so utterly useless and hopeless in all his life. All he had wanted was to be worthy of his grandfather's trust in him. But he had let him down. He hated his decision to return to India, he wished he'd never started the movie or met the people he'd worked with. He wished he'd never met Neha. He was a coward and he'd run away from life and its challenges, like the only way he knew how. And he knew everybody hated him for not standing up to the blatant falsehood and sabotage that stared him in the face.

After several wasted days of agonising over his present state, Prithvi brought out the tote that he had packed in his bag. His hands tingled as he touched the gleaming brushes within. He hadn't painted in days but right then, his imagination was caught up by the urge to paint his study walls. He became a man on a mission as he moved the desk, armchair and every little piece of furniture until all the four walls were accessible.

First, he began with spaceships and Avatar-like aliens with long limbs, matted hair and dove-like eyes. He wanted the Avatars to look at him from wherever he sat in the study. He envisioned it to look like a video game where Avatars on alien spaceships fought one another, complete with escape routes, crevices, hideouts and whirlpools.

Soon, he was painting like an obsessed man, drinking cups and cups of coffee, and binge-smoking (he left notes for his staff to get him dozens of packs of cigarettes and regular refills of coffee).

Days passed and his routine was the same. He spent the mornings painting. Then he had his lunch and took a small nap. In the evenings, he tended to the yard outside, de-weeding with his bare hands. At night, he put on the old gramophone and listened to his grandfather's old records till late at night. His grandfather's record collection had old records of Suraiya. Only Suraiya, nothing else, as if his grandfather had been infatuated by the singer. Prithvi hated Suraiya's high-pitched voice, but he still put her on, and let her croon until his heartbeat settled into a rhythm. If she was all he had to listen to, he'd tolerate her. He made himself a drink and sat on the armchair by the window, stargazing and drinking as she sang in the background. Late at night, when he was exhausted, he slept on the floor and stared up at the day's work on the walls until he fell asleep. In the morning, when the sunlight streamed in through the tall windows, he got back to work. He hadn't shaved in days. He hadn't seen or spoken to anyone. He hadn't called his mother or taken any phone call.

Every time he needed more paint, he left a fresh note outside his door.

His walls were looking more and more like a war zone. A raging sea began to take shape on them, forming the backdrop for the spaceships and aliens. For the sake of distraction from the war zone, he began painting a mermaid resting on the rocks. Her face was what he imagined to be the underwater sea spirit from his movie. Except, she was coming alive with every stroke of his brush. While his movie was dead.

More days passed. He made the mermaid look like she was balancing on the rocks with her shiny scales glistening in the light. The mermaid had no eyes yet; he always left the eyes for last. Her hair flowed down to her waist, and as she sat there waiting for him to complete her, he watched her change and grow every day. From the fantasy mermaid that she was, she'd grown to be his companion over the days. Hidden from the spaceships and aliens, she lent him peace when he slept and woke up. Or when he paced the study sometimes late at night, or toiled relentlessly in the garden, not knowing when he was going to stop and return to the real world.

Then one day, he worked on her from morning till night without taking a break. He gave her almond-shaped eyes, big curly lashes and a lovely smile reaching up from her lips to those eyes.

He took two days to finish just the eyes, filling them with an electric blue paint. When he was done, he put down his brush and palette and mopped the drops of sweat from his head. Her big eyes were looking straight at him. Everywhere he turned he found her staring at him. He took a step back from the wall, satisfied with the final picture.

And as he was looking into those hypnotic eyes, her resemblance to the underwater spirit from the movie that he'd have liked to finish stung him. How could it have been, he wondered again, that KD's script and his were exactly the same? It had been such a unique story, which was what had attracted him in in the first place. *How* could the two stories have been the same? How? The thoughts squeezed his chest. Aditya's last words rang in his ears.

Let it be proved that both registered scripts are the same and KD's date-stamp is earlier than mine.

Slowly, like the unveiling of curtains, the cobwebs in his head cleared.

The two scripts!

What if indeed they'd been different all along?

What if KD's original registered date-stamped copy hadn't been this one at all?

Why hadn't he thought of it before? *Of course!*

Suddenly, as if a switch had been turned on, something clicked in Prithvi's brain. It was like the cranking of a lever, the slow rotation of cogs.

If no one had read the contents of the script at the time of the registration, like the usual practice at the Film Writers Association, wasn't it possible that KD had registered a dummy script? And claimed that it was this one?

Prithvi's thoughts were racing now.

KD had been bluffing, knowing very well that the threat of a lawsuit would make Prithvi back off. Nothing could be proved until the dispute went to court. And that's what KD had been betting on.

The initial shock at the deception was replaced by anger and frustration. When it finally faded and he had calmed down, what followed was a newly found sense of determination. Enough was enough! If KD could play this game then Prithvi could too.

What he realised then was the solution to this dilemma had been staring him right in the face all along. He now knew what he had to do. All it needed was for him to take a leap of faith.

He headed to the bathroom, shaved and had a hot shower. He changed into fresh clothes. Then, emerging from his study for the first time in weeks, he called his house help to set up his breakfast in the dining room.

After breakfast, he started making a few calls. It took a long time to find who he was looking for.

By dinner, he had the contact of the person he wanted to speak to.

After the call, he settled down.

Then, he prepared to wait it out although he knew that time was short.

After that, he called home and spoke to his mother. He told her he was fine and was going to remain in this house, taking care of his Kochi plant from there for a while.

He also spoke to Daisy, asking her to call if she needed anything and to keep her ears open for any conversation between his mother and KD. She was to report to him about the developments in KD's movie, anything that she could gather from his mother.

Now that the plan had been set in motion, all he had to do was sit back and watch it unfold.

33

Seated on his bamboo lounge chair on the porch with his legs resting high on the extended armrest, Thomachan took the sweet *paan* from his new wife, Sundari, and smiled at her appreciatively. She smiled back coyly and started folding another *paan* for him, since she knew he liked two of these sweet, rolled, betel nut leaves after a good, heavy dinner.

Thomachan was pleased to have, at last, found a wife. After sulking for months over his ex-love-interest, Indulekha, and his failed movie plans, it was sweet luck that had brought him in contact with Sundari's father.

Sundari's father once owned a dilapidated theatre on the fringes of Chengannur town. And since there were no theatres in and around Chengannur, Thomchan, who had failed at producing a movie, had a brilliant plan to buy the property and own a theatre instead. And in the course of that deal, he'd met Sundari and fallen hard for her. Harder than during the Indu phase. He chuckled as he admitted that to himself. Sundari was younger, fairer and curvier than Indu. Her skin was soft as butter and her long dark hair fell to her hips.

It had only been a month since Thomachan's wedding and he considered himself the luckiest man on earth. After offering the second *paan*, the young and bashful Sundari leaned forward to massage his legs. Thomachan closed his eyes and enjoyed the sensation of Sundari's soft, fleshy palms kneading his calves.

The sensuous massage was interrupted by the shrill ring of Thomachan's cell phone, cutting through the silence of the cool night. Sundari's hands jerked and paused mid-squeeze.

Tsk-tsking about the interruption, Thomachan answered the call, albeit reluctantly. "Hello?"

Sundari looked at his face expectantly.

"Yes…" A long pause, then, "Yes…Yes..." Much longer pause, then, "Is that possible?"

Her eyes widened in the ensuing silence as Thomachan listened intently.

"Okay…Okay…"

While the caller continued talking, Sundari stroked Thomachan's thigh.

"It's a deal," said Thomachan finally, and hung up.

"What was all that about?" Sundari asked, looking confused.

Thomachan's face glowed in the moonlight. "Your dream is about to be fulfilled, Sundari." He chucked her chin affectionately. "We have a secret benefactor, someone who doesn't want to be named. He's helping us make a movie, at last."

Sundari, who had extracted a promise from her wealthy, eager-to-please husband that the theatre, once renovated, would be inaugurated by releasing their own first movie, was pleased beyond words. "Really?" She hugged Thomachan, much to his surprise and shyness at her first-ever, open display of affection.

"Let's celebrate—", he said, jumping up from his chair, eager to milk the good news for all its worth and to make sure the neighbours didn't catch any peeps into the action. "In the bedroom."

Sundari batted her eyelids and followed him, while Thomachan was relieved that for once he was not already half-asleep by the time they reached there.

* * *

Back at home, Aditya gathered from his mother that there was a boy who liked Priya, and was very keen to marry her. Ever since Priya had finished her final exams, there was an unending line of prospective suitors who came and went. One, however, seemed to have stuck on. He was coming again to visit her the next Sunday. Malathi had been told a day before that the boy was coming to meet Priya, and she had to be at the house before sunrise for the lunch preparations in anticipation of the boy's visit.

On the next Sunday, a white Mitsubishi Lancer purred into Raman's drive around mid-morning. A tall, handsome man wearing shades emerged from the car and made straight for the house.

Raman called for Priya but she was nowhere to be seen.

"Where is she?" he asked his wife.

"She's gone to the temple."

The boy waited for what seemed like ages. His prospective father-in-law, Raman, and he, took their seats in opposite corners of the living room, Priya's mother took up another corner, and nobody said a word. It was almost lunchtime when Priya sauntered in and nodded slightly to the boy. They all sat down to lunch where hardly anything was spoken. After lunch, Priya said she had to finish a project and escaped to the library. The boy waited until tea when Priya briefly popped in again, before she was gone in a few minutes. At last, it was late evening. For the whole day, the boy had probably got just a moment or two to have a glimpse of Priya. He left and promised to come back the next weekend to meet her again.

The next Sunday, the boy was at Raman's house again and the routine continued. Priya tried to evade him as much as she could, but the boy waited for her return from wherever she had disappeared to. It was late evening again before he left.

Raman was tired of watching the same thing repeat week after week. Malathi was tired of cooking up a storm every Sunday. Priya's mother was tired of giving her husband company the whole day, and just chatting with the boy. Priya was tired of having to find a place to hide every weekend. But what to do? The boy seemed adamant in the hope that Priya would spend more time with him.

Aditya woke up half-heartedly on the day of his interview. It was probably the twentieth since he'd given up the movie. He'd attended all sorts of interviews, from that for a radio jockey to a night watchman. Today's was for a college lecturer's post, which he hoped matched his educational qualifications and his personality.

His mother was busy in the kitchen making his coffee and breakfast so that he could get to his interview on time. "Adi, breakfast is in the kitchen. Wake up and get ready," his mother hollered from the kitchen before she was off to do her chores at Raman's house.

"My father has started getting suspicious about every marriage proposal for me getting rejected," Priya said to Aditya, as she sat sulking on the stone slab in the temple compound, where he'd asked her to meet him after his interview. They were meeting after a long time.

"How was every proposal getting rejected?" Aditya asked, curious.

"I told the boys that I was secretly in love with someone and they'd usually reject me themselves. I also tore up all the letters that my father got by post. But then, he is very suspicious nowadays."

"Then why is this boy coming every week?"

"He said he'd marry me even if I had a boyfriend. He doesn't seem to be interested in backing off."

Aditya smiled sadly.

"Sitting here talking to you is also not appropriate anymore. That means I can no longer meet you here."

Ever since he'd turned down her father's job proposal at Bharatmata College, Raman had practically refused to see him. "I wish I could whisk you away from here," Aditya said, looking longingly at her hands that he wanted to hold. "But I don't even have the face to ask for your hand."

A lone tear slid down Priya's face.

He looked at her, ashamed, and rose to leave. Perhaps this was the last time he'd see her if she got married before he found a job.

There was nothing he could say or do to make it any better than it was, and he'd rather leave her with things unsaid than with any hope that he himself didn't have. May she forget me, he thought, refusing to say goodbye to his childhood sweetheart. May she find someone worthy!

"Adi," he heard her whisper to his back.

But he continued on, leaving her sitting there, feeling numb.

Outside the temple gates, he bumped into none other than Thomachan.

Aditya had never seen the devout church-going Thomachan outside a temple before. "You?"

"Ah, there you are!" Thomachan said, slapping him on his back. He noticed Aditya's bewildered look. "This is all my wife's doing," he said. "I come to the temple to drop and pick her up."

Aditya hadn't heard about Thomachan's wedding, much less about his Hindu bride.

"I wanted to meet you," Thomachan said. "What are you doing these days?"

"Just finished an interview for a lecturer's post at a college," Aditya replied brusquely.

Thomachan laughed derisively. "You? A lecturer?" He stopped shaking with laughter and looked at him more seriously. "Heard about your movie. I should have produced it. If I had a wife then as I have now, I would have."

Aditya gave him a half-smile. "Well, it's not going to happen."

"It can happen," Thomachan said, confidently. "I'm telling you it can happen."

Aditya stared at his feet. Thomachan could continue to boast some more if he wanted to.

"I am building a new state-of-the-art theatre," Thomachan said, puffing up his chest. "It will have digital projectors, Dolby stereo sound and AC auditoriums. I want to have that movie ready for release by the time my theatre renovations are complete."

"No, you can't. The story has been stolen. Somebody else is making the movie and we've lost the chance."

Thomachan tsk-tsked. "You've lost your courage, Aditya. If I were young and dynamic like you, I'd have pursued it. You must finish the movie."

"You didn't hear me the first time," Aditya said, louder. "The story has been stolen. KD is now directing and producing the movie."

Thomachan rubbed his belly. "Well, then in that case, it will be a race to the finish."

Aditya looked at him, perplexed as to what that meant.

"The one who releases it first wins," Thomachan explained. "Once we release it, what does it matter if someone else has the same story? It's their loss."

"What if they go to court?"

"We'll worry about that later. First, let's finish the movie."

Aditya was not so sure after being let down the first time. He doubted Thomachan's ability to stick with it to the end. What if this was another of his ploys to further some ulterior motive? "What's your stake in this? Why do *you* want to make this movie? How can I trust you again?"

Thomachan cocked his head. "This time it's different. I'm doing this one for my wife, Sundari. It's been her greatest wish that we inaugurate the renovated theatre with the release of our own movie. And what better opportunity than this." He nodded his head and smiled coyly. "I want to give my Sundari whatever she wants."

Aditya shook his head slowly. "No. It's probably too late now." He started walking away quickly, before Thomachan could stop him.

"Hey! Hey!" Thomachan called from behind. "Stop! We can work this out. I'll give you ten percent."

Aditya paused for a moment, but moved on. He didn't want to waste his time when he knew it wouldn't work.

The next morning, he woke up to the sound of a car driving into Raman's compound. It was a white Lancer. A tall, handsome man got out of it and strode towards Raman's house. Aditya's heart blipped. So this was Priya's groom-to-be. He looked smart, dashing, well-to-do. Everything that Aditya wasn't.

He called out to his mother but she wasn't at home. She'd already gone off to prepare the meal at Raman's. She'd left his coffee, now cold, and breakfast at the table.

34

Thomachan had been anxious all night. All his hopes were going to be shattered. After promising Sundari that they'd be able to inaugurate their theatre, he'd hate to tell her that he'd spoken too soon. That idiot Aditya had refused. Not only had he refused but he'd walked away, turning a deaf ear to Thomachan's pleas. Nobody had ever made him look as ridiculous as that.

Just as he was sitting, head buried in the newspaper the next morning, looking but not really reading, Thomachan heard the sound of a bicycle enter his compound.

It was Sundari who let out a cry when she saw who'd come. "It's Aditya!"

Thomachan could have let down his guard and screamed excitedly like her, but he wasn't a fool. He wondered why Aditya had come.

He came out to the porch and settled down on one of his bamboo chairs. "Hmmm?" he said, gruffly, as Aditya came in. "What is it?"

Aditya scratched his head. "We'd have to start the movie all over again!"

Thomachan looked at him, surprised. What was the lad saying?

That he'd do the movie or that he wouldn't? "We don't have to start again."

Aditya groaned. "But whatever we've shot until now belongs to Prithvi."

"Not to worry about that," Thomachan said in a calm voice. "I'm rich enough to buy the rights from him. I'll buy his share."

"What if you back out again?"

Sundari interjected, "No, now he won't!"

"I could sign a contract," said Thomachan, reluctantly. "Besides, now I'm determined to finish it. For Sundari's sake. I have the finance, relatives owning theatres in most metros, and distributor contacts. Plus, you'll get your share. Think about it. It's a sweet deal."

Sundari nodded vigorously in support of her husband's claims.

Aditya looked at Thomachan and Sundari's expectant faces and shrugged. "Okay! I'll do it!"

Thomachan face lit up like a million-watt tube light. "Deal!" He whooped and lifted Sundari, and did a little dance of sorts. Sundari beamed and kissed him on the cheek.

When Aditya went back home that day, he left another note for Priya under the hibiscus bushes. "Not joining the college. Going to finish the movie."

Priya's reply the next day read: "I don't think I can hold back any longer. The boy's family is pressing for marriage."

When the shooting resumed, they ran into yet another problem. A priest was required for the climax scene. The man they'd selected before had moved on. "We don't have anyone for that role now," Aditya told Thomachan.

"Well, can't you find someone else quickly?"

"We've done some auditions but no one was satisfactory."

Thomachan thought about that for a moment, then slowly looked at Aditya, his eyes shining as if a brilliant idea had occurred to him. "If KD's film has Lal, then we should at least have Vasu, don't you think?"

"Vasu?"

"He'll be a real crowd puller. Many still remember the old thespian."

Aditya was baffled. The problem was that Vasu was an alcoholic. "He can barely stand! How is he going to act?"

"He's a seasoned actor. If we can pull this off, we'll be on top."

"It will take long to get him in any condition to act. It won't work."

"Give me two weeks," Thomachan said.

Although Aditya was doubtful, he decided to let Thomachan work on the idea, while he decided to continue with the rest of the shooting.

Thomachan knew he was taking a chance, especially since his secret benefactor had insisted that this movie be completed as soon as possible. But now he was determined to get Vasu to do this crucial scene.

To get Vasu to shoot for a scene, however, was not going to be easy. His alcoholism had almost ruined his theatre company, which ran no shows for months on end. He was happy living off the scraps made from his marriage broker business. He was usually so drunk that he could barely stand straight after mid-day. Getting him to shoot for a scene was unimaginable. But that was where Thomachan got his kicks from. He was a force to reckon with when the impossible had to be done.

To make the plan work, Vasu had to agree to do the scene. And that was not the only difficult part. He had got so used to taking to his bottle early in the day that his legs would wobble and his hands would shiver if he didn't drink. Once he started drinking, he couldn't stop. To get Vasu to do any scene, Thomachan had to get him off the bottle first.

But before that he had to prep him up to agree to do the shot.

Thomachan started thinking about the plan for Vasu's de-addiction and decided that there was only one way to tackle this.

***

Vasu searched every nook and cranny of his ramshackle house—inside the cupboard by pulling out all his clothes, under his bed, below the mattress, in his meagre kitchen, shaking and rattling every pot and canister, even in the shed at the back of his house, but came up empty-handed. He could have sworn he had a bottle hidden in there somewhere.

Ever since Thomachan had got it into his head to have Vasu play the part of the priest in the movie, he had searched Vasu's house, taken away his complete stash of alcohol, and moved in to keep an eye on him.

"Just until you can be sober enough to do the shot," he'd said, as consolation, but it had only been a few days and Vasu shook so much without his bottle that he could barely stand, let alone face a camera.

"Where is it?" he raged, kicking at the things he'd thrown on the floor in his search. "I need something to stop this trembling."

He stumbled out through the rickety main door in search of his archenemy.

Leaning over the broken well, his pot-belly squished on its rim, Thomachan was in the backyard, when heard the commotion inside the house.

Vasu staggered up behind him. "What are you doing there?"

Thomachan was still bent over the well. "Trying to get some water to go to the bathroom, you idiot! The bucket has fallen in."

Vasu slapped his forehead and lurched towards the well. Then he leaned in too. "Where?"

Thomachan looked up in alarm at Vasu almost bent at his hips over the edge of the well, dangling precariously, and dragged him away. "Get away from there! I'll find something else to draw the water out."

Vasu wobbled and collapsed to the ground. "Where the hell is the bottle?"

"You will not get a drop until you finish the shot," Thomachan said, his hands on his hips as he glared at the fallen Vasu. "Even if I have to stay with you for a month to get it done."

A week went by. Vasu was in an excruciatingly slow and painful recovery, hardly in any condition to shoot for a scene. For many days, he wasted away, searching for the bottle, refusing food, and sometimes crying for a drop of whiskey. "You're punishing me for no reason," he pleaded. "I don't want to act. That's why I gave it up all those years ago."

But Thomachan was not one to budge. Just like he'd convinced Aditya to take on the movie, he was now hellbent on getting Vasu to finish his movie.

Vasu spent his days on a bamboo cot, in and out of delirium. "There's no reason for people to remember me," he called out in his half-dreamy state. "Don't think for a minute that this movie will run because of me. It won't!"

"Leave that for me to decide," Thomachan said firmly, forcing some gruel into his mouth. "This is what you need more than a bottle. Do this for me, my friend."

For a man who'd been pampered throughout his life in a huge palatial house and lately, by his wife's cooking, Thomachan stuck to his latest challenge with patience and fortitude. This movie meant the world to him and he'd go to any lengths to make it work.

Thomachan made sure Vasu was under watch for twenty-four hours; he was made to eat his meals on time and wasn't allowed to go out or have any visitors. It was impossible for him to get a drink under Thomachan's hawklike vigil.

Finally Vasu made it to over a week without touching alcohol. He gradually came out of his delirium. And one day, he woke up to the smell of hot coffee brewing in his kitchen. Thomachan's delivery boy brought hot egg curry and rotis. The compulsion to look for a bottle first thing in the morning was no longer there. His stomach grumbled and he actually felt hungry. He took a hot bath, and put on fresh clothes. Thomachan arranged for a barber to trim his hair and nails. He felt a cleaner, stronger man than he'd felt in ages.

A few more days passed, and when Thomachan was sure that Vasu could stand and think straight, he arranged to call for Aditya to explain the scene to Vasu and get him ready for the shot.

35

The cold winter of Bangalore was giving way to an early spring! Ria was almost done with the school year. Her final exams were approaching soon, and she was looking forward to summer break. Neha, too, was happier, spending her time between being with Ria at her parents' home and doing up her new studio, which she hoped to inaugurate soon.

She was reading a book one afternoon when she got a call from Aditya.

"We're restarting the movie," Aditya said excitedly and told her all about Thomachan buying the rights from Prithvi.

She felt a sharp pang when she heard his name. She had missed him, and often worried about him. "What about KD and the script?" she asked.

"I think we're still ahead because we had a good start." He told her what Thomachan had told him.

Neha was relieved.

Then he told her all about Vasu and they had a jolly laugh about him turning into a teetotaller.

"Where are you going?" Ria was ready in the morning for her school and Neha was already dressed up. These days, she had noticed, her mother was dressed up to go out every morning. What was she busy with? Ria wondered.

"Home," Neha said. "Got some cleaning up to do."

Ria was not convinced. "But you also went yesterday."

"The house is really dirty."

And that was that.

Her mother didn't say much these days but she seemed happier than she'd been in a long time. Although, Ria knew she hid her tears and sometimes cried herself to sleep. She sensed that her mother was still heartbroken and had nobody she could talk to anymore. She missed her father terribly too.

She continued to go to school every day from her grandparents' house. Sometimes Shweta and Niru visited to cheer them up. But life was indeed boring. She wished she could have back her old room but she didn't want to go back to the empty house. It had been eight months ago, that her father had died. Some days she felt almost normal. And others, she missed him so much!

There was also something else that made her feel guilty, and she hated herself every time she thought about it. She hoped she never would have to tell anyone about that. Even though Shweta had begged her to open up her heart and tell her everything.

* * *

Vasu emerged from the changing room, ready for the shot, dressed as the local priest, in white robes. His long, silver hair and flowing beard were neatly trimmed. There was that twinkle back in his eyes. When he rose to stand at the pulpit, Aditya was mesmerised by the transformation, by how realistic an image of a priest he cut.

They were now ready for an important scene in the movie.

Aditya explained the shot to Vasu. He was to address the congregation, the cast for which consisted of the whole village. He was to ask them to think about how they had blamed Manu and opposed his family. What it meant for the village and the heads of the community to have cast out Manu's family and let the real culprits go free. In the end, he was to confess that he was indeed Manu's father and was ashamed of himself for not having supported Manu's mother through her ordeal. It was a memorable speech that was meant to evoke strong guilt and shame within the community, and teach them about doing the honourable thing even in the face of adversities.

At the clap and "Action" Vasu transformed magically. Gone was the drunk who could barely stand straight let alone say a single line of dialogue.

Aditya stood transfixed at what he saw through the monitor.

Vasu improvised at the last minute as he revealed that he was Manu's father. He suddenly had real tears in his eyes. Aditya gestured to the cameraman to continue to roll even when Vasu broke down in the middle of his lines, halted to control his emotions and then continued again from where he had left off.

During the shot, Aditya could not take his eyes off the monitor for a single moment. Unbelievable! Only a veteran like Vasu could infuse so much passion and clarity into it to make it so emotionally poignant. The camera continued to roll until the very end of Vasu's lines.

Claps resounded as Aditya finally called "Cut!" Bravo! The shot was completed in a single take and Aditya was thrilled with the outcome, sure that he'd have a masterpiece once he edited the tearful breakdowns.

Thomachan rushed forward and enveloped a tearful Vasu in a bear hug, amid claps and cheering at the completion of the most important scene of the movie. It also marked the end of the film.

A wave of joy spread through the entire team. Neha, who had done her part of the shooting, was sorely missed.

The shooting was now officially complete!

* * *

The dubbing, sound and foleys took almost two months. Aditya spent a long time at the studio rushing with the post-processing.

At last the day arrived when the final print was ready, and the editor at the studio called Thomachan because Thomachan had asked to know when Aditya had okayed the final cut.

"Hold on. I'll be there right away," Thomachan said, hanging up and immediately rushing to the studio. After about two hours, he was out, his face flushed with excitement.

The movie was called Adhrishyan. *Invisible.*

The publicity and promotions began in full swing. TV channel ads, hoardings, newspaper inserts, Thomachan had plunged into every possible publicity stunt, no-holds-barred. He'd even held a press meet for Vasu.

Vasu gave a stirring speech about the movie, how the youngsters had not only displayed their capabilities but had also shown an old man a thing or two about making a comeback. The movie, he said, had helped him imbue his life with purpose, once again.

The audience broke into cheers. Thomachan clapped the loudest of all.

Meanwhile, at another important press conference, Lal, flanked by KD, and a few other honchos from the industry, were assembled to talk about Lal's latest movie. It was all part of the publicity drama to create hype about Lal's next project, months before it was released.

KD beamed as he watched Lal seated in front of the mic. He couldn't help thanking his stars that Lal, the superstar, was starring in his mega movie. Lal's security guard stood right beside him, while his PA moved around the stage with an important air.

"What is special about this movie, Sir?" a reporter holding up a mic asked.

Before Lal could reply, KD pulled the mic closer and cleared his throat. "Let me answer that. As you know, Lal only does one movie at a time, and this one appealed to his uniqueness funda." He laughed, then continued. "We are all very happy that this movie has a fantasy element, which is a unique concept in Malayalam films. I don't think a single movie so far has this kind of story. And, this is also a family entertainer. So these are its USPs."

Another media reporter stood up with a question just at the moment when Lal's PA moved across the stage and whispered something into his ear…

Lal's face darkened as he listened. "Excuse me, folks!" he said, leaning towards his mic. "This press meet ends here. I don't think I will be doing this movie anymore."

As KD's mouth fell open, Lal got up and made a hasty exit amid ripples of shock that spread through the podium. KD mumbled a quick, "Sorry, I think there has been a misunderstanding," and jumped from the stage and out of the room, rushing behind Lal.

"Sir!" A young reporter ran behind KD and managed to grab his hand in an attempt to get an exclusive comment from the leading producer-director.

KD turned around, jerked his hand free and gave the reporter a resounding slap. "Who the hell are you?" he yelled. "Get away from me before I call the security."

The young chap looked at KD's retreating back in shock.

KD looked around for Lal. But by then, he'd lost him.

Back in his office, KD tried desperately to contact Lal.

On his third try, he reached Lal's phone.

"What?" Lal barked into his receiver.

KD was taken by surprise at his tone. "What the hell was that about not doing the movie? Are you out of your mind?"

Lal's voice was grave. "If you haven't heard already, Adhrishyan will be out this weekend. And it so happens it's the same story as ours."

"That's not possible," KD blurted.

"Going by their press release statements, they started shooting the movie long before us. And I don't need to make too many wild guesses as to how that script came into your hands."

"Rubbish!" KD retorted. "Don't believe the stories. I'll go to court to prove that the story is mine."

Lal scoffed. "It doesn't matter what you do now, KD. I quit and I do not care for your explanations."

"But—"

"You bastard!"

"Please!" KD begged.

"I will never be a part of anything that tarnishes my reputation," Lal growled, as KD tried to calm his breathing. "I dare you to take legal action against me, KD. As far as I'm concerned I'm not a part of this project anymore. You can do whatever you like."

KD buried his head on his desk after Lal hung up. How did it get to this? He knew he couldn't do anything against an actor of Lal's stature. Nobody in the industry dared to alienate Lal.

KD had no option but to give in. The money he stood to lose over Lal's backing off would run into crores, after all the shooting that they had already completed. The thought left him reeling. As far as he knew, he was financially finished after this. And he only had himself to blame for it!

He clutched his chest as a knife-edge of pain shot through it suddenly, and gasped for air. He couldn't seem to find the strength to call for help. He remained there, in that curled, limp position on the desk, until he was found.

36

April! The month of new leaves, new flowers, new beginnings! Neha's drama studio was also almost ready and she couldn't wait to start her dream venture. Everything was good except for the fact that Ria still hadn't said a word about wanting to come back home. Neha was beyond ecstatic as time neared for the release of her movie that weekend.

She was back at her house for cleaning up, just a few days before the weekend. As she was clearing up in the kitchen and her maid was up on the ladder, wiping down the fan, the doorbell rang.

"Who can it be?" Neha muttered to herself, putting away the rag in her hand and going over to the door.

It was Daisy, showing her buck teeth, her hands on her hips. "When did you come?" she asked, peering inside. "Who's there?"

"It's my house help. Did you run out of something?"

"Oh no, Kuttan Sir's mother wanted to speak to you. She wanted to come over. I told her I'd check if you're here."

"Yes, I'm here. Shall I put on some tea?"

"Is it okay to talk now? Daisy pointed to the maid who was busy cleaning, and humming a tune.

Neha nodded. "Sure, we can go out on the terrace."

Daisy returned, with Vinodini in her wheelchair.

Neha smiled and welcomed Prithvi's mother. She'd never come here before. Neha wondered what she wanted to talk about.

"Hope I didn't disturb you?" Vinodini asked, her teeth clicking as she spoke.

Neha blinked. "No. Daisy told me you wanted to speak to me."

"Yes."

There was silence until Vinodini cleared her throat. "Weren't you part of Prithvi's movie?"

It was a long time ago! she heard herself thinking, feeling her cheeks growing hot. "Yes...Well I was—"

"Then there was a problem a few months ago, am I right?"

"Yes."

"Do you know what happened?"

Neha hesitated. If Prithvi hadn't told his mother, then why hadn't he? And how much did Vinodini know?

"Prithvi already told me everything," she said proudly, as if she understood what Neha was thinking. "So, you needn't worry about that. Since I didn't believe a word of what he said then, I want to hear it again from you."

Obviously, she hadn't heard everything. She didn't know that Prithvi had since sold his movie to Thomachan. Would she believe her if she told her all about KD and his master game plan using Ramu?

Vinodini cleared her throat again. "I heard about Ramu."

So, he'd told her everything and she'd refused to believe him because of her connection with KD? If only she'd believed Prithvi then—

"Tell me everything, my dear." Vinodini seemed impatient. "I have to know the truth."

Neha started with the problems during the making of the movie. Vinodini's eyes grew wider as she told her how Prithvi had caught Ramu trying to take pictures of the changed script that Prithvi had left in Aditya's room. It was obvious she hadn't heard of all the troubles that had beset the movie. Neha wrestled with the thought of revealing

Prithvi's new deal with Thomachan, but finally just said, "The movie opens in two days."

"I saw the ads and you were in the trailers. So I realised it was the same movie. But I thought Prithvi had dropped it because KD…" She looked a little confused.

"It's no longer Prithvi's movie," Neha let on sadly. "He sold it to Thomachan."

Vinodini's eyes grew round like saucers. It was obvious she hadn't heard.

"I want to go and watch it anyway," she announced.

Daisy looked at her in bewilderment. "But how will we go, Ma'am? Should I call Kuttan Sir and tell him to take us?"

Vinodini waved her hand. "No, Kuttan is not to know anything. I want to see it." Her eyes misted. "I should have trusted him. It was my stubbornness that led to this. If Priyamvada has closed down, it would all be my fault."

"Please don't blame yourself," Neha heard herself say, suddenly feeling sad for the frail, old woman before her. How her heart must be bleeding now!

Vinodini shook her head. "I have to go. I want to see the movie that almost became a part of our family's legacy."

Neha had already planned to go with her family in a minivan. "I can take you." Surely they could accommodate two more people. But would Vinodini be able to travel like that? "Will you be able to come in the van with us?" she asked hesitantly.

"You don't worry about me. I've sat easily for ten hours cramped in a car. I won't be bothered by a thing."

That settled, Vinodini and Daisy returned to their apartment. Neha shut the door behind them and heaved a sigh of relief. That hadn't gone as badly as she'd feared.

She couldn't sleep that night or rest the whole of the next day, anxious about the film's opening. Her family, Vinodini and Daisy left by evening so that they could be in Chengannur in time to watch the very first show.

By the time they were all packed in the minivan, it felt quite cramped. Ria was not used to long drives and they had to stop several times along the way so that she could get some fresh air.

At last, when they checked into a hotel at Chengannur, it was already late night. They went to their rooms and just crashed. Neha was in jitters all of the next day. She was unable to eat anything at breakfast or lunch. Thoughts of the movie weighed heavily on her mind, and by evening, Neha was a bunch of nerves, as they drove to the special inauguration and first show of the newly opened AC auditorium in Chengannur town, Thomachan's Sundari Theatres.

Nobody had expected that Vasu's return would cause such a lineup of viewers at the theatre. Veterans of the past era, old men and women in tow with the newer generation showed up in large numbers. There were also families with children because this was a family entertainer. The Friday show was completely booked.

Sundari Theatres, the first of its kind in Chengannur, held a grand inauguration.

Sundari, bedecked in a silk saree and flowers in her hair, stood proudly beside her husband, Thomachan, to welcome movie lovers to their theatre. Amid sounds of the *nadaswaram* and drums, Sundari and Thomachan cut the ribbon and declared the theatre open.

Among the special invitees for the inauguration and screening were Aditya's mother, Manu's family, as well as Neha's family. Thomachan was very happy to see Prithvi's mother and gave her a very warm and special welcome. She accepted it wholeheartedly, apologising for coming uninvited, but Thomachan would hear none of it. He wheeled her into the auditorium, himself. All the special invitees had front row seats.

Neha sat between Ria and Shweta and looked on anxiously, praying that the audience, and especially her family, would like her performance. The movie commenced, and Neha could hear her own heartbeat.

Neha noticed Ria looking at her in awe during some of her scenes. In one of them in which Neha single-handedly took on the villagers and refused to give up the house in spite of their threats, the audience applauded wildly. Shweta grabbed Neha's hand. "Awesome, sis!" she whispered into her ears. Neha's eyes grew misty. Her heart swelled with pride; there were several people she had to thank for this movie, starting with her sister who'd pushed her to go for it. Her eyes also misted thinking about Mohan. How proud he would've been of her had he been there! She shut her eyes tightly and felt a sadness sweep over her when suddenly Shweta held her hand, giving it a soft squeeze. She gave Shweta a grateful glance and pushed the sad thoughts away, thinking about how much her life had changed. Here she was, feeling blessed, peaceful and happy.

For some reason, she also missed Bobby today. She wished he were here to see how the audience clapped at his comic scenes. The audience seemed to be enjoying every bit of it, whistling and whooping with laughter.

She looked to where Manu sat. His father was beaming proudly at the performance of his son, the hero. Priya glanced coyly at Aditya sitting by the side. Her fingers were tightly crossed in her lap. Her marriage to Aditya hedged on the outcome of the movie.

To everyone involved, this movie was symbolic of the struggles they had faced.

As the film ended, there was resounding applause from the audience. Towards the very end of the credits, the name PRIYAMVADA PRODUCTIONS showed up on the screen.

Surprised, Neha slid a glance at Thomachan. At the same time, the lights came on. Thomachan caught Neha's glance and gave her a wink.

37

As they filed out of the auditorium, there were many congratulatory hugs all around. Raman congratulated Aditya and for the first time, Aditya could see pride in Raman's eyes. He only hoped it would help his cause in wanting to marry his daughter.

Thomachan had tears as he hugged Aditya. He squeezed Sundari's hand. "See?" he told her, "we finally made it."

Sundari was pouting. "But your name didn't show up in the very end."

He chucked her chin. "Sundari, did you not see Executive Producer Thomachan, flashing just before the end."

She nodded, smiling shyly.

Thomachan rubbed his belly. "This whole plot was masterminded by me. Remember the night we got a phone call. It was Prithvi. He is known to Vasu since childhood. When he suggested I run the show on his behalf, I grabbed the opportunity with both hands."

She looked up at him with pride.

He glanced at her lovingly. "Next time, Sundari, for our next movie, you'll see your name." He stretched his hands sideways, as if to display the credit line. "SUNDARI PRODUCTIONS." He looked at her for approval. "It'll be our next movie. How does it sound?"

She hugged his hand with joy. "Yes!"

Thomachan's phone rang continuously. According to the minute by minute reports from his relatives who were distributors and theatre owners in other metros like Kochi and Thiruvananthapuram, the publicity had worked. The first show was a hit everywhere. Congratulations were piling in non-stop. Thomachan beamed from ear to ear as he thanked each caller profusely, and remarked that he knew this movie was going to be a hit all along. He had his fingers crossed over word-of-mouth now helping to fill up the rest of his shows.

Prithvi was headed outside when he saw his mother, wheeled in by Daisy, at the front of the auditorium.

He rushed to her, surprised. "What are you doing here?"

"What do you think?" she said, her eyes twinkling. "I came to see my son's movie."

Prithvi laughed. "But you didn't know that it was your son's."

Tears welled up in her eyes. "Didn't matter. You started it and I wanted to watch it." She leaned forward and held out her hands to embrace him. "Well done, son!"

When he wheeled his mother outside, he was met with many surprised looks. Nobody had known that he was coming. He had come in through the back entrance a little after the movie had started, so nobody had seen him enter. Happy to see him, Thomachan once again explained to the gathering of enthused team members, how it had all come about.

Aditya saw Prithvi and hesitated for a moment. He hoped Prithvi had forgiven him for being rude and not willing to trust him. His phone rang just as he was about to walk over to him.

"Bobby?" he exclaimed when he recognised the caller's voice.

"Congratulations!!!"

"Congratulations to you too, my friend!" Aditya said. "Your performance was very well appreciated."

"All thanks to you."

Aditya was thankful that the misgivings about Bobby had been cleared.

"I heard a few things about Ramu," Bobby said, tentatively. "Was it true?"

Aditya laughed. "We realised it was Ramu pretty soon. But you'll hear everything when you come home."

"I'm not coming back unless they throw me out!" Bobby said, laughing.

Bobby hung up after a few more updates about how the movie had fared. Aditya finally summoned the courage to talk to Prithvi. When he went up to him, feeling the need to bare his heart and talk, he found himself unable to speak.

Prithvi turned around and looked truly happy to see Aditya. "At last! We did it."

The smile that radiated from his eyes made Aditya swallow and he slowly put out his hand for a handshake. "I'm sorry for not trusting you."

"It wasn't your fault," Prithvi said, his eyes kind. "It was a thoroughly confusing time for all of us. If I've been able to do something about it, it was all for you. I owed it to you."

For the first time after he'd walked out of Prithvi's movie, he felt his chest lighten. It was as if a load of guilt had been lifted. But the question he'd been meaning to ask, still burned inside. "How did you know KD wouldn't file a suit? How did you not fear losing everything?"

Prithvi put a hand on his shoulder. "I knew. Just knew from the bottom of my heart that he was bluffing." His gaze was steady and confident as he looked Aditya in the eye. "For the first time I knew exactly what I was doing. If it wasn't for the support I got from all of you, I would never have been able to prove it."

And, if it hadn't been for Prithvi's kindness, Aditya himself wouldn't have been able to stand so proudly in front of Raman today. He owed everything to Prithvi. His work, his life, his worth.

Manu also joined them as Prithvi related the story of how he'd got Thomachan to play a crucial role in misdirecting KD. They laughed as if back in the days of the shooting. The air had been cleared between them. It felt simply perfect, standing outside Sundari Theatres and reminiscing about the moments they'd shared together as a team.

They were soon surrounded by fans.

Prithvi moved away quietly, letting the young boys soak in the glory of their success, and went over to his mother.

Vinodini was excitedly waving at someone. "Isn't that Vasu?" she asked Prithvi. Vasu was standing next to Thomachan and accepting a bouquet of flowers.

Prithvi wheeled her towards him.

Vasu turned around to her in surprise. "Vinodini Bai!"

She chuckled at the recognition. "You were brilliant!"

He bowed. "I tried."

As they talked and caught up on old times, Prithvi caught a glimpse of Neha standing next to her family. Their gazes caught and she waved.

She was smiling as they walked towards each other. "You did it!"

He saw the pride in her eyes and warmth spread through him. "As long as it was all worth it in the end, I don't feel guilty."

"I'm sorry if I said some hurtful things."

He dismissed it with a wave. "Sometimes one needs someone to beat the fear out of you." Just seeing her smile had been enough. "That's what it was, the fear that I could be wrong."

She gazed into his eyes. "Then, I'm glad it worked."

"Now that you're a movie star," he asked, taking the liberty to tease her, "will you do Thomachan's next?"

Her eyes shone with excitement as she told him all about her new studio. She was childlike in her enthusiasm. "I want to be with Ria and take care of my drama school," she said.

"So you'll never act again?"

"Only if I like a role that much." Her smile was infectious. "But, mostly, no. I'm happy with my school."

He was proud of her accomplishments, her non-pretentiousness. That she had found her bearings. She spoke about her new school, her new life. It felt as if nothing had changed. And yet everything had. She'd turned her life around. She seemed peaceful and content. The most heartening thing for him, was that she had forgiven him. The days that he had spent without any hope of seeing her again had been torturous. It meant the world to him that she was talking to him once more.

He sensed a hint of sadness though when he asked her about Ria. How he wished he were someplace quiet with her alone so that he could find out what was bothering her.

She bit her lip and gazed at her feet, hiding the regret that he'd just glimpsed in her eyes. "Ria wants to continue to stay with my parents," she said.

He'd heard from Daisy that their house was pretty much locked up now. "Has it something to do with her father's—"

Neha nodded with a sigh. "She misses Mohan. I think the house, its emptiness, haunts her. I don't know what to do about that. If I knew what would work. I would do anything in the world for her."

"I'm sure Ria will be happy to come back soon."

Her eyes misted. "Anything to make her happy. She's turning thirteen soon."

"When?"

"Two Saturdays from now. I'm planning a little celebration at home."

"I would like to come too," he said and watched as Neha's face lit up. "I hope you don't mind if I bring her a small gift?"

She shook her head, her eyes soft with gratitude. "She'd be delighted."

Just then Ria came over to where they were standing.

Prithvi waved at her.

"Hi, Bruce!" She gave him a bright smile and they shook hands.

"Where have you been?" he asked her.

She avoided his gaze. "My grandmother's."

He patted her head. "Well, I'll see you soon for your birthday."

She looked up at him delightfully. "Really?"

"Yes, but you mustn't forget to invite me. I have to go now." He turned to Neha. "Thanks for bringing my mother. I'll take her back with me."

Neha and Ria waved goodbye and went back to the rest of their family.

Vinodini was still continuing her hearty conversation with Vasu when Prithvi joined her. He'd never seen her so happy. She turned to Prithvi. "I'm so glad I came today. Brought back great memories of when I was a young woman."

It was almost an hour later when they finally bid good bye to Vasu, and Prithvi wheeled his mother back to his car.

38

One day, a week later, Raman came rushing into his house and hugged his wife, Ambika.

"What happened?" she said, giggling. "Why are you so happy today?"

"Our son has passed his final exams. I'm distributing sweets to the entire neighbourhood."

"What about Priya?"

"She has passed too. In fact, I just called Vijay to tell him the good news! I've invited their family over this evening to fix the date for the wedding. But first things first. Where is Manu?"

For Manu, life hadn't changed much after the movie. He'd been confused at some of the offers he'd been getting, the first of which was Thomachan's very own home production, and he didn't know which to choose. On the other hand, his father was of the strong opinion that he should join his rice business.

"It will help with sales if they know you're driving the business," his father claimed. "Make hay while the sun shines, so to speak."

Manu sauntered out of his room wondering what the hubbub was all about. Did his father get a cheaper deal in Chennai or did he make a great sale this month?

"You passed," his father said, patting him on the back. "I'll buy you the new bike and you can start at the warehouse tomorrow."

"But I'm an actor now," Manu said, complaining because his father never took him seriously. "I can't be keeping count of sacks of rice and handling the accounts of income and deliverables."

Raman peered into his eyes. "Okay, let me put it this way. The day you get a very good offer, you can leave."

Manu had nothing to say against that because he really believed that a really good offer was almost around the corner. And that meant he didn't have to stick to the rice business.

Priya walked in at the same time, back from the temple where she'd gone to offer a coconut for passing her finals.

Raman congratulated her on her marks and announced that Vijay would be coming over in the evening. "I'm so happy that things are falling in place. At least now I can peacefully enter into old age, and my children will be settled and happily married. There is no bliss on earth like that!"

Priya twiddled with the end of her dupatta and gave him a weak smile. Just then, Aditya walked into the house. He also looked like he was coming from the temple. A smear of sandalwood paste glistened on his forehead.

Raman's happiness bubbled over multi-forth at having an audience to recount the day's good news.

"I can't thank you enough," he said, rushing to shake Aditya's hand. "All this, especially Manu's passing his exams, is because of you."

Aditya cleared his throat and straightened the creases of his shirt. "Sir," he said, with all the courage he could muster. "Since you're so delighted today, I hope I can propose one more good news."

Raman beamed. "Of course! Today all news in the world is good news for me."

Aditya hesitated a second and then took the plunge, his words tumbling out in a single breath. "I'd like to marry your daughter if I can have your kind permission, Sir."

The smile on Raman's face dissolved. "What?"

"Please, Papa," Priya jumped in. "I've always only wanted to marry Aditya."

Aditya pressed his palms together. "I've loved Priya for a long time."

Raman sank into the nearest chair.

Ambika dashed into the kitchen and brought him a glass of water. He gulped it down and then let out a long loud sigh.

He looked at the family gathered around him and then looked long and hard at Priya. "So, this was what rejecting all those boys was all about?"

"Sorry, Papa. I didn't know what else to do." Priya shot a desperate glance at her mother.

"Give them your blessings, Raman," Ambika said, touching Raman's shoulder. "Aditya has proved himself now."

Raman clapped his forehead. "What about sending my daughter to Dubai? What about exporting rice to the Gulf through Vijay's contacts?"

Ambika sniffed. "As if all that is more important than our daughter's happiness!"

"But happiness is in the wealth and comforts of a good life," Raman argued with his wife. "Money is what matters in the end."

Ambika's eyes flashed, and Raman retracted sullenly. "Okay, do whatever you please."

Priya whooped in excitement and hugged her mother.

Aditya came forward to touch Raman's feet and Raman looked at him mock-angrily. "So, this is what you and Priya were doing behind my back, eh?"

Aditya lowered his gaze respectfully. "No, Sir! We were always concerned about the reputation of this family."

Raman looked at the eager faces around him and sighed, finally relenting to the pressure from his family.

✳ ✳ ✳

Mrs. Poonam Sharma came over to Neha's house and went gaga over Neha's movie, claiming to have applauded the loudest in the audience when it ended. "Thank God there were subtitles!"

Seated on Neha's couch, she tucked into her second samosa and groaned with pleasure. "Even the samosa in this house tastes better now." She smiled apologetically and chewed away.

She couldn't hold back her curiosity any more. "What are you going to do about this house?" she asked. [Mrs. Sharma-speak: *How come you're not living here anymore?*]

Neha sighed. "Nothing as of now."

"Come on, if you leave a house unopened like this, the furniture starts to rot, you know? That's what happened to my aunt's house in Jalandhar."

Neha gave her a nod. "I'm not going back to my mum's now. My studio is ready. Classes will begin soon and the commute from here is easier."

"And what about Ria?" [*Is it true that Ria is not staying here at all these days?*]

"I don't know, Mrs. Sharma," she said, not bothering to mask her irritation. "I shall tell her you asked."

Mrs. Sharma's mouth gave a slight twitch. "Of course, of course, and do give her my love. Her birthday is round the corner, isn't it? Aren't you going to have a party?"

Neha rose. "I have to go now, Mrs. Sharma. I'll let you know."

Mrs. Sharma took the cue. Rising from the couch, she waddled towards the door. "Okay then. See you later."

Neha heaved a sigh of relief, as she left.

39

May 12th!

The happiest day of Neha's life—when Mohan and she had welcomed their new bundle of joy. How ecstatic he had been that day! Both of them had been unable to take their eyes off their first born. Her eyes misted at the memory. Then she shook her head and concentrated on all the chores that still had to be done.

Neha had invited Shweta and Niru, Prithvi, and about fifteen of Ria's closest friends for Ria's birthday. Today was the day that Ria was turning thirteen and Neha wanted to go the full mile to make it special. While she hoped Ria would be ready to move back home now, she also wanted it to be her own choice. She'd rather not force her to do anything she didn't want, and yet she wondered if Ria wanted to come back. She didn't know what would make Ria change her mind but she prayed for a miracle. She hoped Ria would find the new studio interesting, and would want to get involved in its running. They would make a great team, together! And, it was summer vacation now. Maybe she could get involved in the summer camps or start her own Art Summer Camp. May, June, and July—before the schools reopened— were the best months. She made a mental note to suggest that to Ria. Mohan had insisted that Ria study the International curriculum from eighth grade, so it meant she would have vacation until August. Oh, how Neha longed to see the gleam in her baby's eyes, that sunshine smile of joy, and hear her musical laugh ring through the house again.

Shweta had promised to bring Ria for her surprise birthday party. Neha had been going crazy trying to juggle everything—getting the house neatened up, putting up the decorations, baking the cupcakes…

She was almost done hanging up the huge pink and white, tissue pompoms from the ceiling when her cell phone rang. She let it ring for a few minutes, pursing her lips as she struggled to make the last pompom stick. Then she climbed down from the ladder and picked up the phone.

Shweta chirped into the line. "Hey, how's it going, so far?"

"Don't ask," she said, letting out a long breath. "The oven just pinged, so I guess the second batch of cupcakes are done. Besides, I'm done with the brownies, the pink and white marshmallows, the chocolate dipped strawberries and the oreo pops."

Shweta whooped. "You seemed to have cooked up a storm. What's left to do?"

"I hope Niru has got the cake ready and you guys will be on time."

"Of course, we'll be there," Shweta said. "And we told Ria we're taking her out for dinner at the restaurant and then for a late-night movie."

Neha's heart clenched. "Didn't she say anything about coming home?"

Shweta paused for a moment before answering that. "Well, we told her we're coming to pick you up for dinner and she was really excited about that!" she said, as if to make Neha feel better.

Neha felt like crying nevertheless, because her sweet darling still hadn't talked about coming back home. What could she do to make it any different? But of course, she didn't want to spoil the mood of the day. She sighed. "Okay, hope she likes my crazy ideas for this evening."

"She will," Shweta said. "She's going to love the surprise."

Neha hung up and went back to her decorations with a glimmer of hope that Ria would be totally surprised by what she saw.

By five P.M. Neha was dressed in a casual top and a pair of jeans. She'd tried to add to the celebratory mood by wearing her long, pink, dangling earrings. The bell rang. Butterflies danced in her stomach as she opened the door.

Ria saw the decorations and her mouth fell open.

Gorgeous white and pink pompoms hung from the ceiling as did patterned paper buntings and a huge silver star with THIRTEEN written on it. In the centre of the room stood a table covered in white lace, laid out with mouth-watering treats.

Her eyes popped out when she saw the assortment of cookies, donuts, cake pops, cupcakes, marshmallows and a large jug of punch on the table. Her mother had gone all out and added lace curtain backdrops for the table, and put flowers everywhere. Marigolds and roses were pinned to the walls, blooming in every corner.

Ria looked around her in a daze. Neha came towards her, arms open to welcome her.

"Ma," Ria screamed with delight and rushed to hug her mother.

Neha squeezed her in a tight hug. Pulling back, she gazed into Ria's face. "Do you like the surprise?"

"It's great!" Ria said, clapping her hands in glee.

Niru came in with a huge two-tier cake decorated with her favourite *Enchanted* movie characters as fondant figurines. Shweta entered with a huge smile on her face.

Neha looked at Shweta. "Well, what do you think?"

"Perfect!" Shweta said and pulled out the dress she'd had specially made for Ria—a peach tulle gown with a matching, glittering strapped bodice and tiara.

Both Neha and Ria gasped at the outfit.

Ria went to change before her friends arrived. The doorbell rang non-stop after that. Ria's friends kept pouring in and finally, after the oohs and aahs at the fancy decorations, they all settled down to cut the cake.

Neha suddenly remembered that Prithvi was missing and tried his phone.

"Hi, sorry," he said, picking up at the second ring. "I'm still caught up at work. I think I will be a little late."

"That's okay," Neha said, although her heart sank a little. She wished he'd been here now. But there was no more time to waste because Ria's friends were impatient to get the party started.

"Let's begin," Neha said to everyone.

Ria's friends gathered around her as she blew out her thirteen candles. The happy birthday song followed and then the confetti and whistles as Ria cut her cake. The kids heaped their plates with the treats, talking nineteen-to-the-dozen as they polished off the food.

It was almost dinner time when Prithvi arrived. The kids had all gone home and Neha had arranged a special dinner just for the five of them.

Neha had managed to portion off the terrace into a fancy dining area with table settings for five. When she switched on the fairy lights, the terrace transformed into a magical place. She lit thick candles at the centre of the table and everyone took their seats.

Just before they started dinner, she pulled out Ria's gift. It was a heart-shaped locket. "Open it."

Inside was a picture of Mohan and her with baby Ria in their arms. Ria was overcome with tears and hugged Neha tightly. "Thanks for making this birthday so special, Ma."

"Ok, enough of the mush," Shweta said, teasing. "I'm already hungry."

"What?" Neha said, grinning. "After all those snacks?"

"Well, I'm dieting. So I didn't have any snacks. I'm famished now."

Niru laughed. "Let's dig in, in that case."

They filled their plates with the soft, fluffy, layered Kerala parathas, koftas, and crunchy sago crisps, all of which were Ria's favourites.

"Now, it's time for my gift," Prithvi announced, after dinner.

He went to his house to get it and came back a few minutes later with a box tied up with pink ribbon.

"What is it?" Ria asked, her eyes shining.

Prithvi handed her the box. "Look for yourself."

Ria's accepted it, her hands shaking. "It's heavy!" Her eyes danced in excitement as she untied the ribbon and peeped in.

She gasped and everyone around her gasped as well, as she scooped up what was in the box.

An adorable, tiny, brown and white ball of fur with a pink, stone encrusted bow on its head, looked up at her and made a delightful sound.

"Aw!" Ria cooed with delight and cradled the Shih Tzu puppy in her arms. The little guy snuggled in close and licked her chin.

"You're so sweet," Ria said and kissed his little nose.

Neha, Shweta and Niru oohed at the sight of the puppy in Ria's arms.

Ria beamed at Prithvi with a thousand-watt smile. "This is the best gift I've ever got." She gazed up at Neha. "Can I keep him, Ma?"

Neha squeezed her shoulder. "I know I'd said no pets, Ria." She watched her daughter's face fall. "But in this case, I'll say yes only if you promise to walk, feed and take care of it. He's totally going to be your responsibility."

"I will!" Ria squealed.

The conversation continued at a higher level of excitement after that, everyone laughing and talking over each other's heads across the table.

Neha's heart fell when it was time for Shweta and Niru to leave. To her surprise, however, Ria showed little interest in leaving with them when they made for the door.

By then, Ria had seen the pink balloons hugging the ceiling in her bedroom and the little basket for her new friend, for whom she hadn't thought of a name, until then. "I want to stay here with PomPom," she said, stroking the puppy's head lovingly.

Neha slid a surprised glance in her direction.

"I like that name," Shweta said.

Neha's heart was dancing wildly. Had she heard her daughter right? She couldn't be happier but she only hoped Ria had meant what she'd heard. "Stay here?" she asked again, just to be sure.

"Yes!" Ria's eyes gleamed. "In my pretty pink bedroom with all the balloons floating over my head and my cute little friend for company."

Neha just couldn't contain her joy. "Of course!"

Ria turned to Shweta and Niru as soon as they had reached the door. "Thanks for bringing me and can you tell Grandpa and Grandma I'm going to stay here now?"

Turning back, Shweta rolled her eyes. "And I suppose, I'm supposed to bring back all your clothes and books?"

"Yes, please," Ria said, laughing.

Prithvi rose to leave too. Ria hugged and thanked him profusely for the lovely gift, waved a sleepy goodnight and happily sauntered off to her room.

"Thanks for everything," Neha said to Prithvi at the door. "This wouldn't have been possible without you."

He waved, his eyes crinkling. "Good night!"

She leaned against the shut door, exhausted. Happy that the day had gone so well. Her daughter was back, she now had her own school and she was glad it had all turned out the way it did. .

She couldn't have imagined anything better.

A little later, she peeped into Ria's bedroom. Ria's was curled up in bed, and PomPom was asleep across her stomach. Neha entered the room and tiptoed to her bedside.

Her daughter looked so adorable, her hair fell like a smooth black wave over the pillow. She stroked Ria's hair and gently pulled up the blanket to cover her.

"Ma!" Ria's eyes suddenly opened and she gazed at her.

Neha chucked her under her chin. "Happy birthday again, love! Are you afraid to be alone tonight?"

"Not anymore."

"Well, sleep tight. See you in the morning."

Neha was almost at the door when Ria called her back. "Do you think—"

Neha went back to her.

"Do you think?" Ria tried again, with difficulty. "Papa's going away had anything to do with what I said to him that morning?"

Neha's heart skipped a beat. "What did you say to him that morning?"

"I screamed and threw a fit," she said, looking so sad, it hurt. "I accused him of being a terrible father because all my friends had iPads and I wanted one too." She wiped the tears slipping down her face. "I said I hated him because he was not like all my friends' dads. Could it be that he took it to heart and—"

"Oh dear!" Neha said and enveloped her in a hug. "What happened that morning was not your fault." She grabbed her shoulder and for the first time, the enormity of what Ria had been going through hit her. "Look at me, Ria. Do you understand?"

Ria nodded, her face still downcast.

She had to make this alright for her daughter right now. She wished Ria had confessed this to her earlier. "After you left for school that day…" she started to say to Ria, softly. It made Ria look up and listen. "Papa said he was planning to buy you an iPad for your birthday. By refusing to get you one immediately, he was trying to teach you to be patient." She ruffled Ria's hair. "He was proud of you. Don't you doubt that even for a moment."

Ria squeezed her eyes shut as more tears ran down her cheeks.

"Was that what was bothering you—?" *She wished she'd known earlier.*

Ria hugged her mother tightly, almost squishing the air out of her lungs. "Thanks, Ma!"

Neha let out a deep breath. "Now, off you go to sleep without those creases on your forehead, okay?"

Ria nodded and closed her eyes, hugging PomPom closer to her.

Neha shut the door behind her slowly, leaving Ria snuggled up with PomPom. The two formed the perfect picture of bliss. She couldn't have thanked Prithvi enough for that bundle of joy in their lives.

At last, she had her daughter back. And it was all because of Prithvi.

40

Vinodini had a racking cough, yet she wanted to visit KD in hospital. "Please," she insisted. "I owe him that much."

Do you now, Ma? Prithvi thought. KD didn't deserve anything for what he'd done to him.

Vinodini's stubbornness was nothing new. Prithvi found out the hospital that KD was admitted to and took her there, dressed in her fine cream and gold saree, her hair neatly combed back and a bouquet of flowers in her hand, half covering her face.

As Prithvi wheeled her into the room that KD was in, recuperating from a near fatal heart attack, it was evident that he was shocked to see his guests. His face paled and his voice faltered. "Vinodini Bai."

She handed him the bouquet. "Yes, the person you least expected to see."

Prithvi took it from him and stuffed the flowers into an empty vase.

"I'm grateful to Prithvi for bringing me here despite everything you did to him," she said to KD, who looked down, shamefaced.

Prithvi shot her a surprised look. Who had told her?

"Yes, I know," she continued to KD. "In spite of that, there's a reason I wanted to meet you today. There's something I have to tell you before I'm gone from this world. I owe you that much, at least."

Prithvi was as stumped as KD was to hear that. The two looked at her in awkward silence.

"The lives of actors are strange," she said abruptly, her voice breaking the silence. "Some of us live a lifetime of opulence and yet it's a lifetime of dearth and regret." A tear slipped down the corner of her eye, as her gaze pierced KD. "Like the once famous actress who gave birth to you."

KD looked at her, flummoxed. He remembered his father talking about his late mother. He'd said that she had been a struggling star and complications had killed her during childbirth.

"Yes I knew her," she said, watching KD who looked hungry to hear more, longing to be told everything. "She was a wonderful dancer. She was kind and loving and she really wanted to have you."

KD gave in to a sad smile.

"But she did not have the courage to keep her own first child or tell her husband about it after she was married."

KD stared at her. "What—"

Her words piqued Prithvi's curiosity too.

Vinodini's eyes welled up. The next words came out hoarse. "That unfortunate woman was me."

KD reeled under the shock of what he'd just heard. How many times, in his childhood, had he gone to sleep wishing he were laying his head on his mother's lap. When his father had introduced him to Vinodini Bai several years later, he'd adored her, completely taken in by her warmth. He'd almost wished she were his mother. He would have given anything to have her. Now, her words felt like a kick in his gut.

Vinodini had a faraway look in her eyes. "We'd never been married. Nobody knew. I was desperate to become an actress and there was nothing I could do but give you up and move to the city."

Prithvi could not believe his ears.

KD was silent for a short moment. "Bharathan Nair knew, didn't he?" he said, looking up as if he was talking to the ceiling.

Vinodini nodded. "It still surprises me how he found out. But the old man, bless his soul, never told his son."

"But he made sure I was far away from Priyamvada, his son or his grandson."

"I guess that was his way of preventing his son from finding out, and protecting Priyamvada."

"Well, he won," KD said, turning his head away. "Priyamvada is back."

"When Prithvi told me Priyamvada was in trouble again because of you, I didn't believe him. I still don't. My sons couldn't have caused any harm to each other." Vinodini stifled a sob.

KD let out a deep sigh. He felt something like relief that his plan hadn't worked. He'd been a lost cause and now all he had was her pity. He looked into her eyes, watery and grey with age, and wondered why he'd been the only one who was so unlucky. "Prithvi was lucky to get you and Priyamvada," he said, his heart heavy. "According to Freud, 'a man who has been the indisputable favourite of his mother keeps for life the feeling of a conqueror.' I will always be the vanquished. "

Vinodini wrung her hands. "I have always—"

He covered his face with his palms and looked away. "Please leave me alone now. I need to get used to the fact that I have a mother. I need some solitude."

Vinodini's voice was soft. "Please don't punish Prithvi for what his grandfather did."

He felt like he'd been kicked in the belly. For the first time he was angry with the woman he'd once admired. "Can you not be on my side just once? Can you not treat me like your own son after all these years?"

"Forgive me, son," Vinodini whispered to KD. She then looked up at Prithvi, her eyes silently asking him to wheel her away.

To KD, these words felt like a knife twisting in his heart. His resolve to act strong gave way to sobs that racked his body and echoed in the quiet room after his guests had left. To have had a mother all these years, and never known it. To have caused her so much pain, have her beg one son for the other who'd had the privilege of having his mother all to himself. And to find that he had not only lost to Bharathan Nair but also fallen in her eyes. One moment ago he had nobody. Now he had Vinodini Bai as his mother and Prithvi as his brother.

And yet he was alone!

A few weeks later, he was discharged from hospital. He was a broken man but it didn't mean he couldn't make amends.

He held another press meet immediately, rationalising his actor, Lal's walkout, and apologised for not reading his script more carefully and seeing the similarities. Although he didn't admit outright to stealing, he did praise Prithvi's movie wholeheartedly and said that having watched it, he knew it was made much better than he could ever have.

"Priyamvada is the production house to watch for," he said. "For it has once again made its mark in the industry."

Vinodini heaved a sigh of relief when she read his interview in the newspaper for she could see that KD's repentance spoke loud through his actions. Her heart swelled with pride. This was proof that KD's vengeance had melted away.

Prithvi had stormed out in anger that day, and never spoke to her about her revelation, but she understood that it must have come as a shock to him. Although she had never asked Prithvi to make up with his brother and settle their differences, in her heart, she was finally at peace that her sons would live without drawing blood and trying to settle any more scores.

As a mother, that was her biggest joy and pride. She knew that she still had her two sons who loved her unconditionally, just as she loved them.

In her sleep that night, she passed away.

* * *

For a moment after leaving KD's room with his mother, Prithvi had been really angry. It had all made sense now why his mother had wanted him to be close to KD and nice to him. He had not broached the subject with his mother after bringing her home. But at her funeral, he decided he finally wanted to make peace with KD, who ultimately, was his only remaining family. He called KD and told him about Vinodini's passing away. His message had been brief and to-the-point.

Daisy's cries were the loudest at the funeral. Out of control. "She was like my own mother," she cried on Neha's shoulders.

Neha tried to calm her down but Daisy was beyond consoling.

"Who will take care of Kuttan Sir?" she said, blowing her nose. "Who'll take care of his house?"

Grief-stricken, Prithvi stood in a corner trying to control his tears. Neha held his hand briefly in consolation but there wasn't much she could do. Nothing she could say or do would make it all go away.

Suddenly, there was a commotion at the door.

KD walked in. His steps were slow and measured. He went up to Vinodini Bai's body and offered a bouquet by her feet.

His eyes welled up with tears.

I wish I knew you better, he thought. Prithvi was watching him. He wished Prithvi would come and share his grief. His heart longed for consolation.

At last Prithvi walked over. They shook hands. No words were exchanged between the brothers. What was left to say?

But finally when they took the body to the funeral ground, KD joined Prithvi in the ambulance. Although there was no love lost between the two, both her sons were in attendance at Vinodini Bai's cremation.

Prithvi allowed KD, who was older, to light the pyre. That in itself was a gesture KD would never forget. Chanting the scriptures, he circled the pyre and finally held the lighted torch to the logs on which his mother's body rested.

That is the custom among Hindus. That is what the eldest son does. He was proud to have been acknowledged by her family. At last, he was her son.

41

A month later, a card for Aditya's wedding arrived. June 6th was the auspicious day.

Prithvi called up Neha just as she was wondering who to go with. "Will you and Ria join me for the wedding?" he asked.

The drive from Bangalore to Kochi with Ria chattering nonstop in the back was nothing like Neha had ever seen before. Ever since she'd got PomPom, Ria was a changed person. She was livelier, more responsible and happy.

Even though Neha wasn't keen on having a pet at home, this cute bundle of joy had been a blessing. When she saw him curled up on Ria's lap, sleeping blissfully, her heart melted at the sight. Ria was in charge of his bath. She fed him on time too. Neha hadn't seen her happier than this in a long time. And she had Prithvi to thank for bringing Ria back to her...

"What about Joker?" Prithvi was asking her.

"I liked the third movie in the trilogy the most," Ria said.

They were still arguing about Batman.

"I must say I liked the first," Prithvi said, and on and on they went, bickering about their choice of movies until Neha had to stop Prithvi from parking by the roadside to argue his point.

"Will you both just keep quiet?" she admonished them. "I'd like to reach the wedding in one piece if you both don't mind."

"Peace?" Ria asked.

"P-I-E-C-E. Piece. As in without getting into an accident with the two of you going on like that."

"Oh, that piece! Sure!" Ria said, as she and Prithvi cracked up.

The hours spent in the car were pure bliss. It made Prithvi realise what he had been missing all these years—a woman to love and a family of his own. He had grown so attached to Ria that she felt like his own child. This trip had made him realise what his mother had meant all along. He had feared he might lose Neha. Yet now when he saw her frowning because Ria and he were still arguing, and remembered how she had stalked and spied on him, he couldn't help letting out a chuckle. He couldn't imagine what he would have done without her.

Prithvi stayed behind with Neha at the fireworks display that night, after the wedding. Ria had run ahead to get a better view from the front of the lawn.

"Shall we sit down?" he suggested.

The display was spectacular. They sat on the grass, their hands touching lightly, the end of her saree fluttering against his hand. She pointed to a firecracker exploding high in the sky and laughed. He hadn't seen Neha so happy in such a long time. She deserved someone who would love her. Their eyes met and he laughed in sheer joy. They sat there for a long time, close to each other, hands and feet on the soft dewy grass. It felt like the most perfect night ever. He wished he could kiss her under the stars. It was a night he would never forget.

* * *

A few days later, Neha inaugurated her school, Neha's School of Drama. Prithvi, as her chief guest, lit the sacred lamp in the lobby. After he cut the ribbon, everyone clapped and Prithvi and Neha stepped inside with their right foot first. For her, it was a joyous moment, indeed, with her whole family, and friends from the apartment, gathered there.

Everyone was taken in by the place, and was oohing and aahing at the decor that Neha had so meticulously chosen over all these months.

When they saw the adjoining theatre room, more gasps followed. It was absolutely dreamlike, with sheer curtains filtering the mid-morning light and a newly polished, wooden stage gleaming from across the room. Decal stickers of New York City high rises and skyline adorned the walls, giving it a classy-artsy look. Plush carpeting enriched the room.

Lunch was served outside on the porch. While everyone was relishing the tall glasses of iced lemonade and tucking into croissants and sandwiches, Prithvi approached Neha, who was talking to Shweta. "Hello! I see you've been busy?"

"Yes!" Neha smiled happily. "Happy busy."

Shweta butted in. "Hello," she said to him. "So our Amitabh is less prickly these days?"

Prithvi laughed. "Is that what you guys were calling me all these days?"

"I think it's time to do away with that title now," Shweta said.

"You better," Prithvi warned, grinning.

They laughed, talked and ate. By late afternoon, the party ended and everyone went home. Neha was just closing up when Prithvi went up to her. "I've got to show you something." He took her hand.

"Where are we going?"

"Come on."

They walked down the road to the adjacent building. He pointed upwards. On the top floor was a large sign that read PRIYAMVADA PRODUCTIONS.

"Is it what I think it is?" Neha asked, delighted.

"Yes it is." He led her up to the ninth floor by the elevator. As the door opened, right across was a huge office with glass doors. A security guard stood up and saluted. Prithvi nodded and led Neha in.

They walked up to his private office in the far corner.

Her mouth fell open when he let her inside his room, which was almost as big as two rooms. A breathtaking bookshelf and music collection took up an entire wall, and a desk with a luxurious leather chair stood against the opposite wall. Rich rugs were spread on the floor and a large bay window near the desk gave the most gorgeous view of the sky. She clapped her hands over her mouth as she gazed around. "It looks amazing. When did you do this?"

"Recently."

"You didn't tell me! I would've loved to get you a gift."

"You brought me the movie. That was the biggest gift I could have ever asked for. In honour of that, you're the first person to see this office. With Ma gone, I decided not to have a celebration."

"Is Daisy alright?" Neha asked, suddenly remembering her friendly neighbour who had come to say goodbye after Vinodini's funeral and tell her that she had decided to go back to her village.

"I made sure she got work at a friend's."

"I'm glad."

"Neha," Prithvi said, and then waited a beat. "You're the only one who knows how much this place means to me." He ran his palm over his beard. "If there's anyone I know who'd be happiest for me, it would be you."

Neha was touched and taken by surprise.

He took her hand in his and squeezed gently. "I can't explain what I feel but you're special…you're the best thing that happened to me…I'd like us to stay friends. I—"

She raised her eyes to meet his. Though surprised by the sudden touch, she held onto his hand and felt it stir her soul. Since the emotional turmoil in her recent past, *he* was the best thing that had happened to her. It was as if her heart was thawing, his warmth chipping away at the coldness, seeking the love that seemed to have been frozen in there somewhere. She didn't know one touch could evoke such strong feelings in her. She found that she had been longing for it. Longing to look into the depths of her heart to find out what he meant to her, and she to him. She had craved that, yet, in that moment she felt overwhelmed.

She tried to compose herself, but her heart seemed to her to be beating a crazy rhythm. Tugging her hand away gently, she turned to the door. "I've got to get back now. I think Ria must be waiting."

He nodded understandingly.

That night, in the quiet of her home, she thought of Prithvi, about being his friend. She felt deeply about his friendship too. Yet somehow the way he'd said it, it had felt like something bigger than just being friends. Was she imagining it? Was she ready for it?

42

A young man wearing a kurta and holding a thick folder walked toward the tall building at the corner of the street and looked up at the gigantic sign on its mast—PRIYAMVADA PRODUCTIONS, embossed on it in red and gold.

The young man hoped his script would be accepted. When he went up to the ninth floor, he was asked to wait as Prithvi Nair was busy.

Inside his office, Prithvi had just got Neha on the line when his secretary announced that his next appointment was here and waiting for him in the lounge. He held up his hand to indicate that he needed a moment to finish his conversation. It had taken him a few days to call her and he wasn't going to hang up until he'd spoken to her.

"Hello?" Neha said.

His heart lurched when he heard her voice. Why had he not called her sooner? He'd never thought he'd feel that kind of attraction for any woman. Nobody had been able to stir such feelings in him, earlier.

"We can talk later if you are busy," she said.

He felt the yearning return with full force. Why did she affect him so strongly? Why did he feel that inexplicable pull towards her? He had to stop being such a coward. It had to be now or never. He cleared his throat. "I'd like to ask you to dinner tonight."

There was hesitation in her voice. "I'm…I'm afraid I can't leave Ria by herself."

He hadn't considered that problem. But luckily, it wasn't a big problem, either. "What if it's right next door? My place?"

There was such a long pause that he thought she was going to refuse.

"And please get Ria too," he added.

When he hung up, the joy bubbling inside him mirrored the cheerfulness he'd sensed in her voice when she'd agreed. He smiled as he rang for his secretary to send his next appointment in. Today's appointment was lucky, he mused, because he was happy for a very special reason. "What?" he said to the picture of his grandfather on the wall smiling at him benevolently. "Doesn't a man deserve to be happy?"

The door to his office opened and the young man with the folder walked in.

Prithvi was immediately reminded of his younger days. The picture of his grandfather continued to smile at him as he pinged Neha about the dinner timing before he got back to the young man.

* * *

Ria, who was playing with PomPom nearby, noticed that her mother was unusually quiet.

Neha was a lot happier these days. The drama school kept her busy and Ria too had started feeling a lot better with PomPom for company.

It was very unlike Neha to be staring at her phone, when she usually spent her evening either reading or watching TV.

"What happened, Ma?" Ria asked.

"Nothing."

"Won't you tell me what's bothering you?"

"How do you know something's bothering me?"

"If you're staring at the phone screen that's already turned off, then it means you're thinking of something else."

"Come here!" Neha called her and she went over, cradling PomPom in her arms. Neha patted PomPom's head and PomPom licked her hand in return. "I'm so happy you got him," Neha said, laughing at PomPom's excited response at being rubbed behind his ears.

Ria smiled and kissed PomPom on top of his ear. "He's my best friend ever!"

Suddenly Neha's phone pinged and the screen came on.

"Who is it?" Ria asked.

Neha bit her lip. "It's Prithvi. He has invited us to dinner at his house at seven."

"A date?"

Neha gave her a stern look. "Of course not!"

"Let's ask Aunt S what she thinks about it, shall we?" Ria said and grabbed Neha's phone.

"Give it back," Neha screamed and lunged for it, but Ria held it away and leapt backwards. "First tell me, you'll say yes to Bruce."

"Ria, don't behave like a baby."

"Come on, Ma, it's only next door!" she exclaimed. "Besides I have PomPom now so I think you should be kind to Bruce for everything he did for me. You can't let him down."

Neha rolled her eyes at Ria. "Really? Now my little girl is going to tell me what to do?"

Ria giggled. "You better, Ma! Or I'm going to tell Bruce that he should just come here and take you away forcefully." Before Neha could grab her phone back, Ria replied to Prithvi's message with an *Okay*.

* * *

Neha dressed in a sari that evening.

Prithvi had cooked fish and pasta. There was wine for Prithvi and her, and lemon soda for Ria.

Neha's eyes opened wide at the spread. "You can cook?"

"I was into cooking as much as I was into gaming, back in the US. I'll let you be the judge."

Ria eyed the fusilli pasta dish with finely chopped vegetables, in delight. "This looks like a work of art."

Neha concurred.

Prithvi smiled at Ria's appreciation. "Has mom taught you any cooking?"

Ria pouted. "She won't let me anywhere near the kitchen."

"Why is that?"

"Because she's afraid I'll burn myself."

Neha sipped her red wine. It paired well with the spicy grilled fish. "Thank you so much for the trouble you took of cooking for us."

"I also wanted this to be a mini farewell of sorts." He paused to take a deep breath. "I'm going to be gone to Kochi for a few months, maybe a year. I don't know…"

Neha's hand froze in mid-air.

Ria's spoon clanked on her plate. "Oh no! Why? We'll miss you!"

"I'll miss you too! But I promise I'll be back soon. Why don't you visit me there? I'll take you on a tour of the fish packaging plant if you'd like."

Ria screwed up her face. "No, thank you!"

The net curtains, hung across the open balcony to the left, swayed, bringing in a cool, gentle breeze. Beethoven was playing in the background. It soothed the sadness Neha felt inside. She set her wine down and decided she wasn't going to let anything mar the loveliness of the evening. "What are your plans for this place? Is it going to stay locked up?"

"I'll probably keep one room closed and have tenants for the other two. Haven't decided how long I'm going to be away."

"We don't want you to leave," Ria said, pushing away her plate.

"You can come visit me whenever you like. Or stay with me for a while."

Neha looked up in surprise.

Ria's face broke into a smile. "I'd like that very much? During my holidays, Ma and I can come visit you. I miss not having a summer home like many girls in my class do."

Neha and Prithvi exchanged brief amused glances.

Prithvi patted Ria's hand. "Done! Next summer on, you're staying with me."

In the kitchen later, all was quiet. Ria and PomPom had gone back home. Neha and Prithvi were almost done rinsing and wiping the plates and cups, when Neha cornered Prithvi. "Ria probably took you seriously about the summer visit."

He closed the tap, wiped his hands and turned to her. "I was serious. I'm serious about both of you. I wouldn't joke about something like that."

Neha's mouth opened, involuntarily.

His gaze locked on hers. "I haven't had the guts to ask you directly first."

Neha looked down, her legs beginning to shake as if she knew what he was going to say, and had been dreading it all evening.

"Will you—" he began, willing her to look at him but she couldn't meet his gaze. "It's probably too soon but I don't want to lose you." He took her shoulders in his hands gently and turned her around to face him. "I've never felt this way about anyone before. They say, life doesn't give you too many chances." He cupped her chin, forcing her to meet his eyes. "Will you marry me, Neha?"

She could hear her heart thudding hard. She was afraid that her knees would give way. She was hardly prepared for this.

Prithvi continued to hold her. "I don't know how you feel about me, Neha, but I'd like to know whether you love me back."

She stood mute and still, unsure if her legs would support her, if Prithvi's hands left her shoulders.

"Will I at least get a proper goodbye?"

She nodded, the most difficult thing to do. Too late.

His arms circled her gently, warm, loving. He let out a deep breath as she relaxed her head on his shoulders.

She felt his chin resting on top of her head and closed her eyes. It had been so long since she'd been held. She breathed deeply, savouring her feelings. She wished she could throw worry and anxiety to the winds and allow her love for him, buried within, to stir her back to life. All she wanted was to sink into the warmth of his embrace.

"I'll wait for you to decide," he said, brushing his thumb over her cheek.

She felt a rush of relief at his words. Her arms went around him of their own accord, and she hugged him back, for a moment feeling as if she were in Mohan's arms. It had been almost a year. And she still missed him. But, right here, right now, she couldn't think. Her breath caught in her lungs. She squeezed her eyes shut, and tears rolled down her cheeks, wetting his throat. She felt him stir. He hugged her tighter until the breath she'd been holding inside her came gushing out in a sob, as a wave of desire, love, longing, hope and sorrow swept through her.

He was supporting her now, limp body. "I'm sorry...," he said, cupping her face and kissing away her tears. When she had stopped shaking, he gently pressed his lips to hers. She started at the intimate touch; her tears stopped. Pulling back, she looked into his eyes. He blinked and to her surprise, a lone tear rolled down his cheek on to his beard. He wiped it off before she could linger on in that moment that felt as if she'd been privy to the feelings that he hid in the depths of his heart.

And suddenly she couldn't hold back anymore. She kissed him, tentatively at first, then with a fierce, smouldering passion. As her hands grasped at his neck and pulled him closer, she realised that she didn't want to let go...

She felt his embrace like a magnetic pull that dragged her deeper into him as he slowly responded to her kiss. He was gentle, soft, the way he took his time kissing her, exploring her mouth, ears, the hollow of her neck. His arms held her pressed against him and she felt every inch of her body align with his.

"I've never felt this way before," he whispered in her ears, and it sent a thrill tingling up her spine. She slipped her fingers through his hair, feeling its smoothness, longing to touch more of him. As her hands trailed down his neck and chest, he let out a groan, the guttural sound reverberating through her, making her want to do more to him. Beg him for more. As if on cue, she felt his hands on her waist, his caress burning her skin. Her face turned upwards, her eyes closed, a moan escaped her... and before she knew it, he was picking her up and carrying her back to his room.

In that moment, in the only way she knew how, she let herself go.

He pulled her into him, the expression of his vulnerability showing through his eyes, and the all-consuming intensity of the hunger within them lit her blood afire. The emotions that flowed through her grew hot and demanding until it was like a dam exploding. All the repressed feelings from the past year surfaced and rode upon wave after wave of euphoria. Like the lava flowing out of a dormant volcano, she felt her inner inhibitions break, dissolve and be swept away under the heat of his sensuous caresses. When she came, it was with a cry of relief, as if the months of anguish had been released from within her. Later, as they lay spent and tangled in each other's arms, her heartbeat thrumming in her ears, she heard herself say, "I need more time...Please."

He brushed his fingers over her cheeks and answered with a gentle nod, then stroking her hair tenderly as she rested her head lightly against his chest, he breathed softly into her skin, "Take all the time you need."

Her eyes misted at his patient and understanding way with her. Nestling further against him, her face buried in the hollow of his neck, she let his gentle embrace ease her.

When she finally straightened and moved away, he let her go, and in those moments, overwhelmed by all the feelings that seemed to hit her at once, she crept out of his room, shut his door behind her and went home.

His face swam in front of her eyes as she went to bed that night. She relived his words a thousand times as sleep refused to come. It was difficult to rationalise how she felt, about thinking of anyone but Mohan, or spending a lifetime with Prithvi. Yet, she did love Prithvi. There was place in her heart for all the love she could hold and give, a revelation that jolted her out of the numbness she'd forced herself into. She hugged her pillow, going over the last words Prithvi had uttered as he'd held her close to his heart.

"I love you and I will always be there for you," he had said.

"Thank you," she whispered softly into the night as tears of joy filled her eyes. *I love you too…*

THE END

Thanks for reading!

Reviews are worth their weight in gold to authors! If you enjoyed this book, please take a moment to post a review on Amazon, Instagram, Goodreads, your blog, or simply spread the word. Thank You! :)

Did you enjoy Priyamvada & Co.? Check out the story of Ria and Sid in About That Summer here, or read ahead for a sneak preview.

SUDHA NAIR

ABOUT THAT SUMMER

ABOUT THAT SUMMER PREVIEW

"Roll out those lazy-hazy-crazy days of summer…" Ria had been humming that tune for a month! She'd been dreaming about staying in bed until late in the morning every day, enjoying home-cooked food, and simply chilling over Netflix.

The first day of the summer holidays—and, here she was—with her mother, stuck on the road, surrounded by a dozen fat cows, the Netflix bingeing, the lounging, the dream of unwinding all but dead.

Her mother, Neha, honked so loudly that the cow nearest to the car swished its tail across their windshield and mooed in disapproval.

Neha just slapped her hand on her forehead and gave up. "It's no use unless somebody gets out and manhandles these beasts. Who would let them loose on the main road?" She began honking to get the cows' attention, but they seemed oblivious to the racket!

Neha had finally learnt to drive, and Ria was in awe of her. She was one of those women, who when life had handed her lemons, had not just made lemonade, but a batch of tequila too, while she was at it. Ever since Ria had started college at Pune, her mother had done several things that she had once thought were impossible. She'd bought a second-hand car, started driving lessons, and now wouldn't go anywhere without her car. Her drama school had morphed into an acting school. She'd started conducting acting classes for movie, theatre, and TV aspirants.

They were on their way to the airport to pick up Neha's childhood best friend, Sushma, and her daughter, Tanya, who were flying into Bangalore from Mumbai. Ria was very upset. How could her mother have invited guests over just the day after Ria came home for the summer?

"Oh, but I didn't invite her, na?" her mother said, placatingly. "She asked if she could stay with us for a few days while Tanya completed her course in my acting workshop. How could I say no?"

It had all happened because Sushma's daughter, Tanya, had enrolled for one of Neha's acting workshops. Sushma had decided that she herself could check into an Ayurvedic retreat in Bangalore to lose weight, and it seemed like a good idea for mother and daughter to stay with Neha for a few days until then.

Ria cursed the timing of their visit and wondered why she'd never heard about this Sushma Aunty before, if her mother and she had been such good friends. Maybe, it was because she always zoned out when her mother started talking about her friends. Besides, Sushma Aunty and her mother hadn't met in years.

Pom stirred in Ria's lap. He loved to sleep in moving cars. Obviously, his sleep too had been disrupted by the stalled car. He barked twice and Neha shushed him with her finger on her lips and rolled her eyes. "Not now, Pom."

Pom gave her a doleful look, then looked at Ria for backup. Ria rubbed his head to calm him down. "Ma is right." Pom settled back in her lap, his nose glued to the window, now openly curious at the goings-on outside.

The phone rang just then, startling him. He barked again. Meanwhile, one of the cows inched forward. Neha took the opportunity to manoeuvre the car through a narrow gap that opened in front before it closed again, as the cows closed ranks behind their leader. Neha manoeuvred her car through expertly, finally leaving the herd, and the remaining honking cars far behind.

Prithvi's voice boomed through the speaker just then. "Are you still mad at me?"

Pom's tail wagged excitedly at the sound of his voice. He gave a few strong yelps of delight.

"Hi, Prithvi!" Ria shouted in delight.

Neha, who hadn't realised she had answered the call, looked toward the speaker, annoyed. "I had told you we were going to pick up Sushma and her daughter today."

They heard a click at Prithvi's end. "Oops, of course. But I couldn't wait to say hello to Ria."

Ria turned to her mother and asked in a hushed tone, "Did you two have a fight?"

The car swerved slightly, to Neha's annoyance. She tsk-tsked.

"Just something that happened at last week's awards night. Never mind your mother, my love!" Prithvi said theatrically, catching Ria's question and choosing to ignore Neha's irritation, for the moment. "How was the train ride? All set for the summer?"

"When do I get to see you?" Ria asked, as excited as Pom, whose tail wagging turned hysterical.

"As soon as…" A racking cough interrupted his voice.

Neha frowned. "That cough is still pretty bad, isn't it?"

"When someone ignores me for more than a week, it tends to get worse."

"It tends to get worse when someone doesn't take care of himself."

"Yes, that's what I said."

"I agree."

Ria looked at her mother and the speaker alternately as the two ping-ponged back and forth on what seemed like a lovers' tiff. "Guys, guys, will you please stop? I don't understand what's going on. Prithvi, when are you coming over? Because that was a part of my summer plan." Which looked like it was dwindling down to nothing already, what with guests arriving and Prithvi not coming.

Prithvi sighed. "I want to see *you* too." His stress on the 'you' made Neha let out an irritated sound—a cross between a sniff and a snort—that Ria recognised. "Just a few more days, I think," Prithvi went on. "As soon as this kitchen work at the house is finished, I'm taking the next flight to Bangalore."

Ria and Prithvi teased each other a little bit like always, she about his never-ending renovation projects in his already beautiful home in Kochi, and he, about her learning to cook over the summer so she could eat better at the hostel.

"I'll catch you soon," Prithvi said, his voice breaking as they sped down the highway.

Pom flopped back in Ria's lap and eyed her morosely. Although she'd originally named him PomPom when he'd been gifted to her by Prithvi on her 13th birthday, she'd soon given up calling him by his full name. It was too much of a mouthful to say every time she wanted to scold him, which was often, so she had compressed it to Pom, and he didn't seem to mind.

"You wanted to talk more?" she said to Pom, patting his head. She had missed Pom so much in Pune, but by the way he had welcomed her when she got home, it felt like she had never left. That's why she was never jealous of her mother who got Pom all to herself when she was gone, because Pom never complained, and he was so ecstatic to see her back.

"Now, don't ask me what that was about." Neha waved her hand as she disconnected the call. "Poonam came over the other day with a magazine and showed me a photo of Prithvi with a girl at the awards function. And I…well, I just got a little mad."

Ria looked at her mother who was driving a little faster now, an action clearly triggered by talking about Poonam, their irritating and gossip-mongering neighbour.

"He'll fancy some young girl if you don't grab him soon," Neha mimicked Poonam's tone. "Wagging her finger in my face like he was some prize to be claimed."

"She may be right!" Ria muttered, shifting in her seat and turning on the radio.

"What?"

"Nothing!" Not wanting to start arguing on her very first day back, about how Poonam might be right, she flipped through the channels until she settled on Radio Indigo. If it were up to her, she'd never let Prithvi go 'unclaimed', as Poonam had said. She wouldn't take so long to make up her mind. What was wrong with her mother?

Ria went back to looking out of the window, tapping her foot as Ariana Grande belted out her latest, and patting Pom's head as if to console herself. She would hate to lose Prithvi to anyone. He loved them and they loved him. Why wouldn't Ma just marry him? She was sure Ma had refused him when he'd asked.

Neha was nodding along to the music when Ria glanced at her slyly through the corner of her eye. Ria let the topic slide. She wanted Prithvi with them forever, but she couldn't force her mother into it, could she? As long as her mother was smiling and happy, Ria had no choice but to be content too.

Besides, Prithvi—Ria knew from the bottom of her heart—loved them both to bits. And he would do no such thing as leave them for someone else!

GRAB IT AT

MYBOOK.TO/THATSUMMER

Want More Stories?

Receive an exclusive short and sweet office romance story, LOVE OFFICIALLY (preview ahead), and news, updates, and more, when you sign up to receive my email. Find details at SudhaNair.com/newsletter. Let's keep in touch! :)

LOVE OFFICIALLY PREVIEW

Remember the time when you were young and life was full of confusing choices? What if you didn't know which was the right choice to make? What if your whole life depended on that choice? Take a nostalgic trip down memory lane. Read LOVE OFFICIALLY—a **sweet and short office romance story** *to find out how* **Meera** *faces the challenge of choosing the right man!*

'Hey, want to go out for coffee?'

Meera looked up from her messy desk.

Elbows propped on her office cubicle wall, Vivek beseeched her with puppy eyes.

She threw him a quick 'No!' and went back to rummaging for those client requirements that she'd jotted down after the customer call that morning.

'Oh, come on,' Vivek said, blocking her entrance, his hands spanning the width. 'You need a break.'

She rolled her eyes at him. Did he think she wanted to start the office gossip mills by going out alone with him?

'I was only suggesting a cup of coffee!' Then, 'Hey!' as he moved the tiny clay Ganesha idol out of the way before she could knock it down in her frenzied search. 'Want me to call Shabnam too?'

Shabnam—smart, well-dressed, and always the first to know what was going on in the office—was her bestie at work.

As if on cue, Shabnam came over. 'Hey there, you two!' Her face was flushed, and she couldn't help giving Vivek a flirty smile first. 'Guess what!'

Head bent back over her desk, Meera said, 'What!' Then, suddenly, she found those rogue documents she'd been looking for. 'There you are!' She put them right on top of her to-do box and turned to Shabnam.

'One of us will get that transfer to the US this month.' Shabnam bounced up and down. 'The boss is going to announce it in a couple of days.'

Meera's heart missed a beat. This was what she'd been waiting for. Please, please, let it be me, she said a little mental prayer.

'Well!' Vivek said. 'Another of his marketing ploys.' He turned to Shabnam. 'By the way, Shabnam, do you want to go out for coffee?'

'Really?' Shabnam shrieked. Some heads in the other cubicles turned towards them. Shabnam glanced around shamefaced, then went back to him, all smiles.

'With us?' Vivek's face broke into an amused grin.

Shabnam's face fell but she rebounded quickly. 'Sure!'

Vivek raised his eyebrow at Meera, then stuck out his hand to help her up from her seat.

Without thinking, she nestled her hand into his. Her hand tingled at his touch, sending spirals of warmth up her arm. She jerked it away as soon as she was up.

On the way to the cafeteria, the girls needed to use the restroom, so Vivek went on ahead.

'You see how he can't take his eyes off you!' Shabnam said, as she did an 'O' in front of the mirror and touched up her lipstick. 'You should give him a break.'

A smile played on Meera's lips. 'You want him? He's all yours.'

Shabnam pouted. 'I wish he'd shown the slightest bit of interest in me.' She brushed her hair till it shone while Meera waited. Then she lined her beautiful eyes with kohl. 'He's handsome, eligible and so hot!'

Meera didn't deny his hotness factor. It made her blush, every time she thought about him. He was also a great co-worker, kind, helpful. In other words, perfect! But, she'd decided, she wasn't going to let romance ruin her chances for the transfer that she'd been waiting for, for a long time. 'What I need is that transfer. Then I can get away from home and not have to meet men I don't like.' She let out a long sigh. 'I can't wait!'

'What you really need is a good man who loves you.' Shabnam pursed her lips. 'Like him.'

Meera smirked. 'How can I be so sure he loves me? For all you know, it's just a fling. It's only been two months since he joined.'

'He has eyes only for you,' Shabnam said. "You're smart, attractive and sweet. Only you don't know it yourself.'

'And you're the best friend in the whole world.' Meera squeezed her into a hug.

When they reached the crowded cafeteria, they found Vivek seated at a corner spot.

'I've already ordered three coffees, a masala dosa for Shabnam and two pav bhajis for us,' he said to Meera, as they took their seats at the tiny round table.

'How did you know I love masala dosa?' Shabnam looked up at him and fluttered her eyelids.

Meera loved to watch Shabnam flirt.

He played along. 'Because I have good memory.' Shabnam's slap at his hand made him grin.

The waiter arrived with their food and coffee.

'You shouldn't have ordered pav bhaji for me,' Meera said. 'It's too much!'

'Why? Are you on a diet?' Shabnam winked at her. 'Is someone coming to see you again?'

Vivek choked on his coffee. 'Aw!' His hands flew to rub the quick setting brown stain off his shirt.

Meera wished Shabnam would stop being such a blabbermouth. Vivek's face had grown darker. He was staring down at his coffee. She couldn't tell what was wrong with him all of a sudden.

Clueless, Shabnam egged her for more details.

'It's my parents,' Meera said, shrugging it off. 'I've tried but they won't stop calling suitors home to see me.'

'Do you know who it is?' Shabnam said.

For a moment, Vivek's ears perked up.

'All I could gather was that he works in the US.' She took a long sip of coffee, hoping that that would be the end of the discussion.

'So he can so be your ticket to the US?'

She glared at Shabnam. 'Don't be silly. As if I'd marry somebody just for that.' Then she slid a glance in Vivek's direction. He had gone back to his coffee.

'Talking of the US,' Shabnam started again, 'who do you think is going to get this transfer?'

I hope it's me, Meera thought. That way I can escape awkward meetings with suitors.

'It's going to be one heck of a great experience to work in California,' Vivek said, sounding excited. 'From what I've heard, the assignment will be for three years. I'd love to go but I'm new to this office. I'm sure you guys have a better chance.'

'Oh, you're smart,' Shabnam blurted. 'You do have a chance.'

They discussed a few more likely candidates, and all of their own chances, and then Shabnam had to go because she got a phone call.

'Shall we go too?' Meera said, looking around at the crowded cafeteria and wondering if she recognized anyone that she knew.

He leaned forward and smiled. 'But we haven't finished our conversation.'

She didn't know why but she felt like a deer caught in the headlights. 'What do you mean?'

He leaned closer and tucked a loose strand of hair behind her ear.

'Why are you so afraid of going out with me?'

'Stop that!' She swatted his hand away. 'Someone will see.'

'You're being paranoid,' he said, laughing. 'Just tell me you're not attracted to me like I am to you and I'll leave you alone.' His eyes shone like a baby's.

With how close he was leaning towards her, and his eyes daring her, she just couldn't think straight. *Uff!* 'Don't be so pushy!' She shoved his chest.

He caught her hand and wouldn't let go. 'You're this amazing woman that I want to know better. Won't you give me a chance?'

'Look, Vivek,' she said, wriggling her hand free. 'I don't want this…us to ruin my job.'

He let out a whoosh of breath. 'Okay,' he said, raising his hands in his defense. 'I know you have an independent streak. You're charming and incredibly delightful to talk to.' He ran his fingers through his hair. 'And here it goes.' He held her gaze as he said the words softly, 'I think I'm falling in love with you. All I'm asking is to give me a chance.'

The waiter came to take away their empty cups and plates, and she smiled to herself, watching how he was helping the guy along, impatient for him to leave. Twisting the end of her dupatta, she waited for them to be alone again.

After the waiter left, he looked at her, one eyebrow raised, waiting for her reply.

'I don't think romance at work is a good thing. So, either you'll have to quit or I'll have to.' She shrugged, faking the sassiness while inwardly scowling that both choices sounded terrible. *Did her self-imposed rule about office romance even make sense?*

His shoulders drooped. 'So, do people working together never fall in love?'

'They probably do. I'm just not one of them,' she was quick to retort.

'All this excuse about working together is BS,' he said, calling her bluff. 'You know you don't care about that—'

'I do!'

Just then the waiter sauntered over again with the bill. Vivek pulled out his wallet at the same time that Meera pulled out her purse.

The waiter went straight to him.

'Let me,' he said to her. 'Consider it my best wishes for the latest man who's coming to see you.'

Meera frowned at him.

'Though I really hope he's horrible.' He grinned. 'If you need more time to get to know me, I'm willing to wait.' He winked at her. 'Hopefully you'll change your mind before you or I are transferred out of here.' He chuckled to make light of it but Meera's heart beat so hard she could almost hear it.

Together they rose to leave, with Vivek coming up right behind her. As she took her first step, she felt a strong tug at her dupatta. It pulled her backwards and she fell straight up against his chest.

Strong arms held her steady. 'Sorry,' he said, his breath blowing across her ear, his baritone making her toes curl. Her throat went dry. There was a brief pause and the next moment, he lifted his foot off her dupatta and released her.

'Thanks!' Gosh! She felt her cheeks burn as she looked everywhere but at him. She so wished, after it was over, that she could have snuggled closer for longer.

Subscribe to my newsletter to get the full story at SudhaNair.com/newsletter. Hope to see you there :)

Acknowledgements

Dear reader, your love and trust in me helped me take a giant leap of faith in bringing you this story about hope, rising above a tragedy, and moving on. I hope that it touched your heart and you loved it as much as I loved bringing it to you. I thank you for picking up this book, and if you've come this far, I hope the journey was worth it. Thanks so much for staying with me and I hope that my subsequent books will also bring you joy.

I couldn't have written a story about movie making without the technical expertise and know-how from a dear friend and industry insider. Thanks so much, Kusum Punjabi, for being my guide, and spending so many hours talking movies with me. I'm hugely grateful for what you've taught me. Any variations and tweaks to the movie world for the purpose of this fictional story, are indeed my very own.

I'm incredibly grateful to my beta readers, Priya Gopalan and Mrinalini Menon. I wouldn't have been able to do without your invaluable inputs.

Thanks to my amazingly talented cover designer, Subi Alex, who blew me away with such an artistic and gorgeous looking cover.

Nikita Jhanglani, my ever-insightful and intuitive editor, who remains a pillar of support and full of judicious advice. Big thanks for your faith in me and for answering the tons of questions I had for you.

My partner-in-crime, crossword buddy, reading and writing companion, second-editor-in-command and proofreader—Devika Rajan. Thank you for taking up my book despite your busy schedule. I'm so lucky to have you in my corner. You've been invaluable to my writing life and I thank you from the bottom of my heart.

Thanks, Deepma Jadeja, for coming to my last-minute rescue. :) And also, for your constant support and encouragement.

Thank you, Sanil Nair, for the professional photographs, and the title for this book, which, as in the past, I'm very proud of!

To my seniors, Ruchi Singh, Sonia Rao, Adite Banerjie, Aarti Raman, Devika Fernando, Preethi Venugopala, it's an honour to learn from your vast experience and talent.

Writing has brought me in touch with a whole world of other writers and I'm very lucky and proud to be a part of this generous, supportive and caring community. Thanks to everyone who has been there for me.

To my dad, who is no more: You were in my thoughts at every word I wrote.

This book is dedicated to my mom, who has been waiting to read this book. :) Thank you for encouraging me and for being so proud of me, always.

Thank you Dinesh, Mrinalini, Priya, Abhijeet and Nitya, for always having my back.

A big thank you to my near and dear ones for cheering me along the way. And to the many friends, fellow writers, and family, who have been an important part of this book in myriad ways. I'm grateful for your presence in my life.

Lastly, but to whom I owe the most!

Dear God, I thank You. I couldn't have written this without You.

About The Author

SUDHA NAIR won the Amazon KDP Pen to Publish contest for her debut novel, The Wedding Tamasha—a tale about love, family, values, and traditions. She loves writing stories and creating worlds where she lets her imagination run riot and has fun along with her characters. Sudha lives in Bangalore, India.

CONNECT WITH SUDHA ON:

WEBSITE: sudhanair.com

EMAIL: sudha@sudhanair.com

FACEBOOK: facebook.com/SudhaNairAuthor

INSTAGRAM: instagram.com/sudhagn

www.ingramcontent.com/pod-product-compliance
Lightning Source LLC
Chambersburg PA
CBHW020317160726
47992CB00004B/1584